Christmas Dinner

By

Pat Simmons

@2020 Christian Reads Press/Pat Simmons

Developmental Editor: Chandra Sparks Splond
Proofreader: Kiranshahid966/Fiverr.com
Final Proofreader: Darlene Simmons
Beta Reader: Stacey Jefferson
Interior Design: Kimolisa/Fiverr.com
Cover Design: Ultrakhan22/Fiverr.com

ISBN: 978-1-7338316-2-8

Praises for Pat Simmons Novels:

5.0 out of 5 stars WOOOOOOOOOW.

Just when you think that it can't get any better.....Pat Simmons exceeded my expectations. This book is exceptional. It touched my in so many ways and I could really relate to Robyn because she reminded me of myself. I could just picture her putting her fist on her hips and the sassy way that she would respond to Derek. The proposal was the highlight in the book for me. The reference to Job sent chills over me.—Reader Ceisha Barrett on *Couple by Christmas*

4.0 out of 5 stars Christmas Stories

Pat has a way with scriptures in her stories. I wonder which comes first the scriptures or the stories. I read the Gifts from God series and enjoyed both books but Prayers Answered by Christmas was my favorite. I love the innocence of the children. Well done Pat. I look forward to Coy's story. She needs some love from God too.—Amazon Reader on *Prayers Answered by Christmas*

5.0 out of 5 stars Beautiful Story of Love and Family

Pat Simmons has written a story showcasing the power of love and family. I smiled and cried as Daniel and Saige's story progressed. Pat handles a very emotional issue beautifully and reminds us that God's will is always perfect, even when we want Him to do things differently. I will think about this story for a while as I meditate on how He does all things well. Are you looking for a Christmas story that will warm your heart? You don't need to look any further than *Christmas Greetings* by Pat Simmons. Great job Pat, if I could I would give a rating of 6 stars.—Reader Leslie Hudson

In loving memory of

Nathan Van Taylor
1958–2018

Special thanks to

Readers and book clubs who support my work: thank you reading, encouraging me, telling others, posting reviews, and overall blessing me

To my author sisters. There are *soooo* many to name, but a shoutout to the CBLR and the Fun Friday crew. The sisterhood bond is special

My writing village:

Beta reader: Stacey Jefferson

Consultant: Rose Beavers-Jackson.

Author's assistant: Jackie Roberts

Developmental Editor: Chandra Sparks Splond

Cheerleaders: Husband Kerry Simmons and cousin Darlene Simmons

Love you all

Chapter One

"What am I doing here?" Darcelle Price asked herself as she bundled her coat tighter against the December chill and exhaled the cold air from her nostrils. The outing—daddy and daughter time—had been forever canceled.

Harold Price had been a wise man who had guided Darcelle through life's various tests and triumphs. He instilled values in her to always stand up for herself and let no one take advantage of her in any situation—whether personal or private.

When she mentioned needing a new vehicle, excitement lit his eyes as he announced he would accompany his thirty-two-year-old single daughter on a car-buying spree.

"We'll scope out the Black Friday deals. If we don't find a steal, we'll wait until around Christmas when the dealerships are desperate to clear inventory for the new year."

So, there she was, standing on a car lot—at almost Christmas time—with big red bows arranged on car hoods, twinkling lights looped on massive trees in the lobby, and *Merry Christmas* signs flashing in store windows. The stage was set for holiday cheer.

Darcelle wasn't feeling it.

A link was missing.

Daddy had always been there for her. Faithful. Committed. Loving. The qualities the man she married better bring to the table, a boast that was hard to fulfill. When she was old enough to date, Darcelle realized not many men could measure up to her father.

She blinked away the moisture from her eyes, and everything came into focus. She was surrounded, drowning in an ocean of cars that seemed ready to charge at her any minute.

Darcelle couldn't keep the thoughts of her father at bay as she moved aimlessly from one vehicle to another with enticements to "drive your Christmas present" home. Memories flooded her like a tsunami.

So many monumental memories.

The week before Thanksgiving, her father had died of a heart attack. The Prices buried him on Black Friday. A dark day in the lives of his widow, three daughters, and two grandchildren he left behind to mourn. And Darcelle had mourned and was still grieving.

"This was such a bad idea," she concluded. "I should've never come. I can't do this."

"Have any questions?" Jake, or maybe it was John—the salesperson assigned to hound her for a deal—startled her.

Tucking away the memories into a private place, Darcelle straightened her shoulders and practiced a smile. She spun around to face the man for the second time since she'd arrived at the dealership.

While she shivered under her thick wool coat and cap, he wore a thin jacket halfway zipped and no head covering. Gel fortified his hair against the wind. The crooked grin on his round face and oversized glasses angled on his narrow nose were annoying.

"Not yet." Darcelle was pleasant, but couldn't wait to sneak away as he turned to retreat.

But wasn't that why she left her apartment?

To escape the solitude?

Darcelle had been holed up there for days. *Either refocus or put off making a purchase*, she chided herself. Her dad had advised her that her current seven-year-old car wasn't worth a new transmission.

"Daddy, what should I do?" she whispered as if he could hear her.

Footsteps approached behind her. Gritting her teeth, she had no smile for this guy—again.

"Do you know what you're looking for?" a baritone voice asked over her shoulder.

He wasn't the same guy. His words weren't rushed or pushy. Had the other guy called in reinforcement to up the pressure?

She sighed and twirled around, then she steadied herself against a nearby car. How could she smart off at a man who towered over her five-foot-six-and-a-half-inch stature and whose handsome face was worthy of a second glance?. He was nicely dressed in a long wool coat, and a hat—a Fedora custom designed for his face. His sales bonuses were clearly well invested. His smile mesmerized her.

Mischief danced in his eyes and hinted of a tease. Okay, so he thought he could flirt his way to a commission?

Darcelle wouldn't be intimidated. Lifting her chin, she held her ground. "Like I told the other salesman, I'll let you know when I make up my mind."

"I doubt it." Instead of a retreat, he rocked on his heels. "I've been watching you from over there." She turned in the direction he pointed. "And I thought—*uh-uh*, she's not interested in buying."

His eyes no longer danced but softened. "I'm Evanston Giles. Friends call me Evan. Nah, I'm not a salesman." He scrunched his nose. "Can never trust those guys."

Exactly.

A kindred spirit.

Relaxing her shoulders, Darcelle confessed. "You're right. Although I *need* a vehicle, my heart's not into it at the moment. I can't, not without my dad." Her voice cracked. Better leave now before she broke down in front of this stranger—well, Evan. She moved to step around him.

"Hold on. Your dad might be running late." Evanston took a chance to detain her longer.

"He's not." She shook her head. The disappointment in her eyes, along with the pool of tears, tugged at his senses. "My father died." Her words faded to a whisper.

Usually, an articulate person, Evanston had a word for every occasion. Not this time, struggling to say something besides, I'm sorry.

She stared past him in a trance. "Seems like last night, but it was last month."

A slight breeze felt like a punch to his gut. *What?* "Sorry for your loss." He said it anyway. Still in mourning, the lady shouldn't be making business transactions in her state of mind. "Do you *need* a car?"

"Doesn't matter." She shrugged and began to walk away. "My father was supposed to make sure I got the best deal."

Problem solved. Evanston could recall features on most models that would put a salesperson to shame. Plus, he was a master at negotiation. "I can stand in the gap, but you'll have to tell me your name." Without asking for permission, he grabbed her hand and tugged her toward a car as if they were friends after five minutes.

Stunned, she opened her mouth as if to protest his forwardness but didn't. "Darcelle Price."

"A beautiful name for an alluring woman. I'm not flirting—yet. Stating the obvious." He smiled. Okay, he was flirting, which surprised him. He hadn't dated since… No need to think about past regrets.

Her lips curved into a faint smile until she chuckled. With twinkling clear Christmas lights as a backdrop, her face glowed as if the sun were overruling the sunset. "My dad told my mother he wanted his girls to have beautiful names."

So, there was more than one from where this beauty came. *Stay on task.* "Tell me about your father."

"His name is—was—Harold." She swallowed and sucked in a deep breath. Evanston silently willed her to relax and regain her composure. It worked because she continued. "He was smart, funny, and a family man. When it came to his three daughters, he was a force to be reckoned with."

"No sons?"

"Nope. I've never seen him angry until my older sister got pregnant—twice."

He whistled. Evanston couldn't imagine the fallout. He clicked his teeth as if he were scared. "Yikes."

A memory must have jolted her mind because Darcelle smirked. "You better believe it. Daddy renewed his gun permit. It took prayers and pleading for him not to do anything he would regret."

"I like him already." He admired any man who would protect his family. He had heard of a shotgun wedding, but Evanston had never seen it play out. Suddenly, he felt an allegiance to this larger-than-life family man. "What's your favorite color?"

"Purple." Digging into the oversized pockets of her coat, she pivoted to the left, then to the right as if she were a model. The bold color had gotten his attention from across the car lot, along with the riding boots and a cream cap that couldn't trap her mass of curls. She was definitely dressed for the elements. In a different setting, he might have mistaken her for a model at one of the many cars shows he attended.

He tapped a finger against his lips and faked a frown. "I don't know if I saw any purple ones."

She jutted her chin, and a dimple appeared. He zoomed in on her freckles—three of them. "You didn't say a car. I like maroon or a cranberry shade." Her eyes became bright with expectancy.

Evanston pumped more information out of her like the make, model, and price range. "Let's see if we can find those features in your choice of colors. He pointed to a Ford. She shook her head.

"Okay." He steered her toward a Hyundai and read off what it was equipped with.

She squinted as if she was considering it. "I'm not feeling this one either. Not enough horsepower and Apple CarPlay is a must."

"Ooh, woman," he teased, "you're going to be a hard sale."

She giggled. "Daddy would be proud."

When she hovered near a Buick crossover, he played the part. "This one has automatic high beams and emergency braking—I'm thinking about your safety. You have to admit the big green bow is setting the maroon shade off —" he patted the hood— "plus, this would make your dad happy."

"It's cranberry." The sparkle in her eyes revealed he had picked a winner.

Darcelle glanced over her shoulder. "*Uh-oh.* Here comes Jake, John, or whatever his name is."

"I'll handle him." Evanston stepped closer in a protective stance.

The salesman extended his hand for a shake and introduced himself as Jake. He grinned with a hopeful expression. "So, folks, what do you think? Want to take it for a test drive?"

Evanston looked to Darcelle who shook her head. "I drove one of these a month ago when I needed a rental. Smooth ride."

"Okay. Let's talk numbers, Jake," Evanston used his no-nonsense tone.

Darcelle blinked as if she'd remembered something and pulled Evanston aside. "I can take it from here. I didn't mean to take you away from your car shopping."

He chuckled as Jake waved them forward. "I didn't come to buy."

"What? Why are you here?"

Good question. Was it serendipity, or as his mother always said, the Lord ordering his steps? Why would the Lord be interested in his movements? Not that Evanston was a bad person or anything. It's just that he wouldn't get a perfect church attendance award.

Evanston stopped overthinking it. "I'm a car enthusiast. The dealership's magnificent Christmas decorations made me look and, on a whim, I decided to stop and check out the new models."

"Yeah," She glanced around, "I think the light display beckoned to me to stop here too."

Okay, was that a coincidence—or the Lord causing this detour? He pondered it while falling in step with Darcelle.

Chapter Two

A *m I about to let a stranger with supposedly no ulterior motives broker a deal on a major purchase for me? Maybe he's part of the underground dealership cartel in a scheme to take advantage of me in a game of good guy, bad guy? Is this all a ruse?*

Questions swirled in Darcelle's head as she and Evanston sat side by side in front of a massive desk in the credit manager's office.

Something about Evanston Giles reassured her his intentions were genuine. Unlike earlier, where he was gentle and kind, now he appeared as an intimidating figure as he rested an ankle over his knee—nice socks. He unbuttoned his coat, revealing a rust-color pullover sweater that matched his plaid dress socks as if he purchased them as a set. When he removed his hat, his hair reminded Darcelle of her nephew's thick curls. Making himself at home, he leaned back and spread his arms over the adjacent chairs, including hers.

Evanston spoke with charisma. Clarity. Confidence. "Jake gave us a quote on Cece's trade-in. If you want a deal, let's begin at the sticker price."

Cece? She hid her amusement. His business acumen dared anyone to test him. Had her daddy sent an angel in his place?

Vocal, Darcelle could speak for herself, but why should she when Evanston was so convincing? She believed every word out of his mouth. The man was her hero. After a few back-and-forths, Mr. Greene, the credit manager, begrudgingly, had lowered the offer to a ridiculous amount to move inventory.

It was a duel Evanston had won. He stood.

Wait. You're leaving me?

He must have read her panicked expression. "I'll be in the hall so you can talk privately about money." Evanston gave her a smile as warm as her wool coat.

"Thank you," she mouthed and exhaled. Time for round two. Mr. Greene was not about to make up for the loss on the deal with stacked extras she didn't need, and she told him so without blinking. Satisfied she had the upper hand on the credit terms, Darcelle craned her neck for Evanston.

Leaning against the wall with folded arms, he met her stare. When she nodded, he grinned and pushed off his support and headed her way with an unrushed swag.

"Hi." Evanston took his seat, scooted it closer to her, then waited for Mr. Greene to recite the figures. He twisted his mouth as if he was thinking. "I'm sure you can throw in oil changes, car washes, spare keys, and some other perks, then we'll have a deal." He tapped his finger on his lip. "I'm thinking fabric protection, rust protection…"

Mr. Greene held up his hands. "Okay, okay. You got it. You'll have to come back for the rust and fabric protection." Suddenly, he seemed in a rush to get them out of his office.

When the deed was done, and she and Evanston were out of the office, Darcelle thanked him. "Impressive."

"It was fun to see him sweat." His grin was contagious. "Need help transferring your things, Cece?" His hopeful expression hinted he would be disappointed if she said no.

"Don't stop helping me now." A burden was lifted. She did a quick inventory of what she had in her backseat and trunk—shoes and work binders from the firm. In her apartment, Darcelle was a neat freak. It was a stark contrast to her car—she didn't live in it. Still, she wasn't a slob either.

"By the way, why are you calling me Cece?" Darcelle had not only survived the ordeal but earned an impromptu nickname too. She blushed as he matched her steps to her old car while Jake drove her new vehicle and parked it outside the showroom door.

His eyes roamed over her face, assessing her before he shrugged. "DeeDee isn't you. Darcie is too Jane Austen. Cece is soft and delicate, like you."

Soft. Delicate. How special was his assessment? "What do you know about Jane Austen?"

He met her challenge. "I have a mother and sister who can quote lines from *Pride and Prejudice* with little prompting."

"Thank you." She walked ahead, digging into her purse for her car remote to pop the trunk.

Oh, she forgot the zillion gift-wrapped boxes she had stored while shopping days ago and had never taken out.

He didn't comment on her stash or hide a chuckle or two as he inspected her arsenal, which also included unopened jigsaw puzzle boxes for her niece and nephew, empty water bottles, mismatched gloves, and miscellaneous items that shouldn't be there. Once the task was done, he grinned. "Feel better?"

"I do, Van," she teased as he lifted his brow. "I can almost assure you I wouldn't have bought a car this evening." The compassionate stranger, the confident friend—she needed in a bind—and now handsome hunk, blushed. It was endearing.

Evanston patted the hood of her new crossover after she slid behind the wheel. "Remember, stay up on your oil changes and scheduled maintenance."

"I will." Her words seemed to vanish as the cold air swept them away. Darcelle didn't want to say goodbye. She stared into those gorgeous eyes, reliving the hours of contentment. "My father would have liked you."

"The feeling would have been mutual." Evanston tipped his Fedora and turned to disappear out of her life as he had appeared—in a flash. There was no flirting, asking for her number, or anything beyond the moment. This moment. Their moment.

Why was she having separation issues? Unstrapping her seat belt, Darcelle stepped out of the car. It was too late for dinner so what was the best excuse she could come up with? She yelled, "Can I buy you a cup of hot chocolate, tea, or coffee? That's what they say in the corny movies."

He stopped in his tracks and took his time looking over his shoulder before twirling around. "Do they now?" His swagger back to her was swoon-worthy. Towering over her, his expression was unreadable. What was he thinking?

"Hot chocolate's on you." He lowered his already deep voice. "Breakfast on me in the morning. How's that?"

She exhaled. "Bet, Van."

Evanston grinned. "I'll own the name coming from you. There's a coffee shop in the strip up the street. You can't miss it with the Christmas decorations on steroids that give off a small-town feel. I'd say race you there, but I won't." He winked and walked away.

Back in her vehicle, Darcelle closed her eyes and inhaled the newness of the interior before sinking into her leather seats. She exhaled as a realization hit. She'd ask a stranger out. She laughed and checked the rearview mirror. "I can't make this stuff up."

The reward was sweet, and Evanston wasn't referring to her offer of a beverage. Darcelle had no idea how much he didn't want their time together to end.

In all of his thirty-six years, he had never rescued a damsel in distress, but he enjoyed every minute of it. Evanston touched his Bluetooth headphones when his phone rang.

"What's up, Cedric?" he said to an old high school buddy he considered a brother since neither had one.

They had similar interests: working out, love of cars but...definitely not women. Cedric was always on the hunt. He was chasing after an emotional connection that stemmed from his childhood bout with cancer, and his dates came lacking that connection. Evanston had stopped the chase after a bad breakup. It wasn't unusual for someone to mistake them for brothers—same height, skin coloring, and beard.

"What's up with you? Where you at, man? I thought you were on your way hours ago." He grunted.

"Yeah, something came up. Sorry." He bit his bottom lip. He wasn't. "I'll help you with your website this weekend."

"Everything alright? What could have possibly come up between you telling me you're on your way and my house that's less than ten miles away?"

"What had happened was…" It was the introduction to usually a long, sometimes unbelievable explanation. "I was passing by Tillman Butler Dealership when—"

"Hold up." Cedric huffed. "Stop right there. You're buying a new car without going to the car show?"

"Nope. Just lookin'. Now, I'm meeting a friend."

"You only have two—the Lester guy on your job and me." Cedric patted his chest. "Who is this person I'm getting dumped for. Just know I need my website up and running and making me money. This is the holiday season. I want my deposit back."

"Ha." Evanston was amused. "Buying me a drink doesn't cover parts, labor, my pain and suffering." An IT specialist by profession, if it had to do with building a website or troubleshooting, Evanston liked the challenges.

He would give Cedric the details later. Turning into the small parking lot of the strip lined with various eateries, Evanston felt like a schoolboy who had made a new friend. Plus, the storefront windows decorated for Christmas added charm.

What man with 20/20 vision would want to settle for friendship with a woman as stunning as Darcelle? She had resuscitated his numb heart.

He parked and stepped out. Evanston strolled to her vehicle and opened her door. Her eyes sparkled, and her face glowed. Maybe they both had been revived in some way. He squinted. "*Hmmm*. You look familiar."

"You too." She played along, smiling, accelerating his heart rate.

The cafe was more like a bakery. Patrons were sprinkled throughout the dining area, which was festive with red and green tablecloths and Christmas music playing overhead. Although the business boasted Christmas lights outside, the owners didn't skimp on decorations inside. Even the workers wore red-and-green striped holiday hats. She headed to the counter and studied the menu, which included holiday desserts.

After they ordered their hot chocolates—white chocolate for Darcelle, regular milk chocolate for him - Evanston watched as she claimed a table near the window where her car was in full view. A predictable new car owner.

Once he joined her, Evanston slid the cup across the table.

She nodded her thanks, took the first sip, and glanced at her vehicle. "Today, was surreal. Thank you for being there for me—a stranger."

"We haven't been strangers in hours. You have to admit it was fun."

"Yeah." Darcelle blushed from the mischievous gleam in his eyes. "It was. Everything you did and said back there reminded me of Daddy." She changed the subject, So, you're into cars. Classics or new?"

"Both," he said, taking a sip, "but new models charge my engines—pun intended."

"I got it. So, do you work in the automobile industry?" She patted her hands on the table.

"Nope. I'm a boring IT guy at First Trust Bank."

Hmmph. "You'll never be out of a job. I pester our tech support at work all the time."

"What do you do?" He relaxed his shoulders against the back of the seat. It didn't matter what they conversed about. Evanston enjoyed her company.

"I work at Reed and Meeks Brokerage. My background is in accounting, and I majored in finance." Her admission wasn't boastful.

Evanston gripped the edge of the table in embarrassment. "Ouch. The joke's on me." He flexed his biceps. "Here I thought I was the man protecting a beautiful damsel in distress, but you upped me. With your background, you could have secured your deal on your own."

Darcelle's expression became somber. "You are the man, Evanston."

What happened to Van? He liked the pet name she had given him.

"I did need you. I doubt I'd purchased a car anytime soon, but you proved to me life goes on."

He covered her hand with his and slowly slid it back when his heart felt like it would leap out of his chest. He wasn't looking for romance, but he wasn't opposed to it if it involved getting to know Cece.

Bowing her head, Darcelle tapped her cup against the table. "I debated all day at the office about whether I should go car hunting. I circled the car lot three times before I told myself to do it. Van…" A smile curled her full lips, which he admired. "You helped me get the job done. You rescued this damsel."

"Woman, you're saying the right words to make me fall for you." Did he just say that? Yes, there seemed to be no pretense between them. "Seriously, I'll be your hero any time, any place."

"Every woman needs one. For thirty-two years, Harold Price was mine. I didn't think there was another one."

As they sipped and talked through refills, Evanston spied the time and sighed. "I promised you breakfast. How about now?"

"Now? It's almost midnight." Her mouth might have protested, but the mischief in her eyes conveyed she was all for it.

"We can get an early start." He leaned forward and wiggled his brows. "Pancake Place is open twenty-four hours."

"I'm a Belgian waffle type of girl," she warned him.

"That's all I need to know. Let's go, girl." Evanston stood and helped Darcelle with her coat. The night—or morning—was still young.

Chapter Three

*D*arcelle rested her fork on the table and patted her stomach. "A night to remember—the company, the car, and the food. Did I mention I got a new car?"

"I do recall something about a new car." He chuckled, glancing at the clock on a wall above the cooking station. It's definitely a night and morning to remember.

She could have never, ever expected this outcome tonight when she woke up this morning. It was hard to restrain her happiness as she closed her eyes, mouthed a scream, and danced in her seat. She felt liberated from the sadness that had a grip on her. Opening her eyes, Darcelle found Evanston watching her. He had a slight smirk.

"Sorry." She cleared her throat. "I guess the carbs gave me energy. I didn't realize I was so hungry."

"Me neither. The way you attacked your waffles was unbelievable."

Darcelle laughed at herself. Friends for less than a day, their personalities clicked as if they had known each other since pre-school. No awkward moments. No phone interruptions. Evanston had helped her pull off something so monumental—creating a window for her to escape her sorrows.

"Well," she said, patting her hands on the table, "I guess we'd better go."

There was his stare again. The same stare he first gave her in the car lot. Something was brewing in his head. "Will you call me when you get home?"

So he didn't want to cut his ties yet. Darcelle exhaled, and her heart accelerated.

"Are we on a date?" *Hold up. Did I say that?* Was Darcelle Price flirting? What was in those waffles?

"Nah." His eyes betrayed his mouth. "This is breakfast. A date includes dinner, which means I would like to take you out to dinner."

"Sounds perfect." *Now, I'm this woman who's throwing caution to the wind.* His charisma, intelligence, and handsomeness were assets any woman would want. Before meeting Evanston, dating was the last thing on her mind. Yet, Darcelle realized she wasn't opposed as she recited her number as he punched it in, and her phone rang.

He leaned closer. "I think everyone uses that tone."

"You're right, Van. You should have something different." As if they were in profound negotiation, they sampled her ringtone selections until she chose 'Uplift.' She met his stare. "This one. I'll always remember how you made me laugh."

Adjusting his shoulders, Evanston grinned. "Glad I could. Now, for you." Surprisingly, he seemed to know what ringtone he wanted. "I like the soft sound of a harp, which means you have to call me a lot for me to enjoy a mini-serenade."

With the task done, Evanston slid out of his seat, then waited for Darcelle to scoot out of the booth, then he held her coat while she slipped her arms into the sleeves.

As he paid their bill, she nudged him. "I'm not going to be the first to call if we're talking about a dinner date."

"Noted. So you're putting pressure on a brother. Okay. What's an acceptable waiting period?"

She stifled a yawn instead of answering. Outside, the city was quiet, asleep in the early hours of Saturday morning. Only the flickering of colorful lights in windows and outlining buildings were awake.

It felt romantic. She fantasized Evanston would wrap his arms around her waist and tease her lips with a kiss. Again, fantasy. One reality was she would miss his presence.

"Remember: Call me when you make it home," he ordered, then opened her door and waited while she strapped on her seat belt.

"You're going to make me call you first anyway, *huh*?"

"That's the plan." He winked and bit his bottom lip while she started the engine. He tipped his Fedora, and with his confident swagger, Evanston Giles faded into the sunset.

"Wow," slipped from Darcelle's mouth, a yawn followed. She drove her new purchase home, enjoying the comfort as she pushed the speed limit while sleep gained on her. It seemed like forever, but finally, she arrived at the apartment garage and parked in her assigned space. She inhaled the fragrance of the interior one last time before stepping out. After one final inspection, Darcelle headed to her place.

Too tired to carry out her neat-freak routine, Darcelle dumped her things on the sofa and kicked off her boots. Next, she texted Evanston, which prompted him to be the first to call. She grinned in victory. His deep voice made her shiver and wish to retreat into a warm cocoon.

Putting him on speaker, she performed her nightly regimen—something she was never too tired to undertake. They chatted as if they hadn't been with each other less than an hour ago.

"Hold on." In her bedroom, Darcelle muted him briefly while she whispered a quick prayer before sliding under the covers.

"What haven't we talked about?"

"Me tricking you into calling me first." She smiled, feeling herself drifting into a fantasy dream beckoning to her.

"You got me. Night, Cece."

His low, velvety voice made everything fade to black.

Sunlight was not Darcelle's friend when all she craved was sleep. She shifted in her bed to dodge the slivers of rays determined to stronghold her lids open. "*Uh-huh,*" she moaned.

Satisfied, she won the skirmish with the sun until salsa music interrupted her peace. Untangling her arms from the warmth of her comforter, she patted the nightstand for her phone, then realized it was wrapped in the cover with her.

"Hello?" she forced out her greeting.

"Girl, you're still asleep?" asked Shana Turner, her bestie who had almost lost that reigning title after an evening with Evanston. He was certainly ranked up there as one of her favorite people.

"*Hmmm.* Bye." She rolled over and snuggled deeper into her pillow. In her dreams, everything was all right in her world.

Hours later, Darcelle woke and stretched. She glanced around her room and spied the time. After noon. Darcelle hadn't slept that well since her father died and usually she woke in a gloomy mood. Not today when Evanston's face came to mind. She laughed for no other reason than she was happy, at peace with the world.

Throwing back the covers, she jumped up and slid on her knees for a quick morning prayer. It was a habit drilled in her since childhood but, in all honesty, she hadn't felt a connection with Jesus since her father's sudden death. Darcelle was simply going through the motions.

After her shower, Darcelle craved more waffles but settled for a grilled cheese sandwich instead. She peeped out the kitchen window and admired the light snowfall in the common area near the pool. Christmas wasn't the same without snow—at least an inch or two—a dusting didn't count. While munching, she tapped her friend's name on her phone.

"Morning," she said with a ring in her voice.

"You missed that almost an hour ago. And that's still late for you, even if it is a Saturday. 'Bout time you called me back." Shana tsked. "Although I'm glad you got some rest... How did car shopping go yesterday?"

Darcelle snickered as memories danced before her eyes. "I had the best time—"

"Buying a car? Something you dreaded? We were on the phone for hours the other night about whether you should go or wait."

"I know, right?" Good thing her dreamy smile was hidden from Shana, but if her friend picked up on it, Darcelle's wouldn't deny the glee that engulfed her. "It wouldn't have happened without Van who was with me every step of the way. Got me a ridiculous deal and extras I wouldn't have thought about. Van and I sipped on hot chocolate at this bakery, then shared breakfast at Pancake Place—never ate there before. Anyway, I didn't get home until after two in the morning, then we talked on the phone, although I can't remember how long." She rambled until she ran out of breath.

"Ah, excuse me? You don't stay out late unless you're having a good time, which shouldn't be the case without me. You can't function without your eight hours. So, what kind of car did you get, and who is Van?"

Darcelle laughed and finished off her sandwich except for the edges, then she stood and strolled across the floor. She glanced out a larger window, facing the highway that separated her luxury apartment from the elegant homes and condos in a gated community.

They were out of her price range now, but one day, she would buy that dream home she envisioned since being wowed on a St. Louis Holiday House Tours as a teenager with her parents. Darcelle never forgot those homes, decorations, the smell of cookies, or the grand architecture.

From her location, Darcelle could see the elaborate and meticulous holiday decorations. Beautiful. Impressive. Expensive. She had stalled long enough. "I did go to this dealership and was about to leave. This guy who at the time I didn't know how cute he was..." She spared no detail.

"First, a woman always notices a fine specimen. Maybe I should be looking for a trade-in."

Finger-combing the curls in her hair, Darcelle laughed. "Please. Your car isn't a year old."

"Doesn't matter. Apparently, car lots are where the cute guys hang out." Shana chuckled. "Seriously, I'm glad this Evanston guy was there for you. What's his last name? I'll check him out on social media."

"Giles." Darcelle tapped into her own Instagram account and was immediately mesmerized by different poses, photos, and closeups of Evanston. In most of them, he wore a cap or hat. She scrutinized some of his friends— a mix of women and men. "I can't explain it, but it was like running into an old friend who happened to be someone new."

"Of course, that didn't make any sense." Shana's breath caught. "I found an Evanston Giles on Facebook. Whoa, girl. The man is fine. Either he was born with biceps or has been working out since he was in diapers. How old is he?"

"Four years older than us—thirty-six." She quickly signed into Facebook to see what Shana saw.

"*Hmmm.* Married but miserable, divorced, children? What's wrong with him? Wait—I see a guy in a couple of his photos. He's cute too. Does he have a brother? Are you two planning to see each other again? I've racked up a lot of travel points. I can fly in from Austin to St. Louis for a double date."

Darcelle was amused by how fast Shana had changed her tune. "No to all the above, including no brother—

younger sister—so I don't know who this other guy is, but Van is better looking, and, yep, we agreed to a dinner date." Darcelle giggled and told Shana about the whole ringtone pick and who was going to call first. "I texted him when I made it home and, he called me, so technically, I won. I do miss talking to him."

"You can always call him."

"Nope. I'll hold out." Darcelle turned away from the window. "Besides, I'm going to straighten up here before I head over to Mom's and surprise her."

"I'm sure Miss Nellie is going to be as shocked as me that you actually bought a car. You plan on telling her about Prince Evanston?"

"Nah. No putting ideas in her head about a man. The real story is, Mama didn't think it was a good idea to shop for a car without Daddy, but on the other hand, Van was part of the package deal which got me the car. We'll see. Talk to you later."

The memories of Evanston gave her an extra boost of energy to clean in record time. Raiding her closet, Darcelle found a sweater to match her new vehicle. She approved her reflection in her closet mirror and grabbed her keys. Every time she got behind the wheel of her car, Evan would always come to mind.

Darcelle drove twenty minutes to her mother's home in the city. She parked in front of the story-and-a-half house.

Her four-year-old niece and seven-year-old nephew were outside scooping together enough snow to shape a snowball. Their presence meant her mother was babysitting while her sister Valencia worked overtime to bring in a two-parent salary in a single-parent household.

She tapped her horn, and the children looked up with curious expressions. Darcelle stepped out, and JJ and Zuri screamed their delight.

Her mother and her baby sister, a younger version of their mother, opened the front door to investigate. They screamed in shock too.

Darcelle laughed. "Monique, Mama, get your coats. Let's go for a joy ride." Their snowballs forgotten, JJ and Zuri raced toward her.

"You...you bought a..." Her mother, Nellie, didn't move.

"Yep." Darcelle beamed. "Moni, get Mama's coat."

Zuri wrapped her arms around Darcelle. "Hi, Aunt DeeDee."

Darcie, to most, her niece insisted Darcelle be called "Aunt DeeDee." Since Jackson Jr. was called JJ, Zuri wanted to be addressed as ZZ.

"I was worried about you going without Harold. I know we all grieve differently, but I wasn't sure when you would be up to it." Her mother smiled despite the tears that filled her eyes.

Darcelle hugged her tight. "It's okay. I kinda feel like God sent me an angel, or I wouldn't have bought a car. Now, come on. Let's go for a cruise, grab a bite, shop, anything. When it gets dark, we can check out the lights and decorations."

"All I want to know is when can I drive?" At twenty-eight, Monique drove like she was sixteen and scared of the open road. Considered an old soul, a trait she inherited from their father, Monique was frugal. Once in a while, her sister would buy something new. Otherwise, she shopped at thrift stores for almost everything. She lived upstairs in their mother's house, converting it into a loft for herself, and paid rent.

Darcelle smirked. "Right before the trade-in. Come on." While they cruised through several neighborhoods, she filled them in on the details at the car lot.

"This brought me some holiday cheer," her mother said from the backseat with her grandbabies. "Do you think this Evanston would come to Christmas dinner?"

"I'll see." Darcelle guessed she had a reason to call him.

Chapter Four

*E*vanston's finger hovered over Darcelle's number when Cedric Henson's ringtone intercepted his mission. "Hey—"

"You stood me up, man—and for a chick?" Cedric attempted to lay on the guilt trip.

"I'm on my way now." Evanston huffed and swiped his car keys off the kitchen counter. Next, he grabbed his cap and jacket and was out the door.

If he called Darcelle and she wanted to hang out, Evanston might be tempted to make another detour. The sudden magnetism between them was unexplainable, but he wasn't fighting to be released. Evanston couldn't wait for their dinner date.

His best friend lived in Bridgeton, not far from Evanston's Hazelwood home. Both were located in North County—half an hour away with snow on the ground, fifteen minutes on a dry road. The two friends shared the love of car shows. Cedric also had a fascination with motorcycles, and his passion led him to become an entrepreneur for anything cycling.

"Nice of you to visit," Cedric answered the door with a warning expression that hinted he was about to get all up in Evanston's business. "Glad Miss Darcelle didn't require roadside assistance or something."

"She'd better not with her new vehicle. Besides, that's what AAA and the manufacturer's warranty are for. But if she needs help, I would be there in a heartbeat." Evanston shoved his way into the foyer and stomped the snow from the soles of his boots.

"I'm impressed. You have a tree and lights in the windows. Aren't you festive."

"Don't try to change the subject with holiday cheer. I was dumped for a pretty face, nice legs, and a seductive smile. I don't know if I should congratulate you or demand your brotherhood card back."

His friend had no idea how beautiful Darcelle was. "You're fishin' for details?" Evanston shook his arms out of his jacket, snatched the cap off his head, then stuffed it in a pocket. "Haven't seen her legs, but two out of three got me. Seriously, this isn't about looks—" He whipped out his phone and checked his Facebook account to see if she'd accepted his friend request from that morning. She had. "This is Miss Cece." Evanston scrolled through her pictures.

"Whoa. Liar. Since when has it not been about a woman's looks?" Cedric paused and folded his arms.

"With her, it's more than that," Evanston added. "She's attractive with her thick, wavy hair and long lashes—both looked real—and a sprinkle of freckles, three of them on her nose. Once she came alive from mourning, her personality was warm, engaging, and confident."

"Right." Cedric continued to his home office/gym/junk room, and Evanston trailed him. The place was a disaster. Papers, books and products were strewn across a sofa and on the floor.

"Take a seat, if you can find one." Cedric created a tower with papers, folders, and books to the side with no concern about sorting or balancing the stack on the desk corner.

"I wasn't expecting to meet anyone yesterday evening. You knew I wasn't going to leave you hanging."

"Only yesterday."

"Meeting Darcelle was a breath of fresh air—a specialty blend of a warm cup of hot chocolate." Evanston recalled his drink of choice and suddenly had a craving.

After his crazy breakup with his ex, cynicism had seeped into Evanston's soul. He had been honest, respectable…but felt stupid when Phylicia admitted to an affair right under his nose with a coworker. Evanston couldn't believe he had invested and wasted two years into a one-sided relationship.

In hindsight, they both had settled too long. Call it childish or petty, but it irked Evanston that he hadn't called it off first. Call him a fool for wanting to spare her feelings.

His parents didn't seem surprised by the breakup, stating Phylicia wasn't a good fit from day one, but they accepted her because he did. Jessica, Evanston's outspoken, overprotective brat sister by sixteen years, didn't mince words. She was livid someone had messed over her big brother.

Only Cedric knew how discombobulated he was. Evanston hadn't seen it coming. Now, for more than a year,

Evanston wouldn't allow himself to commit past two dates. He wasn't interested—until now. Darcelle just snuck up on him, and they connected instantly, which surprised him.

"So, what's your next move with Darcelle?" he asked as Evanston pecked away on the keyboard to enter the HTML code needed to build Cedric's website.

"Dinner. I was thinking about calling her when you called."

"Glad I saved you, bro. You don't want to come across too eager."

"I'm not insecure. We both had fun and enjoyed each other's company." Evanston had to compartmentalize his thoughts of Darcelle so he could concentrate.

"You're aware I needed this done weeks ago in time to cash in on Cyber Monday sales? People are skipping the stores and spending some serious money online."

"Me too. Best avoid the crowds at the malls and the traffic in the streets." Evanston's solutions was gift cards.

"I'm glad you're feeling me." Cedric leaned over Evanston's shoulder and gave him a side-eye. "I hope to salvage the season sales with last-minute Christmas shoppers."

"Man, stop hovering. You're the one who changed from wanting a simple landing page to a premium website, and you demanded a fast turnaround. Don't work like that, bro. I'm on vacation all week. I can take care of it then."

Cedric secured an uncluttered spot on his sofa and folded his arms. "Nope. I've got to get you while you're still single. I may have to hit the car lots next weekend."

"Hold up. Weren't you the one who said you weren't looking?" Evanston said.

They both burst out laughing. From there, they switched topics to cars, families, and jobs, but Darcelle was never far from Evanston's mind.

Hours later, after going back and forth with his friend about features, Evanston headed out. He wondered about Darcelle. Once he arrived home, he didn't go to bed right away. Instead, he slouched in a chair and got on social media to refresh his memory of her. He admired one photo and decided to save it as his phone's screensaver, then changed his mind. That might come across as too stalkerish, so he closed his phone and got ready for bed.

Sunday morning, he couldn't resist texting Darcelle as he sipped on his coffee.

Are you enjoying riding on the open road? Evan

Minutes later, she texted him back. **In church, Van. Call you later. :)**

I look forward to it, Cece.

Hmmm. Church was one topic they didn't cover. Evanston was a churchgoer, too, whenever he felt inspired or made the time. He didn't have a conviction for the same commitment as his parents. Whether he showed up at Healing Waters Flow Church or not, his mom always welcomed him for Sunday dinner.

He checked the time. Langston and Sheila attended the early service and should be home now. Evanston grabbed his car keys for an early visit to his parents' house.

While he drove, thoughts of Darcelle's smile as they ate breakfast flashed before his eyes. The woman he had first met had been transformed from helpless to powerful by the time they parted.

Not once did he feel he had to build a wall or guard his thoughts. That surprised him. After his breakup, he was wary of every woman's intentions, so he had trust issues about being played.

Why was his ex-girlfriend Phylicia occupying his mind when thoughts of Darcelle were more refreshing? He was minutes away from his destination when she called. Immediately, a smile stretched across his face.

"Hey, Van," she teased in a singsong manner.

"Well, good day to you, Cece. Sorry, I interrupted you in service. I played hooky today. Truth be told, last week too."

"I'm not the church police. My mother trapped me into a commitment when I showed off Vanessa yesterday. I lifted her spirits, and before I knew it, my sisters and I were coerced into going to church with her today. My sisters, niece, nephew, and Mama, rode with me."

"Who's Vanessa?"

"My car, silly." She *tee-hee*d. "She has to have a name to celebrate her birthdays."

Playful. He liked her personality. Darcelle's whimsy was contagious. He feigned a sniff. "My firstborn."

She laughed, and he enjoyed the carefree sound. He had no regrets, coming to her rescue the other day. "I'm almost at my parents' house now. I'm sure I'll get a recap of Pastor Howard's sermon when I get there, whether I ask for it or not. Parents. What would we do without them?"

"Yeah." Her voice faded.

Uh-oh. He kicked himself for triggering her sadness. How careless. Evanston didn't want her to retreat into the place where he had found her. "I'm sorry."

"It's okay. I guess it'll take some getting used to saying only my mother versus my parents. My world is forever changed—like in this simple conversation. Everything. We'll survive."

Evanston wanted to be part of the unofficial recovery team. "You will. So, are you calling me to cash in on our dinner date?"

"Maybe, and nope."

"It can't be both, Cece."

"I know you're probably spending Christmas with your family, but if you get a chance to stop by my mother's, you won't regret sampling her dressing. You'll get a chance to meet my sisters and JJ and Zuri."

"Oh, we're meeting the family already, are we?" Evanston couldn't stop himself from joking around. Still, a first impression mattered. "I'll make the time and leave room in my stomach." He patted his belly as if she could see him.

"Why not? We've stayed out all night," she sassed.

"I'll be there."

"Great." He imagined her eyes sparkling. "Thank you, Van. Then it's a date."

"Oh, no, it's not. A date is a dinner and movie—just us. How about this week? I promise to have you home by bedtime, and I'll even let you drag me to your last-minute Christmas shopping. I ain't scared of hostile shoppers," he volunteered, throwing caution to the wind. Dating was no longer something he felt like avoiding.

It was his mother who suggested he step back from dating. "You're hurting, and sometimes, hurting people lash out to hurt others. And I'm not just referring to physically, which I know isn't you, but I don't want to see another woman pay for your bad attitude," his mother had said one night about his indifference.

Sheila Giles was a wise woman. Evanston was glad he had taken her advice. He wouldn't have wanted to judge Darcelle based on trust issues he had from another woman.

Darcelle's sweet voice broke into his reverie. "I've already done my shopping online, but a midweek movie sounds nice."

"It does, and it'll be nice to see you and *Vanessa* again." They laughed and ended the call. Seconds later, he parked, then hiked the steps to his childhood home.

Before he inserted his key, his sister, Jessica, opened the door. Home from college for the holidays, she was quickly becoming the beauty he and his dad weren't ready for. Gone was the little girl with a couple of freckles whose brother would honorably fight her battles. Now, her beauty could cause a man to brake on the highway.

Darcelle had freckles too.

"Evan," Jessica screamed.

Evanston engulfed her in a hug that lifted her off the ground. She squirmed and shrieked. "Daddy, tell your son to put me down."

Casting an amused expression as Langston descended the stairs, their father waved at Evanston. "Carry on, son. I did the same thing when she walked through the door."

Sibling annoyances like old times.

His mother appeared from the kitchen. "Let go of her and give your mama a hug."

He did and smothered his mother with attention. They were soon at the dinner table enjoying a soul food meal while holding a lively discussion about professions. Out of nowhere, Jessica announced she had a new boyfriend and he would drive to St. Louis for Christmas. "I want you two to meet him." She eyed their parents.

"What about me?" Evanston patted his chest.

"Definitely not you." Jessica pointed with nails as long as claws. "You've scared away enough of my boyfriends, especially the one I really liked my sophomore year in high school."

Evanston *hmph*ed and scrunched his nose. "His hormones were in high gear. He was too touchy, in my opinion, and showed a lack of respect in front of me." A man had a God-given right to protect his family, like Darcelle's father.

The next day, from Monday morning to late afternoon, Evanston tackled the remaining hiccups with Cedric's website before he tagged along with his sister on her shopping bonanza. He would never let go of being the big brother, so his hidden agenda was to act as a bodyguard.

"So, who is she?"

Frowning, Evanston glanced at Jessica. "What do you mean?"

"Idiot, I'm your sister." She rested her hands on her hips and lifted her chin. She always reminded him of a little general when she discharged darts from her eyes. "I know you. You can't play me."

"But it's so much fun to get you riled up." He grinned and ignored her question as he walked ahead.

"Come on, Evan." She stomped her heel. "You're looking at too much girlie stuff for me. Are you dating again?" On the surface, Jessica was sweet like a cuddly toy poodle until crossed, then she became scary as she transformed into a Pitbull with an intimidating bark. "I need to inspect her because nobody's going to mess over my brother. I'll hurt her." She emphasized each word.

"Calm down, Catwoman. Right now, she's a special friend. She invited me to Christmas dinner, and Mama says never go to anyone's house empty-handed, so I'm not."

"I also saw you looking at toys." Jessica rolled her eyes. "How many kids?"

"Two. Jackson and Zuri—not hers. They're her nephew and niece. You know, for children, Christmas is all about the toys."

"Don't let Mama hear you say that. Christmas is for Christ. They made sure we knew the toys came from them."

The siblings entered another store, and a stuffed animal caught his eye. Did a four-year-old still play with stuffed animals? "Christmas is going to be tough for Darcelle because her father died last month, which is how I met her." Evanston gave Jessica a recap.

"Oh, no." She patted her chest. Compassion filled her face. "I can't imagine life without Daddy, you, and Mama. Well, what are we waiting for? Let's find the perfect gifts. You've got your credit cards, right?"

"Oh, boy." Both of them were suckers for children, which they hoped to have after they were married. Evanston couldn't imagine her sister being a wife—too bossy.

Wednesday afternoon, Evanston stood in the lobby of a movie theater, waiting for Darcelle. When a maroon—or rather as she called it cranberry—Buick cruised down an aisle, he took swift steps toward it. When Darcelle stepped out, he was there and, without regard, he swept her into his arms. Darcelle didn't protest, but participated in the hug.

"Ahh. Refreshing as a cup of hot chocolate."

She elbowed him, stepped back and giggled. "How did you know I needed that?"

"The joke or the hug?"

"Hmm." She twisted her lips as if she was deep in thought. "Both."

"Ahh." Evanston grinned as he bobbed his head in agreement. "Because I wanted that, too, and we haven't seen each other since the first time we saw each other."

Darcelle roared. "I like that about you—us. It's not awkward."

"Never. Come on. It's cold out here." He guided her inside and handed over their tickets. Next, she made a beeline to the concession counter. "Did you forget we're having dinner after this?"

"Nope, but who goes to the movies without feasting on a hot dog, buttery popcorn, and soda? Come on. Who does that?" she challenged with a fist propped on her hip, showcasing her figure in skinny jeans.

Evanston held up both hands. "Ah, ah…me."

"Then take notes, Van. I'll treat since you're springing for dinner."

Although her sassy attitude was attractive, Evanston wasn't having it. "When a man asks a lady out on a date, he treats. I don't care where and what it is. Don't insult me, Cece, with this 'I pay, you pay' stuff." He softened his tone, reminding himself this wasn't Jessica he was scolding.

"Sorry, Van. I don't expect much on dates." She shrugged and unbuttoned her coat.

"Then, you've been going out with the wrong men."

Tilting her head, she seemed to study him. "Okay. You brought your credit card?"

What was it with women and plastic? But Darcelle was a tease. In the theater, he munched on her supersized box of popcorn. When she pretended like she was about to protest, he defended himself. "Hey, I didn't want you to eat all of this by yourself."

Darcelle swatted his hand away. "Aren't you going to ruin your *dinner* appetite?"

For the first time, Evanston noticed the seduction in her eyes as she baited him. "I'm saving you from ruining yours."

She conceded, and they finished the box together. As he escorted her back to the car, he asked. "So, what's the difference between going out on dates and dating?"

"You tell me." Evanston opened her door and waited as she slid in and started the engine. "A pop quiz. Have your answer, Cece, by the time I meet you at Tucanos."

Chapter Five

"Christmas won't be the same this year." Nellie shook her head as she arranged the place settings on the table minus one. Even with all the decorations from room to room, festive music in the background, and the table dressed worthy of a photoshoot, there was a missing piece.

At church for the annual Christmas morning service, the men's choir seemed off-key without Harold Price leading a solo. Different.

"Not just Christmas, but life." Darcelle spied the empty chair at the head of the table reserved for her father. She exhaled slowly to control the tears that threatened to spill. Not good.

"At least Harold didn't leave me alone. My girls and grandbabies were his gifts." Nellie forced a smile but slumped and gripped the back of the chair.

Darcelle gave her mother a moment to herself. It was tradition for the Prices to donate coats at homeless shelters, visit the elderly in hospitals, and donate to food pantries.

They did all of this in the spirit of their Savior Jesus Christ during Christmas. This year, they weren't feeling it as they went through the motions.

"And we're here for you, Mama," Monique said, coming into the dining room and wrapping her arms around their mother's shoulders.

Darcelle nodded in agreement. While Christmas meant the celebration of Jesus' birthday, their reality was mourning the memory of a good man.

In front of the children, the adults kept up the pretense of jubilation, but there was no doubt about the void of the patriarch's larger-than-life presence.

The doorbell rang as they were about to sit at the table. Darcelle's heart rate spiked.

Evanston. He came.

"I'll get it." She hurried to the door. Her spirits lifted when she opened it, and he stood on her porch with a stack of gifts against the backdrop of houses decked out with clear or white lights. It was a snapshot for a postcard. His arms begged for assistance. "You came...and with all this?"

"Don't be a Doubting Darcelle. Merry Christmas, Cece."

She lightened his load by taking a few gifts and stepped back. He was so handsome in a knit cap and jacket. This was her third time seeing him, and she was never disappointed with what she saw.

"Merry Christmas to you, Van."

She hid her amusement when he glanced up at the doorframe and mumbled, no mistletoe.

"Nana," Zuri screamed for Darcelle's mother to come. When she appeared, Zuri pointed. "He's got presents." Her niece's eyes were wide with excitement, and she jumped from one foot to the other.

Her nephew seemed just as impressed but stared with curiosity. With a hide-and-seek father, JJ was leery of adult males.

Her sisters appeared to investigate the ruckus as Darcelle guided her guest into the living room.

"Mom, Val, and Moni, this is Evan. He's the one who helped me pick out my car."

The enlightenment on her mother's face brightened. "Oh, bless you. Merry Christmas. It's so nice to meet you. I'm glad you're joining us for dinner." Ushering everyone in the dining room, Nellie gestured for Evanston to sit in Harold's chair.

Darcelle exchanged shocked glances with her sisters.

"Merry Christmas to all," he said in a deep voice with mischief in his eyes.

"Mama, is he Santa Claus?" Zuri asked.

Nellie didn't give Valencia a chance to answer her daughter. "No, baby. Christmas is about Jesus' birth. He gives the best gifts, not a man dressed up and called Santa Claus."

Zuri frowned. "But he's not Jesus, and he has gifts."

The adults chuckled at Zuri's innocence as Evanston fumbled through the boxes and found a gift for her. "You're ZZ, right?"

"He knows my name." Her eyes widened with amazement. Awe was all over her face. Her niece was about to dash off until Valencia reminded her what she should say for the present.

"Thank you." Zuri hugged him as a bonus.

The gesture made Evanston blush. JJ's gift followed, and her nephew thanked him with a handshake, which Evanston encouraged. The boy tried to hide his excitement, but his eyes gave him away.

It was love at first sight for Zuri as she unwrapped her gift to see a plush furry stuffed animal. Her niece bestowed Evanston with another hug.

JJ's face lit up, too, with awe after he unwrapped his present, a marble maze game. "Wow."

Monique and Valencia were just as surprised as Darcelle when Evanston handed them gift cards.

Wow was right. If falling in love was easy, Darcelle was a goner. Evanston was handsome, kind, generous, and chivalrous. *What woman let this treasure slip through her hands?* Darcelle wondered. A guy like him didn't remain single unless he had some serious flaws.

The truth was, Darcelle hadn't thought about a relationship. It had been a while since a decent guy came along. One gift remained.

"My sister says a woman prefers money," Evanston explained as if he owed anyone an explanation. "And Jess had a ball spending plenty of mine."

Valencia choked out her thanks. Darcelle tried not to sniff. Her big sister rarely dated because of the children, so it had been forever since she had attention lavished on her.

"Your sister is a woman after my own heart. Thanks, Evanston." Monique grinned. Her younger sister could be a shoo-in for a model—her curves attracted her choice of male suitors. Monique turned down most of them.

"Now, Mrs. Price, this is for you." He stood and presented a square gift box. Her mother's eyes misted before tears spilled over.

Darcelle dabbed at hers too. She was glad he had remembered her mom, who needed extra doting.

Now all the gifts were accounted for. Evanston had already given Darcelle the best present in the world. He stood in the gap for her father when she purchased the crossover.

Her mother's hands shook as she lifted the lid off the box and gasped. "You're an angel. Why, thank you, Evanston, for your generosity to my family."

"Please call me Evan. Almost everyone does." He winked at Darcelle. "I know you probably have pearls, but I know my mother loves them."

Speechless at first, Nellie choked as she eyed her daughters. "Harold gave me a pair similar to these on our fifth wedding anniversary, but my grandbaby played with them. I never got them restrung after she brought me the pearls in her fist."

Nellie's embrace confirmed Evanston had won her over. He seemed embarrassed by the attention, and Darcelle giggled and mouthed, *You did good.*

Zuri patted Evanston's leg. "What about Aunt DeeDee?"

"Hush, chile," Nellie reprimanded her granddaughter while Valencia sent a warning look that made the girl pout.

"I didn't forget your auntie." Evanston gave Zuri a sympathetic expression as he reached in his pocket and pulled out a small box. He took calculated steps toward her. Darcelle couldn't retreat as Evanston's eyes pulled her to his, and he handed it to her. "Last, but not the least. My favorite."

Lowering her lashes, Darcelle was speechless. She had finished her shopping online and hadn't thought about any more gifts. "I...*ah*... I didn't know you..." she was stumbling over her words as her family watched.

"Saying thank you is priceless, Miss Price." His eyes danced with mischief. "It's for Vanessa." His teasing voice was soft as a coo to a baby.

"Who's Vanessa?" her mother demanded, and her sisters echoed, not seeing the humor.

"Yeah." Valencia stepped forward. Gone was her earlier admiration as her nostrils flared, and she planted a fist on her hip. "I'll cut you with your gift card."

"*Uh-uh.* Not me." Monique folded her arms. "I'm not giving mine back, but I'll give him a beatdown with my three-inch boots."

"Explain yourself, young man." Nellie squinted as her chest heaved.

Opening the box, Darcelle admired the star-shaped glass keychain with Vanessa emblazoned on a gold plate in the center. Cute. She snickered as she attempted to keep a straight face and played along.

Faking an insult, Darcelle put Evanston on the hot seat. "Yeah, who's Vanessa?" She tried not to laugh, but a fit spilled out, and Evanston joined her, keeping her family in a frenzy.

"I don't see anything funny about giving a woman another woman's gift. Now, what is going on?" Nellie raised her voice, forcing Darcelle to stop mid-chuckle.

"Mama," she reached for her hand and squeezed it, "Vanessa is the name I gave my new car."

The exhales in the room were thick as her family fussed and wagged their fingers at her and Evanston.

Somehow, this was going to be the best Christmas ever; Darcelle's jaws ached from laughing so hard, which reminded her of the song "Joy to the World." Even without her daddy, Jesus had brought joy to their house. "O-okay, okay, everyone. Evan started it. I was only his accomplice. Come on. We've all worked up an appetite. Let's eat."

After second helpings, Evanston patted his stomach. The savory meal was the culprit behind his discomfort, almost to the point of misery. Despite a hearty appetite, two Christmas dinners in one day were pushing it, he realized as he scooted back. "You ladies can cook."

Darcelle's family smiled at his compliments. As if on cue, her sisters and mother began to clear the table, leaving him alone with Darcelle.

"Evan, I was expecting you, not all the gifts you brought. Thank you doesn't seem like enough." She choked. "I know Christmas is more than giving and receiving gifts. Your presence tonight reminded me of the spirit of Christmas. The joy, the peace, goodwill, and all the things I was taught in church. Thank God, and thank you."

Her heartfelt words filled him with contentment. Evanston had to glance away to keep from becoming sentimental. Once he commanded his composure, Evanston cataloged her features: pouty lips, three freckles on the left side of her nose, delicate chin, and lashes that God gave her.

Evanston was glad he could be honest with what he felt. "I wasn't expecting to meet you either, so surprises can be a good thing." He stood. "Come on, Cece, walk me to the door."

"You two with the nicknames." Mrs. Price overheard him as she returned to the dining room.

He liked the Prices. The petite women were welcoming, as were the children who preferred to be called by their initials: little JJ and ZZ. Darcelle said she hadn't given him a Christmas present, but she had. Without knowing it, she had unlocked his heart with a yearning for possibilities. It was as if they were destined to be at that car lot on that exact day and time.

Darcelle reached for her coat and stepped outside with him. "Van...thank you for coming. You made our Christmas amazing." Tears filled her eyes, displaying her sincerity.

He swallowed. He had seen her sadness, and they weren't going there. Evanston took her hands and squeezed them. "The best part of Christmas is meeting you." He stared into her eyes, wishing for a mistletoe. "Do you know your eyes sparkle brighter than the Christmas lights on the houses around us?"

"Stop flirting with me." She grinned.

"Never." Evanston blinked when flurries landed on her lashes first, then his. "Merry Christmas, and I'm feeling really confident about a happy new year." He couldn't help humming the melody to "This Christmas."

"Me too. Good night." Darcelle stepped back inside, leaving Evanston eager about what the next months would bring.

Chapter Six

*E*vanston Giles—whew—he had a contagious smile, hot looks, and charisma that had lured the Prices into his fan club, Darcelle being the head cheerleader.

Sometimes people come into your life for a reason, Darcelle mused as she watched Evanston drive off. Her mother would counter, "God orders our steps."

Thanks to Evanston, the "This Christmas" melody danced in her head, so Darcelle sang the lyrics and, at the precise times, mimicked the drums and sleigh bells.

This Christmas dinner, the first one without her father, would be unforgettable in so many ways. The level of her attraction to Evanston was unmatchable. She didn't want to overthink it, but he was the type of man she could fall hard for.

"If that man asks you to marry him, say yes so I can start planning a wedding," her mother said later as the adults sat around the fireplace.

"Mama, let us be friends first." Darcelle didn't mind taking it one step at a time with Evanston. He might turn out to be a felon—or worst. She doubted that.

"Thank you, Evan," Monique said out of nowhere. "Now I know what type of man I want. He showed up tonight and showed out. I'm with Mama: He's the one." She and Valencia exchanged a high five. Her mother stood to get hers, and Darcelle joined them.

"Convincing Zuri Evan wasn't Santa Claus is going to take a couple of days," Valencia said with a side-eye to their mother. They were all spending the night. With daddy gone, their mother shouldn't be alone.

Darcelle wished her father was there so he could meet Evanston. Maybe she should have told him to call her when he made it home. No. That would be too eager.

Hours later, while everyone slept, Darcelle pulled out her tablet to shop online. The plethora of gift ideas for Evanston overwhelmed her. After a while perusing, she decided on an illusion lamp and hoped he had a man cave to find a spot for it.

Before climbing in bed, she whispered her prayers, giving thanks for a good Christmas despite the Prices' loss. Darcelle drifted off to sleep and didn't wake until late Sunday. She reached for her keychain from Evan, the evidence that last night wasn't a dream. Without getting out of bed, she called him. He sounded knocked out.

"Sorry to wake you. Call me when you're up."

"I'm awake," he argued with a voice thick with sleep.

"Liar." She laughed and stared at the ceiling as if it was about to show a replay of yesterday. "But I think it's sweet."

"Brownie point."

"Please, you've got so many brownie points, you can open your own bakery. You upped me last night with your gifts." She snuggled under her cover despite the aroma of biscuits and coffee, making her way up to Monique's loft. "Why aren't you taken? Are you scared of commitment?"

"Nope. I haven't found the perfect one for me."

Hmmm. "What does 'perfect' look like to you?"

The woman he described sounded like her. Really? Darcelle's heart pounded. "Van, I like you, too, but don't play with my emotions. We met barely a week and a half ago, and I'm perfect for you? I'm not buying that."

"A person knows perfection after they've seen imperfection."

His sincerity was making her wonder if she was, indeed, dreaming. "What imperfection are you talking about?"

"No one wants to talk about past regrets."

"If it helps to understand a person, it's worth sharing—please."

Evanston sighed, then explained. "My last serious relationship ended badly. My ego was bruised, which left me bitter. I went through the motions of going out on dates, but I had nothing to give. No, to be honest..." He was silent so long, Darcelle wondered if he was going to answer, so she pressed him.

"Van, tell me." She tried again to coax him.

"I didn't want to give to or invest in another relationship. I felt numb, void of emotions, no desire for companionship—nothing."

Darcelle didn't believe it and was ready to call him a liar. Instead, she sweetened her reply. "That's not the man I met in the parking lot."

"You chased him away." She could hear a smile tugging at his lips. "You swept into my life and recalibrated me, like that." He snapped his fingers. "Christmas dinner was an eye-opener to me that I don't have to chase happiness. She was waiting for me at the dealership. I want us to keep seeing each other after the holidays. I think we can prove we could be more than friends."

This man was voicing some of the things she'd had thought last night. If Darcelle's feelings got in too deep, she would be crushed if things between them turned out not to be true. "I would like that, too, but it's got to be at a slower pace. I'm not a little girl who believes in fairytales," she warned him.

"Understood, so… besides your past boyfriends not making the cut with your dad, why are you still single, Cece?"

She liked it when he called her the nickname. "I haven't been picked in the 'girlfriend' material lineup. The competition is fierce in the dating world, so I refuse to audition for a man's attention. Do I get lonely? Yes, but that's when my sisters and I do things together. Plus, I stay busy outside of work through community involvement with teenage girls. I go to church—not every Sunday, but I go. I guess to be seen and inspired until I go again. And I also visit my best friend, Shana, in Texas."

They had spoken on the phone before, but never about anything as personal as relationships. "Thank you for sharing that with me." She changed the subject to something more upbeat. "I ordered your post-Christmas gift. It will be here in two days."

"You what? Cece, you didn't have to."

She grinned, feeling she had upped him for a change. "I wanted to. Since I'm off this week, I'd like to treat you to lunch when your gift comes in."

"Woman, you're too much." He chuckled. "I'd be honored for the gorgeous Darcelle "Cece" Price to shower me with a sandwich for an hour. Too bad our vacation schedules didn't line up on the same week, so we could do more together. "

"You're silly."

"But I can be that way with you. I'm looking forward to it."

When their call ended, Darcelle reflected on their conversation. There was no glimpse of the man Evanston had described to her. It was a completely opposite personality. Suddenly, she could hear Shana in her ear.

"Enjoy the ride. Go with the flow until red flags appear," her friend would say.

After the call, Darcelle performed her morning regimen, then joined her family downstairs, where praises and questions about Evanston were non-stop during brunch.

Everything they said about him was accurate. Evanston possessed a charming personality. His handsomeness was so intoxicating any woman would backtrack for a second assessment.

That day at the dealership, Darcelle had been too dazed to focus on his features. Not anymore. She had started to notice everything about him in his presence. Each time she heard his voice, she smiled. His eyes were expressive—they teased her, showed compassion, seriousness, and at all times, his attraction was there. Could he see and hear her heartbeat? Darcelle was attracted to his essence and would always make time for him.

On her way back to her apartment, she called Shana to give her a recap of Christmas dinner. "So, what do you think? Is this moving too fast?"

"If you weren't my friend, I'd be jealous, then I'd have to repent." Shana snickered. "Evanston Giles might be the real deal, but a temptation waiting to happen. Sunday's sermon was on watching out for the devil's devices and praying for God's strength to overcome them."

"You know that's deeper than I wanted you to go."

Shana was never preachy or offensive when she offered advice. She always said everything had a spiritual and physical implication.

Whatever. "Evan told you he's been hurt before, so he knows first-hand the heartache. Proceed with caution. Watch your emotions. I don't want to see you get hurt."

"Me neither, but…" She stopped at a light and drummed her fingers against the wheel until the light turned green. "I've never dated a man who I could say I was friends with first—you know, the whole 'friends to lovers' thing. I always felt when meeting a guy, I needed to be seen in my best light. With him, he's seen me at my lowest and still likes me."

"You deserve the best. I'll be watching him from afar. If Evan turns out to be the real deal, I'm praying that the Lord will give me a godly version, who goes to church, for my next Christmas present."

"Evan goes to church," Darcelle defended.

"So do the devil and politicians—and some of them refused to be converted."

Evanston called, giving Shana the last word. "Tell Evan I said hi, and I'll be stalking—I mean watching—him on social media. I strongly suggest he accept my friend request. Bye."

Chapter Seven

*D*arcelle spent her end-of-the-year vacation cleaning her apartment and with her niece and nephew both of who asked, more than once, if Mr. Evan was coming to visit. Of their many gifts, they were attached to the ones Evanston had given them.

Tracking the gift she'd purchased for him, Darcelle met the delivery driver at the door giddy. She couldn't wait for him to open it and called him. "Your gift came. Can you do lunch?"

There was a pause. "I'm working on a project with another coworker. How about a late lunch like one-thirtyish."

"I'll be there at one-twenty-ish," she countered with a tease.

"Even better. You and Vanessa drive safe."

"We will."

As if she had a cake baking in the oven, Darcelle watched the clock and danced in place when it was time for her to get ready. She dressed to flatter him—from her flawless makeup to her favorite black turtleneck sweater and jeans. She had brushed her curls, then set off for Evanston's job in downtown St. Louis among the older high-risers.

Darcelle worked in the opposite direction in downtown Clayton, less than five miles outside the city limits. From her apartment, it was a smooth twenty-minute drive to his building. She was about to double park, which was the norm on Washington Avenue when Evanston strolled out of the entrance with another Black guy who was as built as him. The pair dominated the attention of admirers in their path. Fierce. Strong. Black. *Whew.*

She watched Evanston's face light up when he saw her Buick. He waved and motioned for his friend to follow him. She lowered the passenger window when he drew near and leaned inside. "Hey, stranger. Need a lift?"

One thing she enjoyed was the carefree teases between them. Evanston's sense of humor was contagious.

"If you're my food truck." He looked at her, making her wonder if he was admiring the extra effort she put into appearance for their lunch.

His buddy cleared his throat, and Evanston seemed to snap out of a trance and glance over his shoulder, then back at her. His mischief was unmistakable. "Lester, meet Vanessa and Darcelle."

His friend craned his neck toward the backseat. "Ah, unless I'm blind, I only see one person."

Evanston stepped back and patted the hood. "This is Vanessa, my firstborn, named after me. The chauffeur is the lovely Darcelle Price."

"You named a car?" Lester's expression was priceless when he looked at Evanston.

"She did." Evanston pointed to her.

"Right. We'll talk about your offspring after lunch. It's very nice meeting you, Darcelle." Lester walked away.

Evanston snickered as he climbed into the passenger seat and strapped in. The smell of the new vehicle's interior and her fruity perfume tickled his nose as he grinned at her. "So, where are we going?"

"Surprise." She batted her lashes, checked her rearview mirror, then took off.

"So a kidnapping is underway. I'll play along." Evanston closed his eyes and inhaled. "I never can get enough of smelling the inside of a new car."

When she exited on the highway, he opened his eyes with a questioning look. "Seriously, I'm taking an extended lunch, but not enough time for a road trip."

She giggled. "We're going to Clayton—fifteen minutes. There's a Crushed Red not far from the brokerage firm where I work. I love their salads and hoped you might enjoy their cowpoke salad, which has crazy helpings of steak strips in it."

He bobbed his head. "It's all about the meat."

They arrived and parked. Evanston insisted she wait until he stepped out, then helped her. They shared a smile as they continued inside. Taking her advice, he ordered the cowpoke salad without scanning the menu for other options, while she ordered her usual farmer's market salad.

A man who trusts me. The gesture was comforting,

At the register, Evanston was faster handing over his credit card than Darcelle. She shoved him. "I told you it was my treat."

"And my treat is lunch with you." Evanston's demeanor hinted at his deeper attraction.

It was the first time Darcelle remembered blushing. Once they were seated, she handed him her gift, which she pulled out of her oversized tote bag. He acted like he hadn't noticed the present before they blessed their meal.

Evanston opened the box with gusto, shaking his head. "I wasn't expecting anything in return except your smile. I told you not to," he softly scolded.

"Good thing you're not the boss of me." She lifted her chin.

"Never." They both sucked in their breaths when he pulled the lamp out of the shipping box.

"I figured a person could never have too many night lights," she added.

He reached across the table and covered her hand as their salads arrived. "Thank you. I love it."

Darcelle beamed. "My mission is accomplished."

Unlike sharing breakfast, Evanston was possessive of his salad when she hinted she was about to help herself. "*Uh-huh*. I'll buy you one to go. This salad right here…" He pointed to it with his fork. "Is not up for negotiation."

Evanston strolled back into his office with minutes to spare. As he shook off his jacket and placed his gift box on the desk, Lester twirled around in his chair. A small aisle separated their cubicles.

He smirked and glanced at the time. "I'm surprised you returned. How was 'lunch?'" Lester made air quotation marks with his fingers. "You lookin' too goofy for me." He rocked back before he crossed one ankle over a knee as if they had time to chat.

They didn't; with a meeting in twenty minutes to brief the department heads about the scheduled tests following the installments of the new software.

"Jealous? The food was good, my dining companion beautiful, and her Christmas gift thoughtful. What more can a man ask for? Now, I have enough energy to work overtime this evening."

"Man, you're creating visuals in my head." Lester squinted. "I've never seen you this excited over a woman. Even when you were with Phylicia. I hope this chick—"

"Her name is Darcelle, remember?" he said with an edge to his voice.

Lester held up his hands in surrender. "Whoa. I stand corrected. I hope Miss Darcelle is what you're looking for."

He and Lester were more than coworkers. Evanston considered him a friend. His idea of a relationship was short and sweet. Completely opposite of what Evanston wanted to explore with Darcelle.

"I have plans to find out." He nodded. Darcelle wanted to take it slow. How could he when his heart was kicking in high gear and running red lights?

Chapter Eight

*H*ow you spend your New Year could determine how you face challenges in the upcoming year, Darcelle's mother had often said when she was old enough to date.

Her mother was probably right. Sometimes Darcelle was convicted of being in attendance at the watch night service at church on the last day of the year. Not this time. Her father's death was still too raw, and she had attended the New Year's Eve service. Nothing could have braced her for that.

This would be a New Year's Eve she hadn't experienced in a long time. What would a relationship look like with Evanston, say, next year? Maybe, if he would have suggested it, she would have, but he was too busy working overtime in preparation to take a new system live come January first.

Mid-week, Darcelle had prepared a box lunch for him and dropped it off. The adoration in his eyes melted her heart. She liked him.

Evanston suggested a low-key evening watching movies. He boasted of his cooking skills, but she heard the tiredness in his voice, so she told him to order wings. She offered to whip up her homemade dips—cheesy bacon spinach and artichoke.

Shana Facetimed her while she was preparing it. "What are you and Evan up to tonight?"

"A quiet evening at his place." Darcelle lifted a bowl. "I'm making dip now. I would rather have gone out, but this thing between Van and me is evolving, so I'm curious what a relationship with him would look like in a month. Will it be there, say, in six months? What about a year?"

"Ooh, you're calculating a long term formula on the pathway to becoming a wife and mother. Be careful." Shana gulped from a water bottle. "Men don't use that much brainpower to think that far in advance. They think they have all the time in the world to settle down." Her friend was on a roll. With both of them in their early thirties, they knew there was plenty of competition for good—or bad—men. "Which is why some date several women at one time, so dating doesn't necessarily mean commitment."

Darcelle tapped the bowl to loosen the dip off the spoon, then licked it before tossing it in the sink. "I don't want to stress myself out by asking him to define our relationship. Right now, I won't question whatever we have and see if he wants more."

"Don't forget, you've got to make a decision if you want more than he's not willing to give. Remember, we have too much going for us to compromise. Some girlfriends and I are going to a New Year's Eve party sponsored by our local radio station, but I'm leaving in time to get to church and pray in the new year."

"Double-dipping as Mama would say. Have fun, and put in a few dance steps for me."

"And prayers, too. Hey, we're single, so we have to mingle, but I do represent Christ when I go somewhere. All the ladies don't have dance partners like you." Shana giggled. "Bye."

This wasn't the New Year's Eve Evanston had envisioned with Darcelle, but he was too exhausted to muster the energy to be entertaining.

At the beginning of December, he knew his department had to install the new computer system, and the testing would require long hours weeks before the launch. It was no sweat then. Fast forward two weeks, and things had changed. He liked Darcelle and wanted to get to know her. Although they were doing things backward—meeting the family first. Who does that? Apparently, he did.

She was making a believer out of him that good women, who weren't looking for the trappings that money in a man's wallet could buy, still existed.

Evanston pulled his mind back from his musings so he could leave the bank by seven. That didn't happen when he and Lester had encountered a security risk with the final system installation.

They groaned as Evanston noted the time. He had plans, but he hadn't gotten promotions on his job without his commitment to perfection. "Okay. Back to square one."

"Unfortunately." Lester rubbed his head as his stomach growled. "This is not my idea of ringing in the new year."

"Mine either. Darcelle is coming over."

"Don't rub it in," Lester snapped as they performed another battery of tests without much success before they called it a night.

It was after ten when Evanston walked through his door with his carryout order of wings, chips, pasta, and drinks. He had time to shower, change, and straighten up the kitchen.

The shower and shave were refreshing. He had ten minutes to spare before Darcelle arrived.

When his doorbell rang, Evanston checked his appearance, slipped his feet into his slippers, and headed for the door while surveying his house—clean, fresh and cozy, according to his mother whom he had given full reign with the decorations.

"Hey. You look beautiful." He relieved her of her load as she stepped inside. "You smell sweet." His nostrils flared in appreciation.

"Nope." Her eyes sparkled. "It's my spinach dip."

"I know the difference between a sweet perfume and food." His eyes stared into hers.

"Stop flirting with me, Van." It was a weak protest as she blushed.

"Not going to happen." Evanston closed the door." His Cece was gorgeous, and he felt a sense of contentment he was ending this year in the company of a beauty.

"Okay." She lowered her eyes, then looked at him. "I like your flirting."

"Whew." He had to exhale to tame his hormones. Evanston wasn't the type of man to tell a woman, "nothing is going to happen unless you want to, and then seduce her to consent to wanting more." Nope, that wasn't his character. The physical attraction was there, but he wanted more—a heart-to-heart connection. He cleared his throat and led the way to his kitchen.

"You have a nice place—and very tidy. Give me a tour?"

"Thanks. As the only child for sixteen years, I was spared no chores in the Giles household. When my sister came along, my parents had slacked off." Although he would have preferred a brother, he learned how to treat a lady because of his love for Jessica.

"This is the kitchen." He set her dishes on the counter and pointed. "That is my living room-slash-man cave. The other rooms are off-limits."

Tilting her head, she studied his expression. "A man of honor. Thank you."

"I want to think I am, but these are the only two rooms that are clean enough for entertaining."

She laughed and elbowed in the side. "Honor and honesty. You're a keeper."

He stifled a yawn before he had a comeback. The rejuvenating shower was wearing off.

"You need your rest." Darcelle looked concerned. "We could have done something tomorrow."

Evanston wasn't having it. "No way. I've done the ringing in the year thing alone. After meeting you, I don't want to do that this time." She nodded, and he squeezed her hand. "Once I get some food in me, I promise not to fall asleep on my guest. You're my energy drink."

Darcelle looked pleased. "Well, the old year is running out, so let's fix our plates and relax."

With samples of their party food on their plates, Darcelle snuggled closer to him on the sofa.

He brushed a kiss on her forehead as if it was the norm. Next, he stole a chip from her plate and scooped up some spinach dip. The flavor popped in his mouth, so he smacked his lips. "Tasty."

"Hey, you have your own plate." She faked a frown.

"And your point is?"

"Don't give me that adorable little-boy smile," she fussed, but a smile teased her lips. "I forgot how much you eat. You practically snatched the waffles off my plate the first night we met."

"What? You got that story wrong, woman. You were eying mine." Evanston cleaned his plate, then relaxed his arm around her shoulder and pulled her closer.

Darcelle picked the movie *My Other Mother*, a Black drama starring Jasmine Guy, Lynn Whitfield, and Essence Atkins, saying she'd wanted to see it, then she immersed herself in the plot. It was somewhat interesting. He preferred to study her expressions.

"Hold on." He paused the flick in time to watch the ball drop from Madison Square Garden.

"You know, Candy's love interest reminds me of you," she said, referring to Essence Atkins' character's long-time manager.

"Me?" Not only was there no resemblance between Kendrick Cross and Evanston, but he wouldn't hide his attraction for years like Kendrick did. "How?"

"Well," she said, shoving him. "He knows her, he has her back, and without saying it, he loves her," Darcelle summarized as the New Year's countdown started. "You had my back at the dealership, expecting nothing in return, and since then, you still have my back."

"I do." He leaned closer and captured her lips in a slow kiss as the crowd shouted, "three, two, one."

64

Chapter Nine

"Let me say, we kissed into the new year," Darcelle confessed the next morning to Shana as she closed her eyes to relive the moment. "Where has he been all my life?" She didn't expect an answer. It didn't matter. He was there now. "I stayed to watch another movie. Afterward, he trailed me to my apartment to make sure I got home safe."

"Lord, help me to hold out for the one You have for me."

Darcelle giggled. "I didn't pray for him, but—"

"Well, I've asked Jesus for a special someone, so hand him over." She paused. "On second thought—Nah. I'm looking for conviction and commitment to God. I'll wait, but if Evan has a play brother, distant cousin, or best friend who sounds like a candidate, I expect a phone call." Shana was serious.

"Will do. So, what about you? Meet anyone interesting last night, either at the party or church? I know your preference is a churchman."

"Correction—a godly man, there is a big difference, but the answer is no to both. I caught the tail end to the message 'Stop Playing Hide-and-seek with Jesus. Stop seeking the Lord only when something is wrong in our lives and hiding from Him when we're doing our own thing."

Hide-and-seek? Darcelle didn't get a chance to ask for a recap out of curiosity because Shana was on a roll. "There were a few interesting gentlemen at the party, but no one memorable. I was glad I didn't stay until midnight."

Shana had struck out while Darcelle sealed the New Year with the sweetest kiss she had ever experienced. Darcelle smiled. Last night—or early this morning—when Evanston returned her call, they talked for more than an hour. She was loving her new year already.

"So, how are you and Evan doing today?" Shana broke into her reverie.

"Ah...he and his dad are watching football. His sister's boyfriend is in town, so he thought if I came, I can even off the team."

Shana laughed. "Are you ready for that?"

"No, and I'm nervous. We both talked about our families, but as the only son, he could be a Mama's boy, and I might not pass the scrutiny."

"Like daddies size up our boyfriends. Darcie, be yourself. You're smart, pretty, and confident. If you get the wrong vibes, don't waste time trying to impress them."

"You're right." Darcelle walked back into her closet, eyed her wardrobe selection, and changed. "Let me go. I'm stopping by mom's before I meet him at his parents'."

A half an hour later, Darcelle strolled into her mother's house, jiggling her keys on the key ring Evanston had given her. Now, she could take a part of him wherever she went.

"Happy New Year, Mom. Where is everyone?" The house was spotless and quiet. She spied the living room where boxes were stacked, waiting for the holiday decorations to be tucked until the end of the year.

Nellie appeared out of the kitchen, drying her hands. "Valencia's on her way over with my grandbabies. Come on back. I made sandwiches and a fruit tray. Monique is upstairs asleep. She didn't get home until almost four." Her mother shook her head. "She's grown and pays rent, so nothing I can do but pray."

Darcelle kissed her cheek. "We can never get too many prayers, Mama."

"You all missed a good sermon last night. 'Playtime is Over. Seek the Lord While He Can Be Found.' I was hoping you and Evan would have surprised me and Jesus with a visit." She chuckled.

Hide-and-Seek. Darcelle froze. Was it a coincidence two pastors in different cities had similar messages? "Maybe, next time," she said, reaching for a couple of dollar roll sandwiches, even though she would eat at the Giles. "Evan and I were together—we weren't drinking—" she was quick to add. "We stayed in and watched a couple of movies."

"I like that young man." Nellie smiled, then in the same breath, seemed sad. "I wish both of you had a desire to come to church on your own."

"We do. Van was tired to go from working long hours, but he trailed me to make sure I got home okay."

"A gentleman. Hopefully, he'll ask you to marry him, then I'll get more grandbabies." Her face glowed with happiness.

"Mom, we're so not there yet." She almost let it slip they had shared their first kiss to ring in the New Year.

The lock to the front door turned, and her niece and nephew's voices grew louder.

"Grandma. Aunt DeeDee." Zuri ran full speed toward her while JJ trailed with a slow gait like his father. Valencia brought up the rear and hugged her.

"Happy New Year, sis."

"Yeah, maybe one year," Valencia mumbled under her breath, causing Darcelle to frown.

"Is everything okay?" she asked while their mother was distracted with the grandchildren.

She took a deep breath. "Yeah. I should have gone to church with Mama last night. I needed mental strength when I scrolled through Facebook and stared Jackson posing with his fiancée." She stifled a sniff. "That hurt. Not that I wanted to marry the bum, but why couldn't I find love first? Petty, I know…"

It pained Darcelle that her big sister had fallen for the wrong man. At one time, Jackson Sr. had been the love of Valencia's life. She'd had Jackson Jr., and Zuri was born three years later. Harold Price had had a long talk with Valencia about being under the influence of bad choices before vowing to hunt Jackson down.

Valencia's heartache was real as she struggled with finances, desired a social life, and was a single parent. Darcelle did all she could to ease Valencia's financial burden and babysat, so she could have some quiet time and give their mom a break. Very seldom did her sister complain, and now Darcelle felt guilty being on the verge of her happiness.

Only Monique had a consistent social calendar. She made her appearance, stretching and yawning, then slung one arm over Valencia's shoulder and the other over Darcelle's for a loose hug.

"Happy New Year to you." Valencia changed her tone to mask her hurt as she greeted the baby girl in the family.

Darcelle laughed to play off their conversation. "I'll talk to you both later. Praying for you, sis." She didn't know what else to say. If only Evanston had two brothers—one for Valencia and one for Shana. "I'd better head out. I'm meeting Evan over at his parents' house for a little while."

"Evan?" His name got everybody's attention as if she had blown a whistle to call a timeout.

"He's not coming over?" JJ pouted.

She shook her head, hating to disappoint him. "Not today, but I'll tell him you asked about him."

"Me too, Aunt DeeDee." Zuri jumped in place.

"Okay." Darcelle smothered a kiss in her niece's head. By the time she was out the door, her sisters and mother had sent their greetings to Evanston too.

Sitting in her vehicle, Darcelle didn't drive off right away but took a moment to fulfill her promise to Valencia. "Lord, please help my sister find happiness. In Jesus' name. Amen." She exhaled, then verified the Giles' address in her navigation system and called Evan. "I'm on my way."

"Can't wait. I haven't seen you since—"

"Early this morning." At least he sounded well-rested.

"Right." His voice was deep. "How could I forget that good night and good morning kiss?"

She blushed. "Behave, Van."

"There's a light dusting of snow on the ground, so drive carefully. Seriously, I can't wait to see you."

"I know, me neither." Twenty minutes later, Darcelle parked in front of a long ranch-style house, and sure enough, she spied Evanston in the doorway with his arms crossed, watching her.

Feeling playful, Darcelle called him. "I'm here."

"I know." Evanston stepped off the porch and swaggered toward her. With the backdrop of meticulously positioned decorations in the yard, he stood out as if on a photoshoot dressed in a thick red turtleneck sweater—no jacket—and a baseball cap. He made her shiver despite being bundled in a wool hat, scarf, and coat.

Evanston stood at attention outside her car door. Mischief twinkled in his eyes while he waited for her to unstrap the seatbelt. When she stepped out, he engulfed her in a warm embrace. "You give the best hugs," she teased, wrinkling her nose to inhale his cologne.

"I aim to please. Come on." He wrapped his hand around hers and guided her to the door, where his family was peeping from the doorway.

Once they crossed the threshold, Evanston made the introductions.

Darcelle accepted the handshake from his father and the hugs from his sister and mother. Langston was an older version of his son.

"And I'm Brandon," Jessica's boyfriend said.

"Hungry?" Sheila asked.

She playfully elbowed him in the side when he answered yep for both of them. She didn't want their first impression of her as greedy. "A little."

"Then, I'll eat what you don't." Evanston's smile coaxed her to comply.

"Well, I guess I'm a little hungry, and he's a lot."

Soon, they gathered around the table for a light meal. Evanston was so attentive, Darcelle tried not to blush. Nothing out of the ordinary when around him, but it was embarrassing under the scrutiny of his family.

Finally, the men made excuses to watch the game in the next room. His mother and sister cleared the table so Darcelle could join them in a card game.

"So, what kind of work do you do?" Sheila asked.

"Currently, I'm a community liaison for Reed and Meeks Brokerage. I started off as a financial analyst after college and have been there ever since."

"Yes." Jessica raised a fist in the air. "A woman with money is powerful."

"Except you." Shelia gave her daughter an amusing expression. "That would give you a never-ending shopping spree." She shuffled the cards and nodded for Darcelle to split the deck.

"What do you do in that role?" Evanston's mother was formal in her tone as if she were conducting an interview.

So, the interrogation begins. "I speak at community forums and schools about money management. My passion is mentoring young girls on how to save money and when to spend it."

Jessica tilted her head. "So...Darcelle, what attracted you to my brother?"

Question number five and counting. Darcelle wondered if they had a notebook hidden somewhere to keep track of her answers to review later.

Evanston's eyes were on the game, but his ears homed in on the ladies' conversation in the next room. He wanted them to like Darcelle as much as he did and prayed they didn't find fault with her. When Jessica started to pry into Darcelle's past relationships and the cause of breakups, Evanston stood and came to her rescue.

Darcelle took his cue, announcing it was time for her to leave. She thanked everyone for their hospitality as Evanston walked her to the door.

"It was nice meeting you, Darcelle." His mother's eyes twinkled—the tell-tale sign she meant what she said. "If you two have no plans tomorrow morning, the church doors are always open."

Evanston looked to Darcelle who shrugged. "Invitation accepted, Mom." Grabbing his cap, he slapped it on his head and opened the door for Darcelle.

Once outside, she exhaled. "Did I pass the test?"

"I had no doubt. I hope you don't feel pressured." Evanston wanted to make sure she was comfortable.

Her eyes—those gorgeous brown eyes—seemed to toy with him. "Nope, but once Mama finds out I went to church with you, you best believe she's going to pencil us in at King Jesus Church with her to even the score."

"You're okay with that, right?"

"Of course." She closed her eyes, and the slight pucker of her lips was the invitation he had been waiting for hours to enjoy.

"I can't wait for our next night out," he whispered against her lips.

"How about dinner one evening after work, or something like a movie on Saturday, considering we'll probably be in church two Sundays in a row?" She laughed as he admired her gleaming white teeth.

"All of the above. But none of that counts as an official date." He opened her car door.

"You'd better get to making a reservation, Mr. Giles." She grinned and started her engine.

The year was starting off better than he could have imagined. He smirked and walked back inside to his family, who was raving about Darcelle—except Jessica.

"I like her, but my opinion may change; I'm keeping an eye on her. She'd better not hurt my big bro."

Chapter Ten

"You have crossed the line." Cedric wasn't smiling when he opened the door to Evanston.

Was his friend serious? The guilt trip wasn't working. Maybe Evanston should have skipped this visit while Darcelle was at her Saturday hair salon appointment.

"I get it. I do." His friend sounded anything but convincing as he allowed Evanston entry. "You're into Darcelle, who I haven't met yet, but really, the car show? This has been our annual hanging out with your boy night, and you're cutting a brother out."

"Nobody is cutting anybody out. I'm simply giving you a heads-up that I'm bringing Darcelle." Evanston straddled the stool in the kitchen. "I invited my lady. She accepted, so the three of us will hang out. Cut the drama. Makes you look uglier than you already are."

"Who you calling ugly? Supposedly, people think we resemble." Cedric laughed too as he grabbed bottled waters from his frig. "Seriously, I'd do the same thing if I found someone special, but the car show, dude?" He shook his head in disbelief. "I've got to meet the woman who's led you astray from your best friend."

"Man, get out of here. Cece and I just happened. Be happy that I'm happy. We have our first official dinner date today." He grinned. "I've got a bouquet of flowers, chocolates, and reservations." He was proud of himself.

Cedric almost choked on a swig. "You two have been officially dating since the car lot."

"That doesn't count." Evanston stroked his freshly trimmed beard. "I don't want to skip a beat with her. Wining and dining is part of the process." He told himself he was cool not being in a relationship until he met Darcelle. They were becoming inseparable. "In hindsight, Phylicia and I never were friends."

"You talking real serious, man. Be afraid. Very afraid."

"Hater." Evanston stood. "I've got to go and get ready for my big date."

At home, he couldn't explain his nerves about their first date as he showered, then dressed. He and Darcelle had spent a lot of time together and shared kisses. They weren't strangers.

He stared at his reflection in the mirror, double-checking his appearance. "Thank you, Lord." He knew Darcelle was a gift from God. The messages had come from the pulpit the couple of times they had attended church with their parents. They didn't have a problem with church but weren't ready to commit to every Sunday, which they'd designated as their brunch day.

With keys and gifts in his hands, he left. Twenty minutes later, when Darcelle opened her door, Evanston's knees weakened at the sight of perfection. The makeup, the form-fitting dress, heels...the package. He stepped closer. "You straightened your hair." He ran his fingers through the mass to test its silkiness.

"Yes." She held his stare as her lips beckoned him for a kiss.

She ended the kiss and stepped inside her apartment to grab her coat. This had only been his second time inside. When Darcelle glanced over her shoulder, she lifted a brow. "What do you have?"

"Come closer to find out," he deepened his voice.

It became a game of hide-and-seek as she peeked behind him until he remembered their reservations, and he handed over her presents.

She sniffed the red roses. "Thank you, Van." That earned him another kiss. Darcelle eyed the chocolate and snickered. "Is this for me or us?"

"You don't have to share this time."

"Yay. More for me," she sassed, and he loved her teasing gesture.

Soon, they were on their way to Cashmere & Pearls, a pricey restaurant in the Central West End of St. Louis city.

"Nervous?" Evanston squeezed her hand.

She turned to him. "I am, and I don't know why." She giggled.

"Me neither." He couldn't believe it. It didn't matter though because they had nothing to hide from each other. As they relaxed during the ride, Evanston mentioned the upcoming car show, and she seemed excited to attend. "To be fair, I'll tag along to a girlie event or a knitting convention with you."

She playfully punched him in the arm. "I don't knit."

"*Whew.* Good." He feigned wiping beads of sweat from his forehead.

They arrived at the restaurant, and the valet stood at attention to park their car. He hoped their dining experience was everything it should be to impress his lady—dim-lit ambience, white tablecloths, cozy booths—and company.

Once they were seated and ordered their beverage, Evanston reached for her hands and toyed with her fingers, admiring her rich brownish nail polish.

They paused to give their dinner choices, then flirted and flirted and flirted until Evanston needed to step outside to cool off.

He didn't have too when their server appeared and placed their meals in front of them. After Evanston gave thanks, they feasted on steak, lobster, and chicken.

"Since we're on our first date, we're supposed to get to know each other." Evanston winked.

When Darcelle had enough, she anchored her chin in the palm of her hand. "Let's switch it up, and you tell me what you already know about me?"

Evanston rested his fork on his plated and angled his body so he could stretch his legs. "That's so easy. You love family and God, you're passionate…you're special. And I think you're transparent. I don't know all your secrets because we all have them, but I'm sure you'll share them when the time comes."

"I like that, no secrets between us." She smiled.

"Your turn." He picked back up his fork.

"Okay." Darcelle nodded. "Evanston—my Van—Giles, your kindness and charisma are sexy to me." She didn't blink as he blushed. "While my best friend is praying for

God to send her the perfect man, I got mine. You're good-looking, easy to talk to, caring…"

If Evanston wasn't hearing it from Darcelle's lips, he would have never believed he was the person she was describing. Hands down, this was the best first date ever.

On Sunday, the pair skipped church and opted for brunch. That evening, Darcelle endured Shana's scolding about missing service before sharing details about the "first date" with Evanston.

Closing her eyes, Darcelle smiled as she stretched out on her sofa. "It was romantic. I mean, I knew I was attracted to Van, but the brother took it up a notch. I should have worn a tiara because he treated me like a princess."

"Don't take this the wrong way, but if you get married before me, and you don't match me up with a handsome, single, and saved groomsman, I'm cutting ties with you, girlfriend."

"Noted." Darcelle was amused by Shana's repeated mild threat throughout the years. "Next weekend, we're attending the annual car show."

"Clearly, I'm not praying hard enough for a husband."

"I wasn't praying at all, and Evanston Giles just happened."

"No, I believe God set you two up. It's what you do in that relationship that will allow God to get the glory."

Darcelle huffed. "Don't start getting all churchy on me. Although I haven't kept myself pure sexually, Van hasn't tried to seduce me. Plus, sleeping with him right now would mess up my fantasy about him being attracted to me on the inside, not just the package on the outside."

"Good. I'm glad we had the talk. I'm happy for you. I'd tell you to slow down, but you and Mr. Giles are breaking the speed limit. Bye."

Monday morning, Darcelle had more flowers—red roses on her desk when she arrived at work. She had more visitors stop by in one day than she had all last week.

The next five days were crazy busy with community requests for seminars and managers' meetings. She usually spoke to Evanston at least once during the day, but she barely had time to grab a bite to eat.

Friday evening, Darcelle was giddy about going to a car show. It didn't take her long to shower, repair her makeup, and redress. Evanston arrived on time with a silly grin when she opened her door.

"Close your eyes, Cece."

"What are you up to this time?" Darcelle tried to peep behind his back, but he matched her step from side to side.

"Nope. You have to close your eyes first."

Darcelle stomped boots in feigned protest but complied. She sensed his closeness, then his touch sent goosebumps down her arms as he guided her chin and brushed a kiss on her lips.

"That's my gift," he whispered against her lips. "Ready?"

"I am." Linking her fingers through his, they walked to his car. He didn't break their connection during the entire ride while they chatted about their careers.

"I love my job, my boss, and everything my company stands for. Usually, beginning this month, I visit high schools and educate students about money. When I can," Darcelle added, "I also teach financial security at women's shelters."

"What you do is rewarding. I'm proud of you." He lifted her hand and kissed it as he kept both eyes on the road.

"Thank you." She swallowed and bowed her head.

"What? Tell me." His voice was soft with concern.

"I haven't heard those words in a long time. I know my family is proud of me, especially my parents, but when it came from my dad, it felt personal, if that makes sense. You sounded like him for a moment."

"Woman, you can tell me anything, and it will make sense. Anything." He glanced at her then back at the road.

"Your flattery is addictive." She sighed. "So, is this an annual event?"

"Big time. The St. Louis Auto Show showcases more than five hundred new cars, SUVs and pickup trucks, even motorbikes. If you're into cars or thinking about buying one, this is the first stop."

"Do you have a garage where you store all the cars you've purchased after one of these shows?" she joked, pulling out her mirror to make sure her lipstick was clinging to her teeth.

"Nope. I guess Cedric and I attend these shows like women go window shopping. I've only purchased a car and pickup truck following one of these shows. That's it. I want to see the latest technology and vehicle upgrades. It has to blow me away to make me want to trade. You'll see."

Once downtown, Evanston announced, "It's showtime. We're supposed to meet up with Cedric in about half an hour." As he helped her out of the car, he brushed his lips against hers. "Thank you for coming with me."

"I'm glad you invited me."

Men, women, and children came from every direction with one purpose—the convention center where the auto show was held.

Evanston kept her hand secured in his and by his side as if someone would kidnap her. Inside the showroom, luxury and fancy cars blinked for their attention.

"Wow." Darcelle felt she had entered a whole new world. "The models are as eye-catching as the cars. I'm sure a lot of men would like them to be part of the car's accessories."

"They're more than pretty faces. The models are narrators and take their job seriously. They have to study the particulars about the car they're presenting."

The chill from outside was gone. Feeling warm, she began to unravel her scarf, then remove her coat. Evanston took it and securely placed it under his arm, then quickened his steps. "There she is."

Darcelle thought he was talking about the woman dressed to perfection; instead it was the car.

"Hi. What can you tell me about this beauty?" he asked the model.

Transformed into another world, Evanston didn't take his eyes off the car as he listened. He circled the vehicle a couple of times, tugging her along. "Can we sit inside?" he asked the narrator over his shoulder.

"Of course." The woman opened the car doors with the flair of a model on a game show.

Evanston thanked her and helped Darcelle inside, then rounded the bumper and slid in. He studied the dashboard features, then turned to her with his elbow resting on the wheel as if it were his own personal vehicle. "Do you know how long we've been seeing each other?" he asked out of the blue.

She smiled. "Three weeks."

"And a day." He lifted a mischievous brow. "Glad to know I'm not the only one keeping a record." Evanston took a deep breath and proceeded. "Cece, are we at a place where we can agree to see each other exclusively?"

Her heart melted at his request. "I had hoped we already were, but I didn't want to assume." He inched closer, and she kissed him as if they had sealed a deal.

"Hey, no making out in the car, Evan," an onlooker said.

Embarrassed, Darcelle blushed.

Evanston looked around and laughed. "Stop hating, Cedric." He got out, then helped her. "This beautiful woman is officially my lady, Darcelle Price." The two men slapped hands for a shake. "We go way back."

So Darcelle ID'd the guy who appeared in several photos with Evanston on Facebook. "Nice to meet you, Cedric." The man had the same build and facial hair as Evanston—both were good-looking, but Evanston had a dash of something extra that had captured her attention.

"Man, I thought we were supposed to meet at the Chevy Corner."

"Oops. Sorry. Lost track of time." Evanston looked at Darcelle as if it was her fault before he wrapped his arm around her waist and pulled her closer.

"Have you two been to the Million Dollar Mile yet?" Cedric asked, slipping his hands in his pants pockets and eyeing a gorgeous model who appeared prepped for a car commercial from her timed pivots, smiles, and poses.

The woman's movements reminded Darcelle of the novelty dance moves of the robot. "Wait a minute. Did you say Million Dollar Mile?"

"Yep. Come on," Evanston linked his fingers through hers. She fell in step with the men. "It's the highlight of the show. There are luxurious and exotic cars that only the wealthy and famous can afford like this Bugatti Veyron." He whistled as they strolled closer to the sleek car.

"And the price tag is only one-point-six million dollars," Darcelle mumbled, hesitant to breathe on it. "This is putting my new car to shame."

"Hey, leave Vanessa out of this. She brought us together." Evanston gently squeezed her hand.

As the three continued, Darcelle watched Evanston and Cedric's interaction and fascination with the cars. Feeling like the third wheel, Darcelle wished her best friend was here. Sometimes, when they were together, they would shut out folks and be in their own world.

As if Evanston could read her thoughts, he stopped in their track , not caring about blocking the path for others. He stared into her eyes before he kissed her briefly.

"What's that for?" she asked, feeling as if they were the only two there in the room.

"Do I have to have a reason?" he challenged her.

Darcelle giggled. "No."

"Good, because I might just do it again before the night is out." Evanston winked.

"Oh, he will," Cedric said, reminding them of his presence.

The date ended with four additional kisses, because Darcelle kept score.

Chapter Eleven

*B*liss. That's what Darcelle felt with Evanston. He joked their relationship started as a parking lot fling. Nope. For her, he sealed the deal at the Christmas dinner.

Finally, she no longer had to go through the motions that it didn't matter that she was single. Liar. Evanston made a believer out of her that the right companionship mattered. While they reserved Fridays for dinner dates and Sundays for brunches, mid-week lunches were their bonuses.

He was in her system now. She smiled, recalling how they had slow danced outside her apartment building one night surrounded by the quiet romantic beat of snowfall.

Surreal.

Even if Darcelle wanted to, she couldn't put the brakes on her emotions. Evanston somehow had earned a spot in her family's hearts as well. Her mother expected him at family functions; he even was there with them during the march from Midtown to downtown St. Louis to commemorate the life of Dr. Martin Luther King, Jr., and his sacrifices for equality. JJ and Zuri never left Evanston's side as they latched onto his hands.

"Sis, you've got a keeper," Valencia whispered with their arms linked together as they kept pace with the other marchers.

A sobering reminder that the children craved a father image in their lives, and if there was anything to pray for, Nellie Price was on it—husbands for her three daughters.

"I know. In a way, Daddy brought us together." Darcelle smiled at the thought.

"I don't know about that, but Harold would want both of you to make God a priority in your relationships. That would've made him happy and me too. Don't let that young man ask you to marry him twice," her mother added to their private conversation, which clearly wasn't that secretive. "Your father and I married after nine months."

"That's code for don't get pregnant," Valencia said, looking ahead.

"It's more than that. Lukewarm Christians want Jesus on Sunday mornings after dishonoring Him on Saturday nights in bed without the benefit of marriage."

"Mom." Darcelle said sharply. "Do you need a bullhorn so everyone can hear us?" She and Evanston hadn't been intimate—yet. Would God really judge her if they did?

"Let them hear," she raised her voice, "if it would help save souls."

"Our mother was reminding me I picked a loser to love," Valencia griped.

"Forget him. Who knows when the right man will walk into your life?" Darcelle put her arm around Valencia's shoulder and squeezed. It hurt Darcelle to see her older sister sad, and she had to be mindful not to flaunt her happiness with Evanston in front of Valencia.

"Val," Nellie said, grabbing her hand, "I love you. I hate what your ex put you through. Learn from that heartache and let God pick the next one."

"Like on a car lot." Monique laughed out loud, which made Evanston glance over his shoulder at them. Somehow, he and JJ, and Zuri were a few feet ahead of them in the crowd. Darcelle wondered if he had overheard Monique and their entire conversation.

"Nope. I prefer a mall lot so we can go shopping," Valencia joked, and they chuckled, even their mother.

Later that afternoon, Darcelle was a guest speaker at a forum on money power in the Black community. It was part of the King Legacy agenda to educate Blacks on wealth, housing, and community service. In minority neighborhoods, she served as the success story at Reed and Meeks.

Darcelle conducted these seminars after the marches; usually, her father attended. Her mother's reason was she had taught her girls how to budget when they were teenagers. In the absence of Harold Price, her entire family was there this time, so was Evanston.

Year after year to a different audience, Darcelle gave the same spiel. She ended her talk by handing out her business cards with the company's logo. "Thanks for coming. I'll stick around to answer some of your questions. Otherwise, feel free to email me at the firm. Reed and Meeks welcomes your business."

Darcelle loved having a voice at the table—a tiny voice, but she wanted an opportunity to make more noise.

It was one of the many perks that came with her highly paid position. She had persuaded the board to create annual scholarships for deserving students. After a series of discussions and the budget agreed upon, the program was up and running the following year.

With her livelihood secured, Evanston balanced her in other areas of her life. She had it all, and whether she attended church or not, she always thanked God for her blessings.

Her family gave her the thumbs up, smiled, and waved goodbye to get the children home after a long day. Although she rode with Evanston, he seemed in no hurry to leave as he waited for Darcelle to answer question after question.

As the crowd thinned, Evanston stood and capped off the slow-moving line off to the front. When they were face-to-face, she recognized his adoration. "Did I tell you how incredibly smart, beautiful, and amazing you are?"

"All the time." She inched her lips closer to his, retreated, then giggled.

"I'll get you back for that." He reached for her hand. "Ready?"

After stealing a few kisses and warm hugs from Darcelle before they strapped their seatbelts, he asked if she minded stopping by his parents' house.

"Of course not. I've held you hostage most of the day."

He pulled away from the curb and headed to a stoplight. "Never. I'm a willing participant. Knowing Mom and Dad, they probably attended a church memorial in honor of Dr.

Martin Luther King, Jr. They stopped marching years ago when Dad started to have problems with his back."

"Hey, how's the new software you installed on your job?"

He was pleased that she asked. "A few kinks, but the department heads seemed to have adapted to the new features. The long hours and headache paid off because I got my anniversary review last week. The bosses showed their appreciation with a hefty raise."

"I'm proud of you too."

Simple words, but coming from the right person, they made him feel like a star student. "Thank you."

In no time, they arrived at his parents' and parked. Evanston fashioned his Fedora on his head, then helped her out. With their arms looped together, they matched their steps to the door where he rang the bell instead of using his key.

His mother answered and smiled at both of them. "Evan. Darcelle, it's nice to see you again."

Evanston kissed her cheek before the couple stepped inside. "Where's Dad?"

His mother didn't answer as she led the way to the family room where his dad dozed in his worn recliner. One of his mother's foreign films was playing. No wonder Langston Giles was asleep, he mused to himself.

His father stirred from Evanston's footsteps. "Hey, son. What brings you to visit?"

"We're coming back from MLK festivities—the march in Midtown and Cece spoke afterward." Evanston beamed and removed his coat, then Darcelle's. "I—we—wanted to check in on you

We won't stay long, he mouthed to her.

She nodded as his dad scrambled to his feet from the broken recliner, which he refused to replace.

"If you two have an appetite, I'm sure your mother has dinner already on the stove."

Evanston chuckled. "Mom always has a stockpile of food ready to eat. If not warming on the stove, leftovers are in the fridge." His mother had a kindred spirit to the military—she was always prepared for drop-ins.

Having eaten, his parents watched on as he and Darcelle fixed their plates. After giving thanks, the two dug in.

The couple almost moaned at the same time as they tasted the pulled pork and steamed potatoes. His mother even prepared them a side salad.

"Mrs. Giles, this is so good." Darcelle swallowed and forked up another mouthful.

His mother rocked in her chair, beaming. "How are your cooking skills?"

"Not like this." Darcelle pointed her fork to her plate. "However, I can cook. With three girls in the house, my father sampled our dishes. If he ate it, then we passed."

Everyone laughed.

"Well, you can cook dip," Evanston teased her. It had been homemade, and he could tell the difference.

She elbowed him. "I'll have you know I know how to formally set the table and prepare a five-course meal." Darcelle playfully wrinkled her nose.

"Is that a dare, Miss Price? Challenge accepted," he flirted. Both had forgotten about his parents until his mother chuckled.

When they finished their meal, the couple washed their dishes, flirting throughout the process. "So, when are you inviting me to dinner?" Evanston bumped her hips.

"Whenever you're ready to cook." She smiled at him, and at that moment, Evanston could see Darcelle in his future.

Chapter Twelve

"*I* need a dinner date for Valentine's Day." Evanston teasingly solicited Darcelle's help on the speakerphone as he shaved. Their morning routine was to chat before heading off to work.

"Let me check with Valencia to see if Zuri has plans." She *teehee*d.

"Funny, Miss Price. She's cute and all, but I'd rather have Aunt DeeDee. Since we're officially a couple, you have to let me pamper you."

Darcelle listened to his deep voice—warm and strong. Bliss was not overrated. "My sisters and I are planning to do something special for Mom on Friday night. This whole 'first time without Daddy' is hard. While children look forward to Christmas, Valentine's Day was Mom's favorite, and she prepared for it a year in advance. She always called it the anniversary of their first date.

"This is going to be rough. Daddy spoiled her and always made sure she knew she felt loved, and he made sure we saw it, too, as an example of what to demand and expect from a man who professes to love us."

Evanston turned off his shaver. "Baby, I understand if you want to spend the evening with your mother. We can —"

"Say that again." Closing her eyes, she wanted her ears to record the endearment while her mind captured the word for recordkeeping. Darcelle's brain was on standby, waiting to send the message to her heart. "Call me baby."

Instead of complying, he tortured her with silence before giving in. "Baby."

"Yeah. That sounds good coming from you. Yes, I'll be your date." She blew him a kiss, and minutes later, ended the call.

The rest of the day was a blur as her mind played instant recall of the endearment.

A few days later, on Valentine's Day, Darcelle sent her mother flowers and a card. When she walked into work, a delivery guy with a bouquet of white roses rode up the elevator with her. He trailed her into the office lobby. While Darcelle waved at the receptionist, the man said, "I have a delivery for a Miss Darcelle Price."

Darcelle twirled around as Nan, the gatekeeper, pointed her way.

"Yes. That's me." She accepted them and waltzed to her desk, giddy. Darcelle managed a quick call to thank Evanston but had little time to relish its beauty as nervous investors flooded the phone and emails concerned about the volatile market. Her concentration wavered with every glance at the roses.

Mid-morning, Shana texted Darcelle a breathtaking photo of flowers—the colors popped, and the vase had to be lead crystal. Darcelle's mouth dropped until she read the caption: **I hope this is the last time I have to send myself a hundred dollar floral arrangement.**

Darcelle replied with laughing emojis and uploaded a photo of her roses. A while back, her friend had commented that Evanston changed his status on Facebook to "in a relationship" with Darcelle. Shana had said if a man was willing to let thousands of friends know he was serious, he had her vote.

Shana's support meant everything. Despite the chaos at work, Darcelle skipped lunch to leave the office early. Her first stop was her mother's.

"Thank you for the flowers." Nellie displayed a smile that didn't reach her eyes.

It pained Darcelle. Maybe she should have canceled her date and stayed with her. After all, they—her mother—had so many firsts to endure: Harold's birthday, Valentine's Day, summer barbecues, park picnics with the grandkids, year-end holidays. "Mom, I can stay with you."

Shaking her head, Nellie scrapped the idea. "No. Go. You have a good man waiting. My happiness is watching my daughters find happiness. Monique has a date, and Valencia is going out with some of her girlfriends, so my grandbabies are keeping me company." She beamed. This time, the smile was real.

"Okay, if you're sure." Darcelle gave her a quick hug and left. A few hours later, she opened her door to Evanston whose eyes told her everything she wanted to know. She had wowed him in her short red dress and higher than usual red heels. Instead of Evanston wrapping his arms around her, he kept them behind his back.

Darcelle squinted. "What are you up to?"

"You have to come closer to find out." He shifted his weight so she couldn't peek. Evanston lured her closer and trapped her into his embrace with one arm, gracing her with his kiss. Next, he displayed a stuffed animal.

"*Awww*. Thank you. Now, I have something to hug at night."

"You can always have the real thing." He winked.

With the sparks between them, Darcelle wasn't sure if she could or would fight off the temptation if he asked.

Fight, girl. She could hear Shana in her ear.

Whenever Shana got in her head, Darcelle always second-guessed her decisions. The restraint on his part strengthened her resolve too. Nellie Price would be proud; she always reminded her girls that fornication is a sin against the body and comes with consequences they might not be prepared for.

"Come on. We have a stop to make before dinner."

"Where?"

Evanston gave her no hint until he parked in front of her mother's house and reached into the backseat for a bouquet of red roses she hadn't noticed.

"What are you doing?"

He climbed out without answering and hiked the stairs to her mother's front door. Nellie opened it in surprise. He gave her the flowers. The moment was tender as her mother hugged him and waved toward the car.

Darcelle's eyes misted, and her words choked in her throat when he returned to the car. "Thank you for thinking of her. That was sweet." She squeezed his hand.

"Without your mother, I wouldn't have my Cece."

He knew how to wow her. What were the rules for not falling in love too soon? Darcelle thought she had just broken them. Instrumental music serenaded them on the way to the restaurant, giving Darcelle's thoughts free rein.

From the moment they stepped inside the place, Darcelle's senses were heightened with Evanston's every touch, cologne, and even the sweet sound of him calling her name.

The dining area was filled to capacity with tables for two draped in white linen cloths. A single long-stemmed candle served as a centerpiece. It was the perfect ambiance for the intimate evening. A string quartet, hidden from view, completed the backdrop for romance.

"You're exceptionally beautiful tonight." Evanston coaxed her to meet him across the table. His eyes—whew, those gorgeous brown eyes—revealed his affection and attraction.

When their lips touched, a spark ignited. He trapped her bottom lip between his for a kiss, then did the same with her top lip. It was seductive and sweet.

"Whew." She fanned herself. "You're trying to set the fire between us."

"I know. You think this is easy for me?" Evanston's tortured expression sparked a chuckle.

"Sorry." She giggled again. "You, Evanston Giles, are so transparent, which I find very attractive."

She linked her fingers through his, which were firm yet gentle. "I'll admit, you make it hard for me to be the Christian woman Mama expects. I don't know what is the greater deterrent, indulging in sex before marriage as a sin against God, or witnessing the aftermath of JJ and Zuri's father deserting Valencia."

Evanston didn't interrupt her ramblings.

"It's as if Mama has a spiritual chart of the symptoms of lust vs. love like doctors have health charts of diseases and its symptoms. That's from *Nellie's Book of Wisdom*." Darcelle looked away. "This is crazy and a mood killer. I don't know why I'm saying all this. I do go to church. Maybe it's the lure of romance in this place and being with you."

"Or love." He massaged her hands. "The truth is I have to tame the lust I have for you. I can't credit a church sermon or Bible verse because my attraction to you is stronger than I could ever imagine. It's called love. If you can't feel it by the way I treat you, let me say it: I love you."

Darcelle's eyes watered as she folded her arms across her chest to capture his words. "Yes, I've felt it before now. I love you, too, Van."

Unfolding her arms, he pulled her hands to his lips and kissed them, then he seemed mesmerized at her fingers. "You're a keeper."

The flirting continued, but they were mixed with Evanston's sense of humor as he recanted his childhood antics with his sister, fishing with his father, and more.

"And here I thought I was the man, getting you a good deal on the car, and you could fend for yourself with your finance background."

"You." She shook her head, and he seemed transfixed as her loose curls swept across her forehead and cheeks. "You were my voice and protector."

"Always," he mouthed for her heart to capture.

Now, she understood why Valentine's Day was so memorable to her mother. Tonight, love was in the air.

She had stopped getting her hopes up to meet a man who was marriage material, but if Evanston ever asked her to marry him, she would say yes. Like her mother had known her father was the one, there was only one Evanston Giles.

Chapter Thirteen

*T*here was nothing Darcelle could do about it—
Evanston had to share her the remaining weekends in
February—Black History Month. She had speaking
engagements at schools and churches about Black wealth
from pre-slavery to the present. Of course, Reed and Meeks
took the credit for her community involvement.

Out of sight wasn't out of mind for her and Evanston.
Actually, the timing couldn't have been better. He and
Cedric had planned day trips to car shows in Kansas City
and Springfield, Missouri.

She and Evanston texted each other so much that
Cedric had teased him to call her, so he did. When they
couldn't talk, he left a voicemail. The best part of hearing
his voice was ending their talk with "I love you."

One Sunday morning, Darcelle attended service at her
mother's church. Pastor Clemons' sermon focused on
relationships. As soon as he said that, Darcelle smiled. Hers
was solid with Evanston.

"I'm talking about your relationship with Jesus. How
tight is it? No parent, husband, or friend wants a person to

come to them only for a handout. If we spend time with the Lord, we don't have to ask for anything. Refresh your memory with Ephesians 3:20: *Now unto Him that is able to do exceedingly abundantly above all that we ask or think, according to the power that works in us...*"

Nothing her childhood pastor said was new to Darcelle, but she felt inspired. She would try to attend church more often.

Afterward, Darcelle felt silly that a young teenager served as her armor-bearer to carry her bag to the classroom where Darcelle would conduct the seminar as if she was an outside guest.

She grew up at King Jesus Church under Pastor Clemons, repented of her sins, was baptized in Jesus' name, and God sealed her with His Holy Ghost with His heavenly language. She had done her requirements for salvation. Period.

Without holiness, no man shall see Me. God's whisper was like thunder.

Darcelle blinked and looked at her audience. No one else heard it? *Whoa.* She swallowed.

As she waited for others to come, her mind reflected on the sermon. In her opinion, she had a good relationship with God. Darcelle's personal assessment was she was a good and kind person, and she did go to church.

Once the ladies were settled, Darcelle was about to get started when Sister Mable interrupted, stating they begin their meetings with prayer and she volunteered. It didn't matter church was just dismissed.

After the amens, Darcelle began with her customary opener. "This is Black History Month, and we'll talk about overcoming injustices and rising out of poverty. Don't get me wrong, voting is important, but money speaks volumes."

Familiar faces who had watched her grow up in the church smiled and nodded for her to preach to the choir.

Her mother sat in the front row with her chin lifted as a proud mama. Darcelle smiled. "Growing up, my family wasn't poor, but we were mindful of necessities and what we thought were luxuries."

"That's right," her mother mumbled loud enough for Darcelle to hear.

"Although we're into the second month of the year, I brought these booklets, which you can slip into your purse to keep track of your savings for a fifty-two-week challenge."

"That's one year, Sister Susie," someone called out in the audience.

"I know how to count," Sister Susie mumbled and shifted in her folding chair.

Chuckles filled the air. Darcelle cleared her throat and continued. "Every week represents the amount you should set aside…"

"After your tithes and offerings." The reminder came from someone in the back.

Darcelle nodded and kept going. "You save the amount for whatever number the week is during the calendar year up to the fifty-two dollars for the last week. It takes discipline, but you'll have one thousand, three hundred, and thirty-eight dollars in your pocket."

"More to give to the Lord." This time it was her mother who joined in the free-for-all.

"Right, Mama." Darcelle was about to share the story of a Harrisburg, Mississippi, washerwoman when her phone vibrated in her purse. She smiled. Evanston was thinking about her. She must have hesitated too long because her mother cleared her throat.

"Sorry. I lost my train of thought." Darcelle hid her blush. "Yes, Oseola McCarty lived a simple life but was able to donate more than one hundred and fifty thousand dollars to the University of Southern Mississippi for scholarships, especially for blacks who needed financial assistance. Miss McCarty only had a sixth-grade education."

The lecture was second nature to Darcelle. "Yes, anyone can save. No amount is too small. Get in the habit of saving more than you spend and leave a legacy. Thank you."

She answered questions, handed out her company's business cards and the savings booklets.

"You made me proud, Darcie, and your daddy too." Her mother sniffed and hugged her goodbye.

"I know, Mama. I know."

Education was important in the Price household. Darcelle had studied hard and earned a full ride to the University of Michigan in Ann Arbor.

She returned to St. Louis, because Reed and Meeks had recruited Darcelle with a signing bonus and other perks.

Once in her car, Darcelle adjusted the volume on her phone. She had missed calls from Evanston. She called him back. "Hey. I'm just leaving a seminar."

"Hungry?"

"Tired." She sighed. Darcelle had snacked on light refreshments, but she was too pooped to make a detour to grab a bite to eat. "I'll prepare a salad when I get home."

"I have a better idea. I'll bring you something hot to eat. You've been going nonstop these past weeks."

Darcelle smiled. "Aww, you're so sweet. "

"You're sweeter. I've got a carryout with your name on it. Cedric and I stopped to eat once we made it back from Kansas City. That's when I sent you a text. I got you something anyway, just in case."

"Did you two have fun in K.C.?"

"Cedric's side hustle is taking off. You should have seen him work the crowds at the car show, passing out business cards. Folks were really interested in his accessories for cycle enthusiasts. Hey, I'll leave home now and meet you and Vanessa at your apartment."

"We can't wait." She giggled, then ended the call.

Chapter Fourteen

"*I*'m throwing a party, and you're on the guest list," was Lester's greeting one working as Evanston strolled into the office. "Oh, and Cece can be your plus one."

"What's the occasion?" Evanston unwrapped the scarf around his neck. It was too cold for a backyard barbecue, which was usually the extent of Lester's "parties," aka get-togethers.

"My fortieth, and I'm doing it up big." He pumped his fists in the air as if he had won a lottery. Good thing they were alone in the office for another hour before others arrived for their shift.

Who was this person? How many energy drinks had Lester consumed? He wasn't an excitable person, so to see him this animated was amusing. Evanston flopped in his chair, stretched his legs, and squinted at his coworker and friend. What was going on?

"My guest list is growing. I'm up to sixty invites." Lester grinned, seemingly proud of himself.

"Sixty? Since when did you know more than twenty folks? Are you including everybody you've met since preschool?" Evanston swirled his chair to his monitor and typed in his password.

"Funny, but yeah, I am. My party will serve as a family and friends reunion."

"Cece and I will be there." Evanston turned his attention to the emails in his inbox.

"Nope. You'll have to formally return the invite card in the mail, and there's a dress code."

"Really?" Evanston glanced over his shoulder and did his best to keep a straight face. His friend was going to the extremes. Since when was Lester concerned about fashion and style.

"Yep. It's black tie." He seemed pleased with himself.

Evanston couldn't trap the laugh that escaped. "Who are you? Since when did you go bourgeoise on me?"

Lester balled up a piece of paper and aimed it at Evanston's head like a tennis ball. "You're not the only one who can find someone special. Maya's an event planner, and it was her idea that I do this for myself." He grinned and used his arms to demonstrate how big the shindig should be.

"*Ahhh.* Now, it makes sense. I couldn't see you coming up with this brainchild all by yourself."

"Hater." Lester turned around to answer a call.

Evanston's phone rang next. While he listened to a department head's tech issue, he was still amused by Lester's mastermind event. Maybe he had found his better half because she was transforming him before Evanston's eyes.

Later in the day, he texted Darcelle and received an automatic response she would call him back, but it wasn't until after he returned from lunch.

"Sorry, Van," she sounded flustered. "It's been a crazy morning."

"Everything okay?"

"Yeah. The big bosses will be in town in a few days, so I had to pull together reports and tweak PowerPoints. I'll need a mini-vacation once they leave."

"Just breathe, babe." He listened as she inhaled and released. "Lester, the one you met who works with me, is throwing a fortieth birthday party, and he's inviting us. Get this, it's a black-tie affair."

"Yay. I get to play dress-up." Darcelle didn't hide her excitement, and that energized him too. "When is it?" When he gave her the date, she sighed. "Bummer. That would have been my daddy's birthday. I'm not sure if I'll be the best of company, you know."

Evanston did understand. No pressure. "We can pass."

Silence.

"Cece?" He grew concerned with her quietness.

"No, he's your friend. We should go. I'll do something special for Mama, then attend the function with you."

"Your family is your priority." He saw firsthand how Darcelle grieved her dad. He hoped not to have to witness her pain for many years to come.

"No. Life goes on. You've shown me that. It'll be good to go."

A week later, Valencia called Darcelle at work. "Hey, sis. Can you believe I have a date on Saturday, so do you mind babysitting JJ and Zuri? Of course, if you and Evan have any plans, I can ask Mama, but I wanted to give her a break."

"You know you don't have to ask." Darcelle danced discreetly in her seat. "Yes. I hope he's a good guy."

"He's just a coworker, more like a male friend."

Darcelle's smile flipped to a pout. "You could sound more excited. Evan and I are going to a birthday party Friday night. Why don't you let them sleepover Saturday?"

"That means you'll have to take them to Sunday school, or Mama is going to have a fit. I only go to church for the children."

"Gotcha. It'll be fun. I have some new jigsaw puzzles we can put together." Darcelle's assistant signaled her from the doorway that she had a meeting in ten minutes. Right. She stood and gathered her tablet. "I've got to go. Do me a favor. At least pretend to be thrilled."

"Yay," Valencia mimicked before they ended the call.

On Friday morning, Darcelle woke up and allowed herself to cry for her loss and laugh at the memories her daddy left behind. The day could have gone downhill, but Evanston made the difference with his calls, flowers, and texts.

That night, the excitement built as Darcelle dressed up. She got Shana on FaceTime to get her approval.

"You look stunning," Shana said with awe in her voice.

"I'm glad we didn't pass on the party." Darcelle scrutinized her manicure, then her makeup. She slipped her feet into her heels when the doorbell rang. "Van's here."

"Have a good time, Cinderella."

Darcelle opened her door, and she and Evanston stared at each other. He cleaned up. The man was decked out in a tux with tails, wearing a top hat. When he slipped on the dark shades, she laughed.

"Ah, you think this is funny, *huh?* I've got a pair for you too." He handed the glasses over. "Here you go, princess. You're killing that black dress."

"So now we're rolling in as gangstas. I'll play along." Darcelle struck a pose and spun around in her black gown and long black gloves. Next, she grabbed her black cape and twirled it in the air like a cowboy's rope, then let it drape over her shoulders.

This time, Evanston snickered. "I bet you can't do that again."

Shaking her head, she slipped her hand into Evanston's. "Probably not. You win."

Darcelle stepped out of her building, expecting to see Evanston's car. Instead, a limo was waiting for them.

She looked at him.

He brushed his lips against hers. "Just because."

He made her feel starstruck.

White roses awaited her inside the limo. "Is this making your day better?" he whispered.

With her eyes closed, she nodded. "Much."

They snuggled until the limo stopped at the hotel, then the driver opened their door where a red carpet led them to the entrance.

"This place is packed. There has to be a couple hundred folks here," Darcelle said as they stepped into the ballroom.

Evanston removed the cape from Darcelle's shoulders and kissed her neck. "Yep. I've known Lester for years, and I'm guessing he doesn't know most of these folks, or maybe they're from his kindergarten class like he said." He snickered.

"What?" She squinted and laughed. "Stop playing."

"I'm not," he mumbled as the guest of honor approached with a commanding stride of a king among his subjects and introduced a pretty woman on his arm as Maya.

"Happy birthday," Darcelle and Evanston said in unison.

"You pulled it off, bro," Evanston bobbed his head and glanced around, "you said big. This is it."

"She made it happen." Lester grinned at Maya. "Hey, I see Little John from first grade over there. Excuse us. Celebrate my party. Talk to y'all later." He whisked his companion off in that direction of his former schoolmate.

Darcelle turned to Evanston, "he seems happy. I'm glad I came."

"Me too. Come on. Let's dance the night away."

"Not the whole night, I hope. I've got babysitting duties tomorrow, so I'm going to need energy."

"Need a co-babysitter? I'll order pizza." His grin was goofy as his niece and nephew's.

Would he be an assistant or another kid? Either way, it should be fun. "Add some chicken wings, and you've just got an invite."

With his hand on her back, he guided her to the dance floor where he twirled her under his arm, tilted her back, and they danced to their own music. Cinderella had nothing on her.

They mingled and made a game out of sampling hors d'oeuvres to guess the ingredients. The entertainment and company made it a night to remember, especially with the sweet kisses Evanston had for her at her doorsteps. "Good night."

"Night."

The next afternoon, Evanston arrived at Darcelle's apartment, bearing gifts: food in one hand and a movie in the other. The atmosphere shifted with his presence.

"I should be jealous," she teased as JJ and Zuri clamored for Evanston's attention.

"Never. I have plenty of love to go around." He didn't disappoint her when he smothered her with a hug and a brief kiss because of their audience.

Darcelle never experienced a motherhood craving this strong until now. It were as if she was living someone else's life. A few times, Evanston caught her staring and winked. Yep, he was definitely daddy material.

Before long, the children worked up a hearty appetite and all four of them devoured the pizza, chicken wings, and salad.

Once the table was clear, JJ brought a box to the table and dumped its contents. Evanston's eyes widened. "A three-hundred-piece jigsaw puzzle?"

"Yep. Get busy," Darcelle ordered as she picked out border pieces of the landscape puzzle. At the same time, the children started to separate the colors.

"This isn't too much for them?" Evanston looked doubtful, actually scared at the challenge.

"Trust me," Darcelle boasted. "They have the skill level. I got them hooked early on these, so let the games begin."

It was on as the children exchanged high fives when one matched a jigsaw piece.

They completed the night sky, and now the group was tackling to match the right pieces to one of two mountains. "Yesterday, I heard rumors at work that my boss's boss is retiring, and he's recommending me to fill the vacancy on the company board of directors. This is a big deal," she said, connecting another piece.

"Congratulations, baby. I'm proud of you." He leaned over the children and bestowed a noisy kiss on her cheek, and her niece and nephew yelled, "Yuck."

"So, what will my lady's new title be?"

"Assistant vice president." Darcelle beamed, lifting her chin. "I'll not only become the youngest board member in the company's history but the first African American woman to do so. This is huge." She pumped her fists in the air.

"Yay, Aunt DeeDee is going to be president," Zuri joined in the celebration.

"Not quite." Darcelle smiled. Although the possibilities were endless on all the things she could do, accountability and responsibility came along with that much clout.

Whatever passion you pursue in life, remember to reach back and bring up someone else, her dad had drilled into all three of his daughters. The new position would allow Darcelle to implement her plans to help young girls in communities investors otherwise sidestepped. "I'm going to do everything in my power to shine and not disappoint my boss or my dad's memory."

"Does that mean you're going to be the boss of me?"

"Nah." She stuck out her tongue. "Oh no, I like to be pampered."

"I gotcha, girl." He winked.

Once the puzzle was completed, the children yawned but begged to watch the movie Evanston brought. Piled up on the sofa with a bowl of popcorn, he played the Disney movie. Less than thirty minutes later, the children were asleep, Evanston was dozing, and Darcelle wondered if this is what a family would look like with Evanston.

Chapter Fifteen

*D*arcelle frowned in annoyance. Something wasn't quite right—or maybe it was her imagination. She didn't have a headache or stomachache, neither had she skipped her vitamins, so why didn't she feel like herself? Work had to be the culprit, stressing her out.

For weeks, Darcelle had no desire to eat, as if she had lost her sense of taste. Now her energy was zapped. It was barely six on a Saturday evening, and she needed a nap before she collapsed, so her mind could run a self-diagnostic test. Seconds later, she drifted into darkness.

Why was somebody dancing in her head, disturbing her rest? She couldn't drown it out, Darcelle registered it was her phone playing Evanston's ringtone.

"*Huh?*" She glanced around her living room to regain her bearings and spied her phone. She grabbed it before it defaulted to voicemail. "Hello."

"Hey, babe. Are you asleep?" Evanston didn't hide his surprise.

"Yeah. I guess so." She yawned. "It's been a long week, and I'm mentally and physically exhausted."

"Oh. I had hoped we could do a movie or something low-key to cap off our workweek."

Any other time, Evanston wouldn't have had to ask. It was a given the weekends were theirs—even if they had other commitments, they still touched base but not tonight. "I'm drained. Raincheck for tomorrow?"

"Sure, babe." Evanston's tone was easygoing, but she picked up on his disappointment. "Sorry. Love you." His whisper was soothing to her ears but didn't eradicate the uneasiness settling on her.

"Love you so much more." That happy thought sparked a smile.

"You are so wrong about that, lady. I fell in love with you first." He chuckled, and they said their goodbyes.

Darcelle rolled over on her sofa and closed her eyes. Sleep evaded her mind despite her body's protest. She stared at the twinkling skylights outside her window in the distance, hoping they would lull her to sleep. Darcelle grabbed her phone again.

"Hey, Mom."

"Hey. What's going on?" Alarm rang in Nellie's voice. "Are you sick? Do I need to bring you soup? Did you have your flu shot?"

"I'm tired. That's all." Her mother's bantering drained her even more.

"You're usually with Evan. Is everything okay with you two?"

"We're perfect." She remained silent as her mother continued to quiz her about whether it was her job, Shana, or something else. "I don't know, Mom. I just don't feel like myself." She shrugged. It was hard to put a finger on it.

"I should be happy, but I'm not. I'm kind of sad—depressed."

"Depressed? Hush, girl. You'd better count your blessings. You have a good man who loves you, a good job that's about to promote you, a loving family, a nice car, an apartment…and Jesus loves you. You should be ashamed of yourself, thinking that kind of foolishness."

Whoa. What did I say to deserve this tirade? Now Darcelle was getting annoyed with her mother's uncalled-for scolding. If she couldn't confide in her own mother, then who?

Me. God's whisper faded.

"You know what's sad? Losing my husband after forty years. It's been almost five months since your daddy died, but Isaiah 26:3 says, 'God will keep us in perfect peace with our mind stayed on Him,' so I've focused on Jesus, and He is my Comforter. You need more Jesus. Come to church more often, and let the sermons minister to you because there's no room for depression in the life of a Christian."

Nellie paused. "The devil is a lie. Don't you ever speak that nonsense again. Now, you and Evan are practically joined at the hip. Maybe you two should slow down. A good night's rest should help."

Yeah—sleep, something she'd been chasing lately. "You're right." *Whew.* She had no idea her feelings would be a sore spot. Darcelle brushed off her melancholy and accepted her mother's counsel. She was tired and yawned as if to prove it.

"Where's Cece?" Cedric asked as he exchanged a handshake and pat on Evanston's back when they met up at a sports bar. "It's Saturday night, and I know I'm not your first choice for a date."

Evanston straddled the stool at the counter-height table. "She's tired, so my better half decided to stay at home and rest."

"Aren't you the perfect gentleman?" His friend seemed amused. "Sounds like you're a hubby in training."

"Not ruling it out." Evanston rubbed his chin. "This may sound corny, but I'm not in sync without her."

"You sound like a greeting card. Might as well be married—I mean y'all been dating—how long?"

"Four, five months. She says I was her Christmas present, but—" He smiled. He thought about how they had gone tit-for-tat about whether the gift of falling in love started at the dealership or Christmas day at her mother's house. "It's the other way around. Darcelle was the surprise in my life that evening."

"Don't I remember?" Cedric bobbed his head. "This has been a long time coming, my friend. You were bound to meet the right one." He took a sip from his glass as the server approached to take their orders.

"She's the one, and I'm thinking about doing something about it."

"Are you serious?" Cedric sat straighter on the stool and rubbed the back of his neck, mumbling a profane word: "Wow, so y'all been talking about it?"

"Not yet—" Cheers from Cardinals fans drowned out Evanston as their team hit a two-run homer to take the lead in the sixth inning.

"Man, this is a good game."

Evanston agreed but didn't take his eyes off the extra-large flat screen. "Yeah, we'll talk later because she is definitely the one."

The next day, he stopped by his parents' house for a visit and a meal. As he sat across from his father indulging in his mother's cooking, his father eyed him as a slow smirk stretched across his face. "You're really in love with Darcelle. I can see it."

Evanston grinned like an embarrassed schoolboy. "She's so easy to love. She smiles when she's sharing something with me. I love her giggle. Cece's unique, refreshing, and…everything I didn't know I wanted in a friend and a lady."

His father snickered. "Sounds like you've found the one."

"I think so. Every time I'm with her, my heart is shouting, *Don't let her get away.*"

Pushing back from the table, Langston went to the stove and swiped a cornbread muffin from the pan. He took a bite that left less than half remaining. "How does she feel?"

"The same way."

"I know I shouldn't compare Darcelle with your ex, but I don't think Phylicia was ever the one for you."

"Now you have an opinion." Evanston grunted with mixed feelings about the revelation. "I wish you'd have shared that sooner and saved me the heartache. It was humiliating to think while I was contemplating a forever, she was devising a plan of escape. I can't believe I got duped like that."

"It was one of those life lessons. You needed a taste of what love wasn't. I think your sister took it worse than you.

She didn't like anyone messing over her big brother. Although she likes Darcelle, I can tell she's waiting for her to make one false step."

Evanston shook his head. "My miniature pit bull. Jess needs to stand down. Cece and I clicked from the beginning. I was smitten the first time I saw her. What I have with her is something special. I'm sure my lady will win Jess over too."

"The way you're grinning, I can tell you're up to something." Langston smirked.

"Yep." Evanston had a plan to stay on a steady course with Darcelle until he felt confident she was the one he couldn't let get away. Standing, he shook his father's hand. "I'll never kiss and tell, but I'll kiss my mother on the way out."

Darcelle snuggled deeper into her sheets and exhaled. Yes. She purred as she drifted into slumberland again. Too soon, Evanston's ringtone jolted her awake.

"Hey, my sleeping beauty. Wake up. I brought you breakfast."

Darcelle's drowsy voice gained strength. "Where are you?"

He chuckled. "Outside your door. Don't keep me waiting."

"What?" She disconnected and leaped out of bed. Although she loved his surprises, not today. Darcelle washed her face, brushed her teeth, then freshened up before grabbing her sweatshirt and pants.

She hurried to the door and was met with the warmest eyes. "Van." Her mother was right. She was blessed beyond measure. She fell into his chest, and he wrapped his free arm around her, then kissed the top of her hair.

"Took you seven minutes, Cece."

"Good thing I'm hungry." She giggled. "Otherwise, it would've taken me fifteen if I had showered and fixed my face." She stuck out her tongue and grabbed the bags.

At the table, he said grace, then they dug in. She usually liked blueberry crepes from this bakery, but it was as if her taste buds were switched off. She went through the motion of forcing herself to enjoy them so as not to hurt his feelings.

"What did you do last night without me?"

"Hung out with Cedric. Guess what I did when I got home." The pride beaming from his face was unmistakable.

Tilting her head, Darcelle didn't have the mental energy to guess but strained her mind anyway. "I give up."

"I tackled some Sudoku puzzles."

"What?" Darcelle was shocked and pleased. "Look at my big, strong man. You ain't scared. I'm proud of you." She had mentioned the brainteasers in passing, not knowing he had paid attention. "So, how many did you get right?"

He bowed his head like a reprimanded child. "One out of eight."

Darcelle couldn't stop laughing, and he joined her. It felt good to release some of the exhaustion.

After they finished eating, he cleaned her kitchen, which included loading the dishes from the previous night into the dishwasher as she showered.

A meticulous housekeeper, Darcelle never would have retired for the night without her place spotless or allow Evanston or anyone to see her messy kitchen.

Since Sunday was their low-key day, Evanston didn't leave her side as they watched movies and tried some sudoku brainteasers together. She even dozed a little bit.

"It's getting late," Evanston announced so they could get ready for work the next day.

She was tired from the smiles, laughs, and kisses they shared, which was a good thing. Darcelle looked forward to sleeping like a baby.

Chapter Sixteen

*D*arcelle and Evanston parted ways on Mother's Day, so they could spend time with their own mothers. The Price family, minus Harold, filled a pew at church. It wasn't the same, though; her daddy's absence would forever be noted.

Pastor Clemons' sermon from Deuteronomy 5:16 was perfect as he preached on "Nothing Like a Mother's Prayer."

Nellie's prayers had carried her family through good times and bad. They were the answer to whatever problems ailed them, except...well...since her mother said nothing was wrong with Darcelle, there was nothing to pray for. Her mother was clear, not to mention that topic ever again—depression wasn't an issue in the life of a child of God. The Prices were strong and could endure anything. Period.

After service, she and her sisters prepared dinner and smothered their mother with love and gifts. Valencia was overcome with emotion by her children's gift—a photo she had taken with JJ and Zuri that Darcelle made into a jigsaw puzzle.

"You can play with us, Mommy." Zuri wrapped her arms around Valencia's neck and squeezed. Even JJ added to the group hug without being coaxed.

While Darcelle visited, Evanston had flowers delivered for Nellie and Valencia. His thoughtfulness was amazing.

"That man's a keeper." Her mother blushed and wagged her finger at Darcelle.

"Oh, don't I know it. I'm not giving him up." She kissed everyone goodbye. In her car, she called Evanston as she drove home.

"I was hoping to see you and get my Cece fix before we start our workweek." He didn't hide the expectancy in his voice.

Closing her eyes at a light, Darcelle envisioned them sitting on a park bench and resting her head on Evanston's shoulder. Sounded perfect. A horn honked behind her, and she blinked back to reality. "Name the place, and you can steal me away for an hour, then I really have to get home."

"How about Pito's Place for dessert? I'll save us a seat when I beat you there. Love you."

"Cool. Love you more."

"Woman, what have I told you about that? Impossible for you to love me more than I love you."

Their call ended as Darcelle smiled. Yep. Her man was most definitely a keeper.

Evanston leaned on his car hood, arms folded, watching and waiting for Darcelle to turn into the parking lot. When her vehicle drove down the aisle, searching for an available spot, he waved. His strides were swift as he made his way to her door. Her face glowed when she stepped out.

"My better half." Evanston wrapped her in an embrace and rubbed his lips in her hair as if he were trying to leave an imprint.

She welcomed his embrace with a sweet, slow kiss. After a couple of pecks, she mumbled against her lips, "I'm your best half."

"You'll get no argument from me about that." He tweaked her nose and guided her toward the patio seating.

They ordered a slice of key lime pie to share and two cups of coffee. Scooting her chair closer to his, Evanston stretched his arm around her shoulders and guided her closer. "So, when is the V.P. retiring? You've been doing a lot of double duty. Our mid-week dates have become hit-or-miss. It's driving me crazy."

She was Evanston's energy drink on Tuesday or Wednesday evenings. The weekends were too long to wait to see her. The FaceTime didn't count. As a Black man, he was sympathetic to her woes about the old boy's network and breaking through the glass ceiling. He reassured her and offered his opinions on how to navigate around the isms—sexism, racism.

Their carefree moments were slipping, replaced by reruns on repetitive conversations. It was becoming frustrating, but he would never tell her that.

"Mr. Jeffries is leaving at the end of the month."

"Good." He brought her hand to his lips. "Jess will be home from school next weekend. Her boyfriend secured an internship here this summer. How those two masterminded that is beyond me. Anyway, I'm hoping we can double date with them a couple of times, basically, giving me an excuse to keep an eye on the dude." Seemed like it wasn't long ago when Evanston chaperoned his baby sister's dates.

Glancing up, Darcelle's eyes seemed to smile at him. "I would like that."

Chapter Seventeen

"I haven't seen you this excited in a long time." Evanston eyed Darcelle as they drove to the airport. His woman glowed with happiness that had him smiling.

Shana had announced she was coming home for Memorial Day weekend, and Darcelle was hyped about her visit. "I haven't seen her in a long time—since Daddy's funeral last November."

Darcelle had told him a while back how the two been friends since high school. Close as sisters. Distance didn't cut their ties while Darcelle studied in Michigan and Shana at the University of Texas at Austin.

"Reed and Meeks lured me back to St. Louis after graduation with a signing bonus and a promise to put me on a management track for promotions as their shining star in the world of finance. It was a win-win situation—my family and job security."

Evanston added, "I won too."

Her company was making good on their promise, so why was his woman stressed? As he turned into the airport garage, he could feel Darcelle's excitement build.

"I can't wait for you to officially meet her." She was animated, waving her hands in the air. "Now, are you sure you're okay taking a raincheck to go sailing on the Lake of the Ozarks?"

"Yes…this time."

She leaned over and pecked kisses on his cheeks.

"You light up my world, and I've missed that while the firm has overworked my baby."

Darcelle bowed her head. "Sorry. I've proven my worth with my past promotions. I'm doing the same for this one. There's a lot of perks and authority that comes with the appointment, so it's worth the extra effort."

He slid into an open space, turned off the ignition, and rested his arm over the steering wheel. He parted his lips and gritted his teeth before he revealed his thoughts. "True. I get it that blacks have to work twice as hard to be on 'equal' footing—" he used air quotations— "with our white counterparts, but you said the company has groomed you for upper management since they hired you. It's yours."

This was a big-time position for Darcelle that came with a voice. The opportunity to become the first African American of anything was an honor, even if the responsibilities were intimidating.

"There's a difference between being confident and overconfident." She tilted her head from side-to-side. "Besides the ridiculous salary bump, a Black woman will finally have a voice at the table. I can't give back to the community if I don't have a say in what we want."

"I get it, babe," he said it and winked, but she wondered if he really did. "Now, let's go inside and get your partner in crime."

"Yes." Darcelle unfastened her seatbelt.

Evanston got out, rounded the bumper, and opened her door. "I'll get the balloons in the back." He grinned that crooked smile, and his eyes shined bright.

"No. I want to carry them."

"Okay. My kid in a candy store." They laughed before he brushed a kiss against her lips.

Linking her fingers through his, Darcelle leaned into his shoulder as they strolled to the crosswalk, then waited at the curb for traffic to clear before proceeding inside the terminal.

Minutes later, Darcelle broke free when she saw her tall, fashion-conscious friend. The highlights in Shana's thick natural twists accentuated her beauty as they fanned from her head like blossoming flower petals. They screamed their greeting before hugging and swaying from side to side.

"It's been forever."

Shana stepped back. "Look at you. You're drooling with happiness. Wow." She glanced over Darcelle's shoulder. "Hi, Evan."

"Nice to finally meet you in person." Evanston stepped forward to shake her hand.

Typical Shana, her friend swatted his hand away and hugged him. "No need for that. Take care of my friend," she whispered, then added loudly, "or I'll cut you, then repent."

Darcelle turned away to snicker. They hadn't used that threat since they were in high school and were fearless when they came up against bullies. Shana's cousins had taught Shana and the Price sisters how to kick butt.

"I have my best friend and my best man." Darcelle danced in place. Happiness never felt so good.

"For the record," Evanston said, staring into her eyes and lifting a brow, "I'm your only man."

"Oh." Shana struck a pose, and with dramatic flair, positioned a hand on her shapely hip. She topped her stance off with a roll of her neck. "We're going there? Well, if that's the case, I'm her only best friend."

Laughing, Darcelle looped her arms through theirs and wanted to skip down a yellow brick road as the trio headed to baggage claim to retrieve Shana's luggage. It was going to be a great weekend.

On the drive back to her apartment, Evanston was his charming self. Shana had given Darcelle the thumbs-up when he wasn't looking.

"You ladies sure you don't want to grab something to eat before I drop you off?" Evanston's brown eyes widened with hope.

"Nope. I stocked my fridge, so we're good, sweetie."

"Okay." His mimic of a pout was adorable. When they arrived at Darcelle's, he took Shana's suitcase inside. "While you're having fun, remember this..." In slow motion, he bestowed a soft kiss on Darcelle's lips.

"Whew. I will." Closing her eyes, Darcelle enjoyed his embrace and the reminder.

Shana cleared her throat. "Bye, Evan," she said in a singsong manner and wiggled her fingers. Before Darcelle could close the door, Shana screamed, "I'll take one of him, same height. A dark-roasted blend—and a DNA clone of his looks. I thought he was good-looking through FaceTime, but *girllll*, I almost passed out, along with other female passengers. And he seems like a sweetheart."

"Thanks, Shana," Evanston shouted from outside the door.

Busted.

The ladies giggled and made sure the door was airtight. Once Shana settled in, the pair stuffed themselves on Asian cuisine, which Darcelle had cooked earlier in the day. It was Shana's favorite food. In no time, they collapsed on the sofa in front of the TV. Darcelle didn't reach for the remote.

"You are doing it—new car, new man, a soon-to-be new position. As Miss Nellie says, you are blessed."

"If only Daddy were here to see all this."

"You've got Evan. He's got your back now."

"Yeah, but—"

Shana gave her the side-eye. "But what?"

"I know that man loves me, and I have his support, but I think my career aspirations are testing his patience." The thought pained her, but this was her life's goal. "I hope he doesn't have a problem when I have to attend more functions, travel, or asked to sit on more boards."

"Stop worrying about it. Plus, I believe Mr. Price would've given his blessings before Evan would have asked for it to propose. Just sayin'." Although Shana called her mother Miss Nellie, she wouldn't call her dad by his first name, even with a mister in front of it. That's where her friend drew the line.

"And I wouldn't mind him asking." She exchanged a five-high with Shana.

"Darcie Giles—or should I say, Cece Giles." Shana snickered.

Darcelle blushed. "Either way, I like the name. Maybe I should practice signing it, but we could date for years, and he could never propose."

"This isn't college. A four-year campus love doesn't count. Kevin thought graduation meant your relationship was finished too—jerk."

"And I was crushed." The pain had lasted for years. Kevin had been her bona fide first love.

"I was mad." Shana cracked her knuckles, then winced. "Guess I'm getting too old to fight. Just kidding. Now the Lord will fight my battles."

Darcelle hoped the Lord was on her side with the job situation. She snickered, recalling a handful of fights they'd averted when Shana cracked her knuckles, then wrapped them in gauze as if she was a boxer in high school. "Yeah, Daddy was ready for a road trip to confront Kevin, but I learned a lot from that relationship and life. If it's meant to be, it will happen."

The more they talked about old times, the more Darcelle's mind drifted to Evanston. She hoped their love would lead them to the altar. She'd survived the breakup with Kevin Spencer in college. That was a trial-and-error relationship. Evanston was the real thing and an essential part of her. No one survived heart surgery without a heart.

Chapter Eighteen

*E*vanston had to ambush Darcelle into a midweek dinner date, because after Shana returned home, Darcelle seemed to revert back into her work mode.

"You're starving our love, baby, and I've never been demanding, or at least I don't think I have. What we have is special, so I hope I'm just as important as your job—if not more."

She gave him an expression he had never seen before. "Is this the quiz where choice A is my man, and choice B is my career? Because I always thought I had both."

Evanston's breathing slipped as her loving eyes went blank. Maybe he had pushed her too far, but he'd wait her out.

"I choose C, Evan. I need a healthy balance of you and my livelihood until my status in life changes."

Darcelle might as well have called him Evanston with the tone she used. So he had gotten himself in the doghouse. Now what? When she gave him a tender smile, it erased their tit-for-tat—maybe. "Noted."

At her door, Evanston pulled her into his arms and kissed her with longing. If they could only talk about future plans that didn't entail her job.

"I love you, Van." Her words were soft.

"I love you more, Cece."

On Saturday morning, Darcelle's sultry voice teased him awake when she called him. Her ringtone always made him smile. "Hey, baby." Eight wasn't early when they were out late on Friday, but he was surprised she was up already.

"I'm hungry, and I want you to treat me to breakfast." Her demand was unmistakable and comical.

It had been a while since they'd dined out for bacon, eggs, or waffles. "How long will it take you to get ready?"

"Ready and waiting."

Whoa. Her sassiness propelled him out of bed, and he caught himself from tumbling to the floor. "Clock me. See you in fifty minutes." He ended the call and rushed through his morning routine.

An hour later, he rang her doorbell. When she opened the door, he had a bouquet covering his face.

"You're late, but forgiven." She playfully snatched the flowers from his hand and giggled, then stepped back so he could enter.

They indulged in a morning kiss before her stomach rumbled.

His own stomach expelled a roar. "We're hungry. Come on. Let me feed my woman."

Her purse and jacket were waiting on a chair at the door. She grabbed it, and they left. While driving, he glanced her way a few times. "Why is my lady so hungry this early on a Saturday morning?"

"I was up early to go over minutes from the fourth quarter shareholder's meeting."

Work—again. Should have figured. Why did that tidbit cause his heart to play dead with disappointment? Darcelle couldn't leave work at the office to enjoy life. Now, he focused on the road. He tightened his jaw to keep from saying the wrong thing.

Darcelle turned to him. "But, I'm done, so the day is ours."

"That's what I'm talking about." Evanston couldn't keep from grinning. "I guess we'll enjoy lunch and dinner too." Evanston made sure the day was unrushed. They shopped—well, Darcelle did. He made himself comfortable and watched her model clothes for him. The only thing she allowed him to pay for was a wallet. Otherwise, she paid for her own purchases, and he carried the damage from her dollars. For lunch, they dined at an outdoor cafe with a lake view.

While heading to their next adventure, Darcelle suggested a detour. "When Shana was here last week, we house hunted—more like condo counting." She pointed to new construction. "I want you to see this place I plan to buy once my promotion goes through."

"Cece, I don't recall you mentioning moving or buying a condo." Evanston followed her directions to the plot of land. He scratched his head slowly, as if to uproot his thoughts. Was he wrong to feel left out of the loop?

She waved her hand in the air. "Oh, I hadn't given it much thought until Shana and I passed by these exquisite homes. Curiosity got the best of us, so we decided to check out some of the display models. I envisioned me going over the top with Christmas decorations like houses I've visited on holiday tours.

"Next thing I know, I'm having a serious conversation with the sales rep about the amenities, floor plan, and phase one closeout deal. I put down a deposit to hold my lot. There were only three left."

Seriously? Evanston didn't care if his outside voice was louder than usual. "Who are you, and what have you done with my woman? Since the time I've known you, I don't recall you ever making a split decision like that. What did Shana say?"

Darcelle laughed and fanned her hand in the air. "It was her idea to look, but my idea to buy. Although Shana thought it was perfect for me, she suggested I wait." She looked at him.

"I was hoping we would go house hunting together," he said. *Silent hint: I'm wanting a forever with you.*

She shrugged as if it was no big deal and glanced out the window. "It was a spur-of-the-moment thing."

Did she not get the clue? "But I've been the voice of reason or gotten you a better deal like when you brought the car. You know I have experience with protecting you from high-pressured sales reps." He grinned. "Plus, I wanted to talk about our future together."

"I like the sound of that." She smiled and closed her eyes. "I know you're my protector, but I was lucid this time and negotiated extras in the closeout price." Facing him, she puckered her lips, and he delivered. The kiss was sweet but did nothing to heal his bruised ego caused by leaving him out of her decision-making.

What if they were to marry within the next few years? He was willing to sell his house, but he sure didn't want to live in her condo.

On Sunday morning, Darcelle wasn't up for church or brunch, so Evanston defaulted to his parents' church. They were glad to see him. Even Jessica and her boyfriend were in attendance, outshining his solo appearance.

While Pastor Howard preached, Evanston picked up bits and pieces of the sermon, but he couldn't remember one keynote after the benediction. In truth, he was confused. Was Darcelle using her job as an excuse to pull away from him?

Her eyes and kisses didn't back up that theory. He thought they shared and talked about everything. Darcelle's decision to purchase a pricey condo on a whim without mentioning it to him had him feeling a sense of betrayal. Was he no longer her confidant?

He trailed his parents back to their house, craving a man-to-man talk with his father and his mother's meatloaf and mac-n-cheese. "Am I being overbearing?" Evanston asked as they reclined in the family room.

Langston was slow in answering. "What's really the problem, son? You own a home. She's living in an apartment and wants to be a homeowner too. Maybe you're overthinking this."

"Maybe." He tugged the hairs on his chin. "Folks don't buy a pricey house as a starter house. I'm annoyed, but I don't know why."

"Have you discussed future plans with her?" His mother stepped outside the kitchen door onto the veranda. "Women today are independent. They're not waiting on a man to marry them to live their lives."

"I've hinted of a future. We've had surface discussions about the topic, but nothing deep."

"Hints about a future don't work for women." She shook her head. "Young people today are clueless about what love is and isn't. When I was in my twenties, couples knew when they found the one and married within six months, sometimes sooner. Women today settle for living together. That wasn't the norm in our day, right, honey?"

His father nodded.

Darcelle had never mentioned buying a condo. No, he wasn't her husband, but he thought she would have valued his opinion, or did she think he wasn't going to ask her to marry him?

"If Darcelle is the one, snag her before another man does—"

"I thought I had, Mom." He and Darcelle never had a problem communicating. Maybe they did need to talk about the future. "Thanks, Dad, for listening." He stood to leave. Instead of a handshake, he hugged his father.

Chapter Nineteen

"Noooo." It had to be a recurring dream. Evanston groaned when Darcelle told him the company had pushed back the announcement for the promotion until late July. The madness of her working late into the evening continued.

He missed the times whenever they would drop whatever they were doing to see each other. Their mental connection had become fragile too. He and Darcelle had a good handle on reading each other's body language and mood. However, Evanston was no longer privy to her thoughts. Their emotional connection was fading fast.

Although they had honest talks, maybe their honesty wasn't deep enough. After seven months, he was looking at permanency with Darcelle without fear of competition with a job. He made close to six figures without overtime. As his wife, they wouldn't have to struggle.

The Mrs.

The thought made him smile.

Their upcoming Fourth of July holiday agenda included starting off at his parents' house, a quick trip by Cedric's, then ending at the Prices'. Plans changed when she suggested they take different cars.

"Why would we do that?"

"I need to spend a few hours on this report." The hesitation in her voice made him feel like the bad person, so he consented to keep the peace between them as a storm brewed within him.

So Evanston spent most of the day at his parents', avoiding more in-depth discussions about Darcelle, especially with Jessica. He skipped Cedric's barbecue altogether, but he wouldn't disappoint JJ and Zuri, so he made a pitstop for ice cream.

As he drove to the Prices', he practiced his smile—not too wide or crooked—but he had to show some teeth; otherwise, his disappointment with Darcelle's last-minute change of plans would leak through.

When Evanston parked in front of Darcelle's mother's house, he stepped out of the car with his offering, looking for her car. Not there, and he had given her a thirty-minute head start. He huffed and followed the voices on the path to the backyard.

Valencia waved and announced his presence. "Mom, I see Evan."

Zuri dropped her jump rope and charged toward him as he waved back. If only he had a big brother or older cousin, he could introduce to Valencia. She had a heart of gold, and her children were like sponges, soaking up the attention. No wonder Harold Price was ready to hunt down the children's father.

Although all the Price sisters were pretty and smart, Evanston had the jewel—the pearl he boasted.

With Zuri latched onto his side, he greeted Darcelle's family with a genuine smile—not a practiced one. He held up a gallon of ice cream. "Who should I give this to, and have you seen my better half?"

Nellie had a glimpse of a frown before she perked up. "If Darcelle was here, she would remind you she's your best half."

"And she would be correct." Evanston winked. "So, she hasn't made it here yet." It wasn't a question.

"Nope. Sorry." Valencia shook her head and took the ice cream, then strolled to the food table for two cones for her children.

"Have you talked to her? She's usually the first one here." Nellie frowned. Was that concern on her face too?

"Cece said she was finishing up some work project and would meet me here." Evanston huffed. "I was running late and still beat her."

Monique glanced at the time on her cell phone and shrugged. "Probably lost track of time."

"She's coming," Nellie emphasized, directed at her youngest, clearing her throat. "While we wait, you might as well grab a plate."

Evanston massaged his belly. "If you made your potato salad, Mrs. Price, I'm starved." At his mother's, he'd made sure he left an empty pouch in his stomach, reserved for Mrs. Price's homemade recipe. First, he stepped out of their hearing and called Darcelle. He ended the call when it was about to go to voicemail.

After visiting with the family for an hour or so, Evanston said his goodbyes—a mix of annoyance and hurt. He had called Darcelle twice more—voicemail.

Family, commitment, love—the greatest was love. Reed and Meeks couldn't compete. Evanston doubted the company really appreciated her. "Cece, you're losing yourself to this job."

Forget walking on eggshells about the brokerage firm. Evanston was about to have the talk, but what if something was wrong? This wasn't like Darcelle to miss her own family barbecue.

Fearing the worst, he held his restraint from not going over the speed limit to get to her apartment.

Chapter Twenty

Yes, Darcelle was wrong that she missed the family barbecue, but the argument that followed with Evanston took her by surprise. What was his problem?

First, he leaned on her doorbell like he was some type of crazy man, which made Darcelle fear something was wrong.

"What's going on?" Her tears were on standby, bracing for the news.

"You missed the barbecue—your own family—and when you were a no-show, I was concerned and came to check on you."

"You scared me." She patted her chest. *Whew.*

"Scared you? Woman, you're driving me crazy." He rubbed the back of his neck.

"Why didn't you just call?"

"I did. More than once. Check your phone." Evanston's tone bordered on a demand than a suggestion. He didn't wait for an invitation to step inside, then closed the door, which was a good thing since their discussion quickly evolved into an argument. "Cece, help me understand what is going on here."

She looked at her phone. Her mom, sister, and Evanston had called. *Oh, boy.* She immediately sent a group text and included Evanston to be funny and lighten the tension. **Sorry, I missed the BBQ. Overworked and overslept. I hope Mom fixed me a plate.** ☺

Evanston's phone chirped, and he read her message. He didn't seem amused. "That's it? Since when do you miss a family gathering?"

She had to think.

"Exactly. Your mother said never."

Wait a minute. She didn't like his tone. Was he chastening her? Now Darcelle had an attitude, and she folded her arms to deliver the blow. "You're not my daddy, Evanston Giles, to come at me with a scolding as if I were a child. Do you think my family isn't important to me?" She loved this man, so why were they having an argument over something he had blown out of portion?

Her doorbell rang again. Darcelle rolled her eyes. *Who or what now?* This time it was Valencia and the children. "I just received your text, so you're alive and well. I wondered what happened, so I stopped by on my way home to make sure everything is okay. I see Evan beat me here."

Home for her sister was in the other direction.

"Hi, Aunt DeeDee." Zuri hugged her. "Mr. Evan brought ice cream…"

"You can tell her about it later." Valencia placed her hand on her daughter's shoulder. "Come on, you two. Summer camp tomorrow." Valencia hugged her, then left.

Darcelle exhaled and looked at Evanston. The reprieve had sent them to their own corners in the boxing ring to cool off. Before she could apologize for scaring him and telling him she loved him for caring, her mother's ringtone caused further delay.

She withheld her groaning. *What is wrong with everybody?* she wanted to scream but didn't. "Hi, Mom. Yes, I'm okay. I took a nap, and I guess I was more tired than I realized. Evan is here to check on me, and Valencia just left. Everything's okay. I just overslept."

"Then, we'll talk tomorrow, sweetie."

"Okay, mom." She smiled, ended the call, and swirled around to meet Evanston. Her sister had come and gone, but her man wasn't going anywhere with his arms folded and back leaned against the wall. "See, all is well."

Shaking his head, Evanston pushed off the wall. "But it's not, Cece. You're pushing me away, and clearly, there's nothing I can do about it."

"Van, stop trying to make me feel guilty. Do you even understand the pressure on me?" Her attitude was resurfacing as she positioned her fists on her hips.

"I'm trying to, woman, but you're making it difficult. I'm done here. Call me when you can pencil me in." He huffed, marched to her door, and left without another word.`

Who was that man? She shook her head.

The next morning, Darcelle scooted up in bed and covered her face with her hands. What was going on with her?

A quick power nap she'd craved from her exhaustion turned into a deep slumber. She imagined the tongue lashing her mother, in a sweet voice, was saving for her. Smiles would not reach Nellie's eyes—eyes to the soul that never lied.

Darcelle was starting to feel defeated in life and in her relationship. A position at the firm that was supposed to be sealed shouldn't be this hard to deliver.

When the announcement was delayed, she asked her boss and mentor why.

"It's a formality. You presented well during the interview, but certain board members wanted to review every recognition you earned, quarterly reviews, *yadda, yadda, yadda.* Probably fingerprint samples and a head count of the number of hair strands. It's brutal, but you've got this." William Blair's soft chuckle was missed on her.

Yes, she knew there would be scrutiny. Every Black person was subject to overkill.

Darcelle had met all the prerequisites for the position: a solid work record, unblemished private life—no skeletons—company and personal community presence.

Checkmate.

She sighed. It was a new day, or new God's mercies Nellie would remind her daughters every morning, quoting from a verse in the third chapter of Lamentations.

Darcelle rushed through her shower but dressed with attention to detail. Too bad she couldn't master the slight puffiness under her eyes, despite all the sleep she had gotten.

Her first stop was her mother's. Darcelle rang the bell once before inserting her key. The echo of her heels overpowered the faint sound of the radio in the kitchen. "Mama," she called out.

The hallway ended in the spacious kitchen where Nellie sipped from a cup of coffee—probably her second cup, her mother's limit.

Her body language wasn't readable, and she hadn't glanced up. *Oh boy.* Darcelle swallowed. She took the scenic trip around the table to deliver a loving kiss on her mother's cheek.

"Hi, I can't believe I missed yesterday. I'm sorry." Darcelle was repentant as she sat in front of her mother. To blame it on the job would be useless

Slowly, Nellie lifted her chin and stared at her daughter. She did nothing to mask the hurt. Darcelle could have accepted disappointment better. Hurt took more recovery.

"I can't believe it either."

"I'm sorry," she pleaded. "It was only supposed to be a short nap. I guess I was so tired... It was as if I was comatose because I couldn't move."

Blank face.

"When I woke again, I was still exhausted. I couldn't help but steal more sleep." Would tears help?

Quietness.

"You know I wouldn't miss your potato salad." Darcelle smacked her lips to emphasize as her stomach craved a taste, even at eight-thirty in the morning.

Her mother folded her arms. Finally, some movement. "How is it *your* boyfriend could make it to *your* family gathering, yet *you* were a no-show?"

Nellie stood and padded the table. Double movement. She was gathering her arsenal, and Darcelle braced for the verbal assault.

"I know you have to get to work... Looks like you've lost weight." She *tsk*ed. "I'll make you a breakfast sandwich."

"Thanks, Mama. I'm taking my vitamins," Darcelle said in a childlike voice. Maybe she had overthought things. She exhaled. She loved family forgiveness.

"What's more important than your family?" Nellie huffed as she performed the task. "If you don't re-evaluate your priorities, you'll miss out on a good man who loves you. Evan would be a faithful husband and a good father. My heart bled for him that you stood him up too. Is *that* job *that* important? Are you so greedy for worldly things that you're living beyond your means?"

Those weren't questions.

They were accusations.

"What are you referencing? Is this about the condo?"

Her mother had been happy Darcelle had purchased it at the ridiculous close-out price. Nellie agreed it was an investment when she and Shana had mentioned it to her. Her mother's approval reinforced that Darcelle had made the right decision to put down a sizable deposit.

Her mother didn't answer, so Darcelle assumed it had to be about Evanston. "When it comes to Van, I do love him, and he loves me. We haven't discussed marriage. It's only been seven months. Besides, two people could love each other and never marry. Couples are living together—"

Oops.

Wrong answer.

Nellie's nostrils flared. "Without a wedding ring, you best walk away. Love is more than emotions and physical attraction. Where your soul will spend eternity should be at the top of the list."

How did the conversation go from missing a barbecue to a good husband and now missing heaven? Darcelle bowed her head to hide her aggravation. Forget the sandwich. Any appetite she had was fading fast, but she had to regain her strength to defend herself.

"Mom, I'm sorry I missed the barbecue, but this isn't about me living beyond my means. That's not who I am. I started my career as a financial planner. If I can't budget my investments, what kind of example will that be to others? Reed and Meeks has been good to me. Although the promotion is a given, I can't be seen as a slacker."

Her mother huffed and placed the wrapped sausage muffin sandwich in front of her, but she didn't move her hand. "Well, the point remains you're still working too hard."

Darcelle nodded as she licked her lips. The aroma alone was giving her energy. "Trust me, I'm feeling it too." She'd taken an hour comp time this morning but planned to leave the office on time today. Her body was demanding it. "Thank you."

"Darcelle Caren Price, don't let that happen again. Your job is not a good reason to put your family second." The sternness in her voice served as a warning. "When Harold was alive, you would beat your sisters here. Your daddy is gone now..." Her mother paused. "Family is just as important, if not more."

"Yes, ma'am," she said in a respectful tone and measured her next words. "Daddy's the one who pushed me to do my best and work hard. To do less would dishonor his memory too."

Pushing back from the table, she stood to hug her mother. The old-fashioned clock ticked in the background, keeping count of the embrace. Like the nap last night, it felt good, so she lingered.

Both were slow to part, so Darcelle added a bonus, a kiss to her mother's cheek. "This will be over soon. Once I'm in my condo, I'll have a pool party for JJ and Zuri to enjoy, then you'll see all my hard work paid off." She hoped her mother understood.

"Go on. I'll be praying God's will with this job situation."

"Amen." Darcelle nodded and left.

Chapter Twenty-one

*E*vanston drummed his fingers on his desk, staring at an email that he had read twice but had no clue of the message.

The object of his frustration's name flashed on his phone with the soothing melody of Darcelle's ringtone. It did nothing to settle his emotions. He squinted, debating if he should be petty and let it go to voicemail.

He manned up and answered but didn't hide the edge to his voice after last night's disagreement. "Darcelle Price." The pettiness reigned when he addressed her using her legal name.

"Van, I'm sorry again."

"And why is the woman I love sorry?"

"You know why. We've never argued like that. It wasn't a good feeling. Are we okay? Would it help if I say I love you?" Her soft, innocent voice soothed his bruised ego.

"Oh, it's working, alright." Evanston surrendered to her too quickly as he softened his tone. "Makeup dates and kisses will make it better. How about lunch?"

"I wish." She groaned. "I've got a working lunch at the office. How about us cooking dinner at my place?"

He smiled at the memories. The few times they'd attempted to cook a meal together at her apartment, they made bigger messes playing around. It was never about the food. It was the flirting, the fun, and the love of being together, pretending they lived under the same roof. He wanted more than make-believe.

"Baby, I know the script. I'll be in your kitchen preparing *our* meal while you work." Nope. He wasn't up for that. "What happened to you and me time? It's been a while since we even had a mid-week dinner date."

His woman was as frustrating as she was beautiful, smart, and savvy. Her passion and conviction were the qualities that fascinated him and made him crave her. When they were alone, they were playful, comfortable, and loving. But when was the last time they were in tune?

"Call me when you get home, and I'll have takeout delivered to you." He couldn't keep feeding her work addiction.

"But Van—"

"Love you, babe." He fought off his emotions as he ended the call. Evanston exhaled to push out thoughts of his baby pleading, which would lead him to give in to her whims, but she had to miss him enough to put him first.

Darcelle Price was slated for the position of assistant vice president. Her mentor and department heads had told her that. The other matter was the condo. He had envisioned them house hunting on a cool fall afternoon together. He thought about what his mother had said. If Darcelle didn't have a ring from him, she was the queen of her own castle. Basically, he didn't have to answer to her.

"Hey, you okay?" Lester asked, nudging him.

Evanston hadn't heard his friend return from a morning training seminar.

"*Huh?*" He snapped out of his reverie. "Yeah, well, no." Evanston whirled his chair around. "Am I being selfish because I want some downtime with her?"

Lester took his seat and stroked his chin as he stared at Evanston. He crossed an ankle over his knee and made himself comfortable. "I'm assuming *her* is Darcelle. Nah, it ain't you. Women trip."

Since Lester had broken up with the event planner, bitter was his middle name. "It was bound to happen. You two have been on a honeymoon since day one. Now, reality has sat in, you'll enjoy making up after the breakup." He wiggled his brows.

"Man, get out of here. Nobody's talking about breaking up. She's obsessed about her promotion. At one time, I thought we were obsessed with each other. I feel when she's at work, she belongs to the firm. When we're together, she still belongs to the company despite being with me." He rubbed his head, a gesture Darcelle said he did when he was annoyed—lately, usually with her, but he did need a haircut.

"Sounds reasonable to me, man." Lester changed his tune. "Vying for a promotion takes on a whole new meaning for us." He pointed to himself, then, Evanston. "She's Black, and a woman, and has to work extra hard to prove she's qualified, even if the promotion has her name on it."

"I get that. I do." Evanston leaned forward to plead his case and win his friend back to ***TeamEvanston. He wasn't the bad person here. How could he talk about a future with the woman he loved who couldn't multitask a relationship and career? Wasn't that a built-in skill in women? Evanston waved his hand. "Forget it. I've got a meeting." He didn't bring up her name anymore that day. That didn't mean she hadn't been far from his thoughts.

Apparently, standing his ground caused Darcelle to make room for them that weekend. She greeted him at her door with a brilliant smile that didn't reach those tired brown eyes. He swept her into his arms and lifted her off the floor.

The kiss they shared was unrushed. "Love you," he mumbled.

"Love you more," she whispered back.

"I doubt that." Evanston gave her a few more pecks as if they were exclamation marks.

Refreshing.

"Hungry?" He linked his fingers through hers.

"Of course."

The atmosphere at dinner was relaxed as their meal was scrumptious. Enjoying the time together, the two lingered long after dessert was served and devoured.

With her undivided attention, Evanston shamefully flirted to make her blush until she turned the tables on him. She teased him without saying a word.

Her alluring eyes. Sultry voice. Kissable lips. The way her fingers combed her hair in slow motion. He was a goner.

Whew. Evanston could dish it out, but it was torture being on the receiving end without yielding to temptation. No better time than this to discuss their long-term future.

Darcelle inched closer and coaxed him across the table for a kiss. Her perfume swirled around them until their lips touched. Explosive.

Deep breath.

His heart rate was ready to run track.

Pulling back, Darcelle batted her eyes and playfully scrunched her nose. "Hey, do you mind if I bounce something off you?"

"Anything," he choked. Evanston needed ice water—now.

As soon as she mentioned her company, everything shut down. There would be no perfect time for the "us" talk with this woman as long as the promotion dangled over them like a mistletoe.

"You know that position is important to me..." Darcelle's soft fingers warmed.

He grunted. "You never let me forget that." When she was silent, Evanston had to remind himself not to beat her up about her goals, so he softened his tone. "Babe, all I'm asking for is balance."

"Aren't you the one who encouraged me when I was nominated for the position?" The accusation wasn't lost on him. "Aren't you the one who said, 'Whatever storms come to blow you over, I'll keep you steady.'"

What storm? Did he say that? Evanston couldn't remember. "Actually, Cece, I didn't think going for the promotion would consume you like this. And I believe this is just a preview of what it will be like after the promotion." *Tame your irritation.*

"Evan Giles, there's a difference between consumption and passion. I want you to be my cheerleader," she pleaded.

"I've invested twelve years in this company…" Her voice faded.

Evanston huffed and looked away. Why was it becoming so frustrating when he talked to her lately? "You know I'm the head cheerleader, and your family is the squad."

Darcelle's expression was unreadable, despite her becoming agreeable. "You're right. Never mind. I guess I've been overthinking this." She became quiet, and for the rest of the evening, Reed and Meeks wasn't mentioned again.

Chapter Twenty-two

*T*oday is the day. Darcelle exhaled the nervousness. The wait was over. No more delays. The announcement would be official, and everyone would know the milestone the company had made.

Happy dance. Darcelle didn't need any music. Of course, her mother would call it a praise dance.

Darcelle couldn't believe the torture the board of directors had her endure. She strutted into the office with confidence that she had unleashed. Her steps kept beat with each breath.

Some coworkers greeted her with smiles. Others stood expressionless while a handful in the "Old Boys Network" nodded. She entered the conference room and paused, not expecting to see some unfamiliar faces.

"Looks like we're all here," her boss and mentor, William Blair, announced, and the chatter stopped. He closed the door, signaling for board members and Darcelle to take their seats around the long executive table that could seat twenty easily. Only a few chairs remained unclaimed.

"Good morning, everyone." William began. "Filling Thurman Stephenson's vacancy due to his retirement has been an exhausting task…"

Don't I know it. Darcelle gave an encouraging nod.

"The candidates were highly recommended and qualified," William continued.

An indescribable uneasiness triggered a stampede of sweat down her back. The dampness began to boil on her skin as she impatiently waited for William to bring his congratulatory speech to a close. Finally, he did and introduced Tom Spann, the senior board member, to further the announcement and torture.

Tom stood, cleared his throat, and fumbled inside his suit jacket for his reading glasses.

"Good morning, everyone. Before we congratulate our newest assistant vice president, I would like to read their qualifications."

Darcelle smiled as he boasted of her accomplishments. However, the more he read, the more she wondered where he had gotten the misinformation. She didn't attend Brown University. What was going on?

"Please welcome Mr. Hadley Cunningham…"

Huh? Hadley who? There was no one within the company by that name. Were the board members looking at her for a reaction? Darcelle's body felt like melted ice cream, and she was about to slide out of her chair and spill under the table.

Never let them see you sweat. Her father's wisdom surfaced, so she sat straightened and looked ahead. *Don't blink*, she coaxed herself.

So to her disappointment, the buzz was true. They had vetted an outsider for an internal promotion. Darcelle

155

hadn't worried because no one could compete with her education and experience. Isn't that what the board wanted?

Darcelle had brainwashed herself to believe she would be etched in industry periodicals as the first woman, the youngest woman, and the first African American to be a financial powerhouse in history.

The company's community outreach, which she'd spearheaded, would be reduced to nothing more than a photo-op during the holidays. She had given the company twelve years she couldn't get back.

Darcelle wanted to leap out of her seat and storm out in protest. She didn't. Besides, Darcelle would have mowed Hadley down as he entered the room on an imaginary red carpet to the applause. A little too hearty for her taste.

The formal meeting concluded with the Old Boys Network welcoming the newcomer. She had been too stunned to congratulate the company outsider whose smug smile was cemented on his over-tanned face.

Since her father drilled into his three daughters to be civil even in a hostile atmosphere, Darcelle plastered on a fake smile, lifted her chin and strolled out of the conference room. To say she was crushed was an understatement. She was devastated.

Lost.

Confused.

That explained why her boss had avoided eye contact, then tried to play her with his fake disappointed expression.

No, sir. Not now.

Once out of sight, Darcelle strutted down the hall to her office, grabbed her purse, and announced she was leaving.

For lunch.

For now.

Two days ago? What? Evanston was shocked. Why had it taken Darcelle forty-eight hours to tell him she didn't get the promotion that had tested their relationship.

Correction. She didn't tell him.

Evanston had learned it on his own, because he had suspected something was off when she hadn't mentioned Reed and Meeks for a couple days. Of course, he had no complaints and was not about to bring up the topic to dominate their conversation.

Actually, he feared she would say there had been another delay. Nope. He was keeping his mouth shut.

Big mistake.

Darcelle's demeanor had been too calm reserved, and controlled. Her expressive eyes struggled to blink and her voice had become too monotone.

When she opened up, Darcelle choked on tears. Her cries had been gut-wrenching. A moment he would never, ever forget—ever. His hugs always seemed to comfort her, but not this time. Evanston had heard men were clueless. In this situation, he agreed.

"Why didn't you tell me? How could you hold back something that has dominated your life—our lives—for months?" Evanston thought their relationship was too close to keep this secret.

"I was too numb. I felt lifeless, as if I was dreaming. I was in denial." She shook her head. Her face was flushed in agony. "To say it would have made it real, and I wasn't ready to face reality."

Evanston still didn't get it, but this wasn't the time to ask for clarification on why Darcelle felt she had to hold this in.

As fate would have it, not a day later, Evanston couldn't believe he found himself torn in a similar plight as Darcelle. Instead of him not having access to her, it was Evanston who wasn't available.

Without warning, the bank's computer system was hacked, compromising thousands of customer accounts. Lunch, breaks, and personal phone calls were under scrutiny because millions of dollars of damages were at stake.

The company wanted the tech department to eat and sleep at the bank headquarters—around the clock. Protecting personal data was a priority.

"This is a hot mess." Evanston scratched his head to restore the security firewall on one of three programs.

Lester yawned, nodding in agreement. It was two a.m., and his friend was on his second energy drink. "Who you telling?"

Evanston craved Darcelle and rest—in that order. Was this how she felt—craving to be with him and her family, but feeling the allegiance to her job?

Although his heart ached for his woman, Evanston had to stay focused. The IT department had to hunt the hackers, a cat-and-mouse game, because of the criminal's sophistication level.

The best he could do was FaceTime Darcelle between restroom runs and *shh* her with soothing words as if his lips were kissing her cheeks through the phone in sixty seconds or less. After three days, she hadn't sounded any better.

Evanston hated himself for his lack of understanding in her similar situation. He hadn't cried since eighth grade when he broke his arm, but it healed. Now, Evanston felt he was on the verge of hidden tears for and with Darcelle because he couldn't kiss her hurt and make it better.

It took days for the tech department to complete hundreds of tests after tests to assure investors, board members, and upper management that this type of security breach wouldn't happen again.

Although the damage was contained, his department was pressured to the point where some managers second-guessed the IT's problem-solving skills. All Evanston could think about was some downtime with Darcelle, but he hadn't been able to give her the attention she needed because of the fiasco at work.

Finally, things seemed to be back to normal at the bank. Evanston left on time and headed to Darcelle's apartment. Red lights seemed to be on his side and flashed green for him to proceed. Heavy traffic tried to sabotage his mission, but Evanston knew the detours to her apartment.

He arrived without flowers or candy, both of which would have brightened her day, but he was more eager to get to her. The other things would have to be a raincheck. After what seemed like eternity, she opened the door, collapsed in his arms, and the dam broke again. Had she been crying like this for days straight?

"I'm sorry," he whispered over and over.

Scooping her up in his arms, he kissed her cheek, then shut the door with his foot. He carried her to the sofa where he held her, clueless of what to say to comfort her. When he thought he found the words, her quietness revealed his woman had cried herself to sleep.

Evanston had never felt this defeated about anything. He was mad at himself for the pressure he had put on her.

He was mad at her job. He was mad at his work demands. He would have been mad at God for not having Darcelle's back, but that would be stretching it.

He stayed for about an hour with her secure in his embrace. Finally, he untangled his arms, made Darcelle comfortable, then covered her with a nearby throw blanket.

Stepping back, Evanston stared, helpless to repair her broken happiness. The security threat at work was easier to fix than Darcelle's sadness.

On her worst day, Evanston hadn't seen her disheveled. Leaning down, he brushed a soft kiss on her cheek. Only because he had to be at work early the next morning, he convinced himself to leave now.

The following day, Darcelle didn't seem any better when he checked on her. She was just as sad, which was why he suggested they go out for dinner after he left work. Darcelle didn't sound too enthused, but she agreed anyway.

They had built their relationship on an active social life—dinners, movies, walks, plays, anything where they could be together was welcomed. All that had been put on hold.

"Baby, I'm sorry. I know how bad you wanted the promotion, and I'm sorry I wasn't there for you when you really needed it." Evanston reached across the table and gathered her hands in his, while they waited for the server to bring their drinks. "I'm here for you. We'll get through this. Okay?" He squeezed her hands and looked into her eyes.

Darcelle nodded, but he wasn't sure if she believed him. Throughout his shift, Evanston called rather than texted. Their chats were brief. Subdued. Lifeless.

With the weekend approaching, Evanston planned to devote the next couple of days to her. He called to take her to a movie or on a visit to the aquarium.

She wasn't up for it. "I need some alone time to process this."

He had no idea the rejection would affect her this way. "I can come over; we can order takeout, watch movies, listen to an audiobook, and be alone together." That earned him a soft chuckle, but she still declined.

By default, he drove to Cedric's to hang out for a few hours. He couldn't shake the turn of events this week. Evanston wasn't happy how the company had deceived Darcelle, but a part of him—a tiny part. Okay, bigger than tiny—was relieved the madness was over, but not at the sake of Darcelle's hurt.

Chapter Twenty-three

*D*arcelle still wasn't sleeping well, and when she did, someone called. She woke to her mother's ringtone, then noticed there were two missed calls from Evanston.

"Morning, sweetie. Haven't heard from you. Doesn't sound like you've gone back to work yet."

"Nope."

"Oh." Silence. "I know how hard you worked for that position, but God knows what you needed. That position wasn't for you." Her mother paused. "I'm sure there will be other opportunities. Reed and Meeks has been good to you. You can't get everything you want all the time…"

Not now, she wanted to scream. There was nothing good about that company at the moment. Hadn't been since the day she left for "lunch."

Her father always had a sympathetic ear before giving Darcelle straight talk. Her mother gave it to her straight without a warmup. It seemed like she was never on Darcelle's side when she needed her. Actually, Darcelle felt alone—isolated.

She needed her mom to transform into an intimidating mama grizzly bear, storm into the building, and demand the board turn over the position that was rightly hers. Her mother had that fierceness in her. Darcelle had seen that personality in action when the Price girls were in grade school, and they had been wronged by a teacher or administrator.

That was then. Fast forward to now.

"Mom, I need time to figure it out, and I will. I'm going to get up and fix myself something to eat."

"I'll make cranberry pancakes. Come eat and spend some time with me, and we can talk." Nellie Price had redeemed herself. "I'd like that."

Darcelle craved a hug anyway. "Okay." They ended the call, and Darcelle dragged herself out of bed, stretched, then shuttled her way into the bathroom, where she stumbled at the sight of her disheveled reflection.

God, is that me? Darcelle's own reflection scared her. The thought of returning to her hiding place under the covers was overruled by the stabbing hunger pain in her stomach. She proceeded to the shower.

Not surprisingly, Nellie had lured Darcelle to a prayer breakfast by mentioning the pancakes. No doubt, she needed prayer, but it didn't seem like God had been concerned about her plight. She couldn't connect with Him at the moment.

That night after convincing Evanston she was okay, they ended the call so he could go to a business seminar for entrepreneurs with Cedric. Just as well, Darcelle wasn't in the mood for company.

She called Shana, who had been her constant confidant, night or day, to rant. "It's been a week, and the flashbacks are vivid, giving me every reason to quit."

"Quitting isn't an option for you. You're a fighter, always have been." Shana almost sounded convincing, "Take this time for yourself. I don't care if it's another week or a month. You've got the time. Breathe. Then, with a clear head, we'll devise a plan B, C, or whatever it takes for you to collaborate with this guy."

"O-okay. Thank you," Darcelle whispered. She cringed at images of Hadley's smirk. Could she answer to a man who knew nothing of her accomplishments? She doubted warm and fuzzy vibes would spring forth.

"But imagine all the good I could've done." Over the years, competitors had attempted to lure her away, but no, Darcelle's loyalty had been with Reed and Meeks. "They made good on their promises. They promoted me three times within twelve years. I stayed believing I'd get a voice at the table to expand the mentoring program for minorities."

"You still can. That's a lot of weight on your shoulders." Shana spoke the truth.

"Yeah." Darcelle was numb. "Daddy always said pay it forward. That was my intent landing that coveted position. Like you, he would've coached me how to handle this, and I would follow it to the letter."

"Yes, Mr. Price was a good man. While you're trying to pay it forward, I'm praying it forward that the Lord Jesus will reveal His next step in your life." She added, "As your best friend, it's my duty to give you a daily dose of inspiration." She either quoted a Scripture or an inspirational thought.

Shana was the best practicing Christian among Darcelle's peers. Her friend lived what she talked about, even when they went out. Shana had this unspoken standard but never made Darcelle feel ashamed of her life choices. They had their share of disagreements, but in the end, their friendship meant something.

"Where did I go wrong?" Darcelle's mind wouldn't shut down.

She jabbed her finger at an otherwise thriving plant that was wilting by her window. She had forgotten to water it.

"You did everything right, so don't start second-guessing yourself." Shana broke into her reverie.

"I'm trying. You don't know how hard." Darcelle untangled herself from the throw blanket and padded across the bedroom floor to her kitchen. She grabbed a bottled water from the refrigerator, then put it back, changing her mind.

Evanston's name flashed on the phone, and she sighed. She rejected his call and texted him. **Talking to Shana. Will call you back.**

Much later, she thought, when she got her head together.

"I need you to come back from your mental meltdown," Shana said as Darcelle sent the text. "We're never going to forget how this went down. Gather your thoughts and pride and strut back into Reed and Meeks like a force to be reckoned with. Hold on, I'll FaceTime you, so you can use the look I mean."

Shana struck an expression that caused Darcelle to chuckle—no, it was a laugh-out-loud moment. "You look crazy. You want me to walk in there with a crazy Black woman attitude?"

"Girl, that's the fierce look." Shana shook her head. "Show them you're not only a team player, but they picked the wrong candidate for the position."

Darcelle paced the floor from the kitchen to the living room and ended back at her window seat in her bedroom to stare outside. That new condo she wanted—her first home to decorate for Christmas—had more than two thousand square feet to allow her to breathe and not feel claustrophobic. "You're right."

Shana's pep talk was so lengthy Darcelle should have taken notes. Her friend created responses for every scenario.

"Ready to do this?" Shana asked. "Do you want me to fly in?"

"Nah, you let me vent for..." Darcelle glanced at the time, and her eyes widened. "Three hours."

"Plus, ten minutes, but who's keeping track?" Shana laughed. "We got this. When boyfriends and family don't get us, we do. Never forget that. Remember the time I broke up with James?"

Humph. "I'll never forget that." Darcelle had shown up at Shana's campus and coaxed her friend back to life so she could graduate. "Whew, girl. That was rough."

"Yep, but you and the Lord pulled me through, so we'll come out on top of this too," she said as if she was a drill sergeant. "Now, you got this?"

"Yep." Darcelle gave her a mock salute.

"Good. Then my job here is done. I'm hungry, and I can only re-heat this frozen dinner so many times. Bye."

When they ended the call, Darcelle was no longer angry, not happy either, but sad. She dared say depressed.

Darcelle won't talk to me. Not really. The weekend had been a bust. The atmosphere was different when he took her to dinner and a movie. She smiled, but it never reached her eyes, or he felt it in his heart.

Instead of a hearty appetite, she picked at her food. Sunday morning, he thought a long ride, nowhere in particular, would clear her head, and she'd share her thoughts with him. She didn't. Darcelle never came out of her hiding place or granted him access. He was frustrated. Heartbroken. Confused.

As if a big chunk of his life had been carved out, Evanston found himself spending more time at his parents' house. When Darcelle wasn't reachable, he stopped by Mrs. Price's house.

He was welcomed with open arms. After finishing a glass of iced tea, then playing with JJ and Zuri, he looked at Mrs. Price. She must have sensed his desire to speak privately and sent her grandchildren outside to play.

"What's on your mind besides Darcelle?" She smiled and waited.

"Nobody but Cece." He frowned, not knowing how to proceed. "Is it only me?"

Nellie's expression gave him a glimpse of Darcelle. "You know she gave her all and all to that company, and the letdown was catastrophic. All she talked about was Reed and Meeks. Now she doesn't want to discuss work at all."

She tapped on the table for emphasis. "Sometimes the world's disappointment is the best time to seek God. I've been praying for my baby." Nellie stared right through him, keeping the rest of her thoughts private.

PAT SIMMONS

"I'm just trying to understand the woman I thought I understood." He got to his feet and jingled the car keys out of his pocket. "She's my better half—my best half as she would say. It feels odd not breathing the same breath with her on the weekends."

Nellie nodded. "I'll be praying for you too. 'Although the Lord be high, He respects and has passion for the lowly.' Young people forget that today. Sometimes, people run to Jesus when they're in trouble, other times people forget He's already there at the time of the crisis."

In all honesty, Evanston hadn't thought about that Scripture, nor did he know where it was located in his Bible. "Thank you." He walked out onto the porch and looked up into the sky, feeling helpless over this situation. "Lord, if You're listening, please help Cece get over this."

As he walked to his car and waited for an answer, all he heard was the laughter and squeals from JJ and Zuri playing in the back with no cares in the world. That brought a smile to his face.

Why did love have to be complicated?

Chapter Twenty-four

*T*he wound was exposed and rooted. The healing process had come to a halt. Darcelle had no desire to mingle, so she watched the world from above on her balcony. Anything she needed, Darcelle opted for deliveries.

She gnawed on her chapped lips as if they were her nourishment. When was the last time she'd bothered with any of her beauty regimens?

Evanston's compliments about her natural beauty were an indication he noticed she wasn't as meticulous. "Babe, don't sweat it. It was never about the makeup that attracted me to you." His words were meant to be comforting. Instead, they were a reminder she wasn't the same person.

Indirectly, she was torturing him. Her wound cracked deeper.

Why couldn't she self-heal like auto-correct?

Although the church message gave her comfort and peace, it didn't seem like enough. Once the benediction ended, she walked outside with Evanston and her family.

An overpowering sensation restrained her as if invisible thugs had jumped her. She wasn't equipped—too weak—to fight this spiritual warfare; they robbed her of any victory she received in church.

She had dinner at her mother's with her niece and nephew on autopilot. Afterward, she and Evanston shared a passionate kiss goodnight. She walked inside, and her spirits plummeted.

Going through the motions was draining, so after a couple of weeks, Darcelle told Evanston she wasn't in the mood for going out.

Argument.

Apologies were given and accepted.

His solution was to stay in and watch movies, so Darcelle indulged him. In the middle of a romantic scene, he turned to her. "You're awfully quiet. You know you can talk to me about anything on your mind." His eyes were as warm and inviting as his voice was soft.

Anything? Not so. I'm still hurt about my lost promotion. Yeah, right.

She played along and talked about everything except what was troubling her. Darcelle batted her eyes before brushing her lips against his puckered ones. Ambushed. He trapped hers into a drugging kiss that almost made her forget her woes—almost.

Evanston wasn't about to allow Darcelle's job to continue to wreak havoc on their relationship. He found that easy to declare, but in reality, it wasn't easy when he found himself in a similar situation at work.

He had no say to mandatory overtime because of the system breach. It was consuming—both body and mind. This is what Darcelle experienced. He got it and apologized to her for not being there, but something told him she didn't believe him.

With the oppressive heat of August, Evanston wanted to prove it by spending the weekends on the lake. Darcelle made excuses until he got tired of begging for dates.

He opted to spend more one-on-one time with Jessica who was getting ready to go back to school. Most of the summer, she and her boyfriend, Brandon, were inseparable.

Resting in the hammock on the deck at their parents' house, Evanston heard voices throughout the house before he felt her presence.

Not one to be ignored, Jessica walked around and blocked his view. "You might as well talk to me because I'm the only sibling you've got."

True, but Evanston was older, wiser, and the one who should counsel his baby sister on matters of the heart. Yet, he was in a place where he felt clueless on how to get his relationship back on track. "It's Cece."

Jessica removed her sunglasses and sat down, rocking the hammock. "I knew it because you've been over here more lately. What has she done? What did you do?"

It didn't go unnoticed that his miniature Pit Bull defender pointed the finger at Darcelle first. Evanston chuckled, but the humor never reached his lips. He shrugged instead. "I love her—"

Crossing her arms, Jessica tapped a foot. "Oh, I get it. She doesn't feel the same way," she stated as if she had assessed his situation in thirty seconds or less.

"Hold on." He sat up to nip that notion. "Something is off between us."

"You mean like when you were with that backstabbing, unfaithful chick Phylicia." Her sneer resembled a growl.

How did her name come up? "Down, girl. Cece isn't cheating on me."

"You sure about that?" Jessica gave him one of those crazy expressions used for memes on social media.

Time to set the record straight. "Very. I'm one hundred and one percent sure. Something special between us is slipping away. I thought it was all about the fallout from her not getting the promotion, but she's taken a leave to deal with it. It doesn't seem like it's helped." He sighed heavily. "Maybe she's been wondering about us."

"Maybe your relationship was built on lust and not love. I've seen the way you've looked at her." She lifted a brow.

He matched her warning glare with one of his own. "Then you should recognize love when you see it. You're starting to cross the line, Jess."

"Okay, okay." She rolled her eyes.

Darcelle had been a damsel in distress when they'd met, and the attraction built from there. He wanted to remain her hero and keep the flame from flickering, but it seemed as if it could be extinguished at any moment.

"Got you thinking, don't I?" Jessica struck a smug pose. "*Umm-hmm.* I don't know why my smart, handsome big brother picks losers. I can hook you up."

"Hold it. I thought you liked Darcelle."

"Oh, I do. She's pretty, funny, and down to earth, but —" she folded her arms— "but nobody messes over my brother."

Why did he bother to have a heart-to-heart with his baby sister? Evanston shook his head. "You have sooo much to learn about relationships, little girl."

"And so do you. I don't know everything that's going on between you two, but, if it doesn't work out, I'll compile a list of suitable chicks that could be potential sister-in-law material."

Loyalty and…immaturity.

Neither worked at the moment. What Evanston wanted to hear was that his Cece would realize their relationship was bigger and more important than any outside forces.

There's nothing bigger than Me, God whispered.

Uh-oh. Was the Lord summoning him to church again?

Chapter Twenty-five

*I*t had been more than a month since she saw the inside of Reed and Meeks. The injustice stung like it was yesterday's bee prick. Darcelle returned to work that morning with her head high and plenty of makeup to cover up her advanced aging process due to stress.

Darcelle had made the decision to go into the office, because sleeping during the day had become her only coping therapy. Each morning brought realization into focus that she had been played. She'd shut her eyes so fast to squeeze out the image in her head. In her sleep, the nightmare waited for her.

Despite Shana's pep talks, Darcelle tried to bounce back, but couldn't. Why did "business as usual" include casualties? She didn't know what normal looked like anymore.

Speaking with her mother and assuring Nellie everything was fine had become routine. Communication with Evanston was on her daily to-do-list, but it didn't seem like either of them had much to say. Her fault—she guessed.

Evanston tried to make her happy with outings, phone calls, and flowers, but Darcelle felt helpless to give him back the love he gave her.

None of that mattered anymore. She made the decision to show her face at Reed and Meeks. The deed had been done. There was no turning back.

That was earlier. The day seemed to turn dark with rain shower minutes before she returned home. If the sun didn't want to come outside and play, Darcelle wouldn't bother with turning on any lights to illuminate her surroundings.

The next night, Shana called her. "Hey. This is your friend check. How ya feeling today?"

"Great, I guess." Darcelle felt a sense of freedom. "I quit."

Silence. "What?" Her voice shrieked, then she calmly asked, When?"

"Yesterday." Darcelle grinned and lifted an imaginary champagne glass in the air for a toast.

"Although I'm not surprised, why am I a day late finding out about it?" Shana waited for Darcelle to answer. She didn't, so her friend continued. "They didn't force you to resign?"

"Nope. As a matter of fact, it felt good that they pleaded with me to stay, be a team player, or apply for a position in another division. It had been a somber moment."

"That's a lot to ask of someone."

"Exactly." Darcelle nodded as if her friend could see her. The Monday after the fatal blow to Darcelle's self-worth, she had called in sick. After her two weeks, her sick time ran out, then she added vacation time to the mix. It took her that long to become numb to face the humiliation.

Humiliation that was unwarranted.

"I strutted into the building as if I was the new assistant VP, greeted friends and foes with a smile—it was fake—and kept stepping to William's office. My boss's face lit up when he saw me. *Humph.*

"William stood to meet me, and I handed him an envelope that contained one paragraph—that's all they deserved—for my resignation letter. No two weeks' notice. They had a month's notice when I wasn't there. I've been officially unemployed for twenty-four-plus hours," she boasted.

Her father would be proud she held to her conviction.

But what about quitting a job without having another one?

"William said I was overreacting, and the decision to hire Hadley had come from the top."

"*Ah.*"

"I know. I sweetly told him he was part of the top, and his voice carried weight. I looked him in the eye and dared him—double dared him—to deny it."

"High-five, girl. Oh, hold. This deserves a FaceTime high-five."

After they switched to FaceTime, Darcelle lifted her hand and touched the screen along with Shana. Her friend's eyes sparkled, and that made Darcelle smile without realizing it. "William told me there will be other opportunities. He said, 'Let's forget about that letter. I'll bump your salary 5K if you just stop overreacting, get over your hurt feelings, and let's work together.'"

"Oh, no, he didn't."

"Oh, yes, he did." Darcelle matched Shana's frown.

Overreacting? She didn't think so. Hurt? He had no idea how fresh her cut was after a month. "What I'm doing is moving on," she'd told him. Pivoting on her heel, Darcelle headed down the hall to her spacious office, which she'd decorated.

She'd said her final goodbye to a fake future with the company. It was like leaving a bad marriage. She took the remainder of her personal belongings, including her plaques and other tokens for her outstanding accomplishments. Now, those accolades held little meaning.

Crossing paths with her competition, Darcelle locked eyes with Hadley. She didn't blink but kept walking. She hadn't realized she had zoned out until Shana called her name twice.

"Unless there's something you haven't told me, I doubt you have another job so soon, so what's your game plan because this isn't something the Darcelle Price I know would do."

Darcelle slumped and sighed. "On point. I don't have one."

"Enough of this nonsense. Since my best friend is unemployed, why don't you let me pay for your flight to Austin?"

"Girl, please. I have the money. I've got my two savings accounts, stocks and 401(k). I'm good." Her eyes teared up. Her situation wasn't dire—yet—but she had put a ridiculous amount of money down on the three-story condo.

"Yeah, maybe financially. What about your spirit? You still seem down. A change of scenery will help."

"I'm going to have to talk myself into it. This weekend may be too soon for me to plan a getaway."

"True. How about Labor Day weekend? That way, I can take extra days off and whip you into shape because this ain't you."

Then who am I? Darcelle glanced around her apartment. She would need to get away, especially after telling her mother, then Evanston that she would miss the last summer barbecue. "You know what? I like your idea. I think I will."

Ecstatic, Shana cheered, and minutes later, they ended the call.

Jobless. Darcelle thought she would feel vindicated once she quit. The thrill was gone as soon as she packed up her things in her office, never to step foot in that building again.

Although she did nothing all day and had spent most of it in and out of bed, watching anything funny she could find, Darcelle's body was aching, her head hurting, and her energy drained from the mental anguish.

She padded across the room into her kitchen in search of something to aid in keeping the pain numb. There was a surprise in her cabinet. A bottle of unopened wine from when she and Evanston had cooked dinner and forgot about it. Was now a good time?

The next day, she and her mother exchanged kisses and hugs at the front door before Nellie led the way to her kitchen where coffee and muffins were waiting for Darcelle. A weekly breakfast with her mom during her sabbatical from the company had become almost routine.

"So have you decided when you're going back to work?" Nellie asked after taking a sip from her coffee cup.

"Ah," Darcelle was slow to answer, "I quit Reed and Meeks."

"You what?" Her mother roared. The lioness had come alive.

"I quit," Darcelle repeated. The deed was done. There was no turning back. Time to move on.

"Darcelle Price, have you lost your mind?" Steam could have come out of her mother's nose and ears from the heat Darcelle felt. "You don't quit a six-figure job because things didn't go your way."

"Okay. How about discrimination? Is that a good enough reason?" Darcelle folded her arms.

Nellie rubbed her temple and took deep breaths. "Sweetie, no matter how good we are, someone out there is always better than our best. This Hadley character had to outshine you in one or more areas…"

Is that what her mother thought? "Mama, that man had nothing on me. I knew that company inside out."

"I'm sorry, baby. I only wished you had prayed about it before you quit."

"You quit?" Valencia echoed from the doorway. "You made a whole lot of money." She walked farther into the kitchen and sat next to Darcelle. Her jaw dropped as confusion lingered in her eyes.

Her sister probably thought Darcelle was crazy, too, to walk away when Valencia worked overtime to provide for her children. Darcelle filled in the gaps financially whenever her sister came up short. That wouldn't stop. She refused to see JJ and Zuri go without, even if Darcelle had to.

Flustered, her mother fired one question after another. "What do you plan to do now? What would your father have said?"

Tears welled in Darcelle's eyes. "I wish he were here to tell me I was right to hold my ground... That other opportunities are waiting for me... That everything will be alright..." She retaliated with a firestorm of things she thought her daddy would say.

"I'm with Mama, sis. What do you plan to do now?" Valencia wrapped her arm around Darcelle's shoulders and squeezed her tight.

"Nothing." Darcelle snapped, then apologized. "Sorry. I haven't been sleeping well."

Valencia didn't hide her concern. "Sis, you look like it. You've never stepped out without makeup and fashionable clothes."

Darcelle wished she was invisible, and her mother must have sensed it as she came to the other side and closed the gap with Valencia as Darcelle cried until she developed a thirst. She had squeezed all the moisture from her body through her tears.

A few hours later, Valencia announced she had to pick up the children at summer camp.

"I don't want you guys to worry. I got this." Darcelle gathered her things to leave too.

Nellie pulled her aside before she walked out the door. "I don't know what's going on with you, but I'm here if you want to talk, and I'm going to be praying God gives you direction."

"I'm starting to pray too." When she's awake at night, and it was too late to call Evanston or Shana, she hoped

God was listening. *Maybe not as long or as loud sometimes as you, but at least it's consistent when I'm not crying myself to sleep.* Darcelle turned around before she stepped off the porch. "Oh, Mom, before I forget. I'm going to visit Shana Labor Day weekend."

"That's the last summer holiday." Nellie didn't hide her irritation with a fist on her hip. "You've missed one barbecue this summer, and now you've picked Labor Day to go out of town? What did Evan say about this?"

"Van? What does he have to do with my decisions?"

"About you quitting? Stop being on the defensive." Her mother shook her head.

Oh. Darcelle wasn't expecting her mother to drop the Labor Day trip that easily. "Sorry." She was annoying herself with her own short temper. "He doesn't know about me quitting yet. He's next on my list to tell." Not today.

Days later, her doorbell rang. She didn't order takeout or groceries, so it had to be Evanston. She wasn't ready for him—physically or emotionally.

Shorts, a T-shirt, and a lose braid. This was her best at the moment when she opened the door.

Evanston's arms were folded, and his legs spread as if he was a superhero. He was her hero, but not today, or yesterday either. "What's going on, Cece?"

She shrugged. "What are you talking about, Van?" She stepped back, and he seemed to contemplate whether he should cross the threshold. After a few moments, he did.

"Something's going on, and I'm unable to read between the lines. I love you. God knows I love you." He paced across her living room floor.

"I love you, too, and you know that." Now, Darcelle was irritated for no reason.

He spun around. "Do I? Because what I feel is you pulling away from me. Did I do or say anything to upset you?"

"No," she whispered and bowed her head.

Immediately, he was there, face-to-face. His thumb lifted her chin, and she looked into his eyes. "Then what is it, baby?"

"I quit my job." She stared to read his reaction. It was a blank stare. "Are you happy now?"

Emotions played across Evanston's face until he blinked. "I'm happy if you're happy."

He was evading the question, and she didn't have the energy to pull the truth out of him. "Are you happy?"

"I'm not, and I don't know why."

His expression seemed to be the same one she saw in the mirror every morning. Confusion.

"Cece, you've been pushing me away. Why? What do you want me to say or do?"

"I don't know."

Turning away, Evanston strolled to her window and glanced out. He was thinking. Moments later, he pivoted on his heel to face her. "Are you still in love with me?"

"Yes," she whispered, "but things have changed, and I don't know if it can be fixed."

"What?" He didn't hide his surprise. "I love you, woman, and I'm willing to fight for what we have, but I can't do it alone. Will you fight with me?"

Tears filled her eyes. She couldn't fight for herself. Where would the drive come from to fight for them?

"Okay." He bit his bottom lip. "Okay. Okay." He started toward the door. His hand was wrapped around the knob. "It's not the answer I came for—"

"I love you, Van. You know that." This was draining her to explain herself.

"I don't anymore, Cece. I don't." Opening her door, he walked out and quietly shut it.

Darcelle wanted to yell after him, but her feet wouldn't move. She was losing everything—her income, her mind, and her man. What was left in this world?

Me, God whispered.

What did that even mean? Darcelle locked her door, then padded across the room. She crumpled on her sofa and cried until she fell asleep.

Chapter Twenty-six

*D*arcelle had regrets. Not about quitting her job, not about not having a game plan on what she would do next when she told her family, not about calling Evanston back to argue. It would have started off as an apology but ended with harsh words. They might love each other, but at the moment it didn't seem like they liked each other.

She had to shake whatever she was coming down with. At least she could look forward to her upcoming visit with Shana, which was a week away, so why was she packing now?

Evanston's ringtone interrupted her musings.

"Hey, babe. I was just thinking about you as I always do." Was this the same man who had argued with her days earlier?

Her heart fluttered, and she thought it would soar, but instead of a takeoff, the flight was aborted, the liftoff delayed. Darcelle twisted her lips.

"Ah, you're supposed to say, 'I was thinking about you too.'"

"Sorry."

Evanston was quiet. "I'll excuse you because I love you. Can I get an 'I love you' back?"

"Of course, silly." Darcelle giggled. "I love you back." Her heart had liftoff. His deep chuckle made her close her eyes and relive the times his timbre had lulled her to sleep.

"What are you doing?"

"Packing for my trip to visit Shana next weekend." She eyed which pair of jeans she wanted to take.

"Next weekend?" Evanston sucked in his breath, then huffed. "And when were you going to tell me that? I had hoped we would have an agenda for the Labor Day weekend." He was either disappointed or annoyed. "With your downtime now, maybe we can make up for the time we were cheated out of."

Downtime struck a nerve. "You know I wasn't prepared for this scenario. Downtime is not a vacation."

Again, silence. Then his words were measured. "It seems like whatever I say, I'm going to be in trouble." Silence. "You could have told me you were going to see Shana."

"Yeah."

"Listen, Cece, I want to be a part of your life. We used to share everything—thoughts, happy times, sad times… You know what, I don't want to argue. I'll let you go."

"Okay," she whispered. She ended the call—or maybe Evanston disconnected first. It didn't matter as Darcelle sat in the chair next to her bed. She reached over her clothes, waiting to be packed, and grabbed a pillow. She squeezed it tight against her chest and closed her eyes. Everything was quiet around her, except for her heartbeat. She was alive but somehow felt dominant.

Opening her eyes, Darcelle scanned the room. Clothes that either needed washing or folding. "Not today." How could a man she loved like crazy suddenly become annoying? "I need space."

I've given you space. The wind carried God's voice.

"What's the plan?" Darcelle yelled, wanting an answer, but nothing else came.

Even the Lord didn't want to talk to her. Darcelle was disgusted with herself. She frowned and ran her fingers through her hair, which demanded a salon visit, but she would do it herself. She didn't want to be around people right now.

Darcelle stood and headed to the kitchen for something to drink. She returned to and pushed aside the suitcase and clothes, then climbed into the bed. She needed a nap. She didn't care if it was one in the afternoon.

A ringtone in the distance grew louder until Darcelle recognized it as Shana's. Reaching for her phone, Darcelle moaned. The nap did nothing for her. She was still tired, and her body ached. Where were all these pains coming from? "Hello," she whispered.

"Hey, the night owl is asleep? It's only ten o'clock."

"I guess," she slurred, not wanting to open her eyes.

"I need your flight information... Are you okay?"

"Yeah." Darcelle rolled over, then it dawned on her Shana had said ten. "I guess unemployment is making me lazy." Her room was dim. She had slept through an imaginary shift.

Darcelle forced herself to get up. There was no need to take a shower since she had no plans to leave her apartment. Whatever she had drank, had knocked her out.

One thing that would always be clear in her mind: Hadley's smug look.

Hmmph. I will bounce back. Maybe after she visited Shana, she could plan another trip. Perhaps as far away as Canada.

She had money saved.

It was time to splurge.

Darcelle had been up all night. She craved hearing Nellie Price's voice. It was after seven, and she knew her mother would be up. After the pleasantries, her mother asked how she was doing and said she had been praying God would give her direction. Then she brought up Evanston.

Somehow the closeness she had with Evanston was lost, and Darcelle didn't know how to get it back. It frustrated her because she wanted to break through a glass to get to him. "Van and I aren't in a good place right now."

"Oh? That man loves you."

"I love him, too, but he's the one who shut me down a long time ago whenever I brought up Reed and Meeks."

"C'mon, sweetie. That's all you used to talk about. It consumed you."

"Guess I should have kept my problems to myself," Darcelle said in a steady voice, masking her hurt feelings. No one was on her side.

Except Shana.

Friends are forever.

After that downer conversation, Darcelle was more determined to finish packing. She needed to get away. Another call came, and she thought about letting it go to voicemail but decided to answer.

"Miss Price, this is Brenda Horne from the leasing office. I'm calling to confirm your move-out date."

"*Huh?* I'm not moving out." She strained her brain to think. Was she?

"You didn't return any of my emails. You didn't renew your lease per your contract agreement regarding the two-month notice with your intent to stay."

Emails? Darcelle hadn't checked them since... She couldn't remember when.

"I can't move now." Darcelle groaned her frustration. She forgot life goes on whether she was in motion or not. Her condo, they were probably breaking ground now. That didn't matter now.

Plus, the bank wouldn't give her the loan to finish the construction without a stable income. *Oh boy.* She forced her brain to calculate her money.

Darcelle could still swing it if she cashed in her stocks, bonds and depleted her savings. That would go against the money sense workshops she taught. Now, Darcelle would lose her deposit. "Is it too late to sign a six-month lease?"

The headhunters who had tried to lure her from the company would have no problem finding her a good position and salary.

"I'm sorry. We've already rented your apartment, and the new occupant wants to move in mid-September instead of at the end. I was calling to see if that was possible."

No, you're calling to tell me I'm going to be homeless.

What else could go wrong? Her world was crumbling, and she couldn't put it back together.

"What am I going to do? Where I had planned to move isn't an option now." She tugged on her hair.

"I'm sorry, Miss Price. If only we had known your intention."

Darcelle was in a losing battle. *Why does it feel like the world is against me?*

If I am for you, I dare anyone to be against you, God spoke and referenced Romans 8 in the Bible. Her mind was too jumbled to read right now.

Shana must have been praying for her. Her mother, too, and probably Evanston, if he wasn't mad at her.

Miss Horne interrupted her thoughts. "My sister-in-law is a realtor, and she rents out small homes on short-term leases."

"Please. I would appreciate it. I had planned to purchase a condo...but now I'm unemployed. I can afford rent only if it's not more than what I'm paying here... until I secure another position," she rambled on.

"I see." The woman was quiet too long before she said, "I'll discuss your present circumstances with her."

After they ended the call, Darcelle stared out the sliding door from her balcony. She blamed her boss for forcing her hand and causing her to quit and be on the verge of homelessness. She wrapped her arms around her shoulders and cried out, "Daddy, I wish you were here. I'm lost and don't know what to do." She sobbed without restraint, surprising herself that she had tears left.

I'll leave the ninety-nine and come after the one lost sheep, God whispered. *Read Matthew 18:12–14.*

Darcelle went back inside. Instead of finding her Bible, she found something to help her sleep and crashed on the sofa.

The following day, Shana called twice. "You're going to be stranded at the airport unless you give me your flight information."

"Not coming." Darcelle moved her lips, but the words came out slow.

"Now I'm getting mad. What happened that made you change your mind? And you sound like…either you're experiencing a stroke, or you're drunk, because your speech is slurred. I'd say the latter. You know what? Stay there. I'm coming to you." *Click.*

Chapter Twenty-seven

*D*arcelle stood from her sofa, which had become her sleep sanctuary, and stretched. It was six in the morning. Smacking her lips, she rubbed her stomach and headed for the kitchen. The smell of rotting trash greeted her. "*Ooo-wee.*" She scrunched her nose. The neat freak inside her had deserted her too.

She looked at the dishes in the sink and the trail of discarded takeout boxes in the living room. Opening the fridge, Darcelle noticed leftover pizza and retrieved two slices, a bottled soda, then sat at the counter. She consumed the food without the benefit of the microwave. She would clean tomorrow—maybe.

Hours later, she dozed off on the sofa, watching a foreign film. Her doorbell rang, followed by a couple of knocks.

"What?" she whined and spied the time.

Who was banging on her door at eleven at night? Not wanting company, she turned over to ignore it, but the knocking persisted. Throwing the covers back, she got up and marched to the door and peeped through the security glass.

"Shana." She opened the door and hugged her for dear life. "What are you doing here?"

Her friend wrestled herself free and pushed Darcelle aside, dragging her carryon on wheels. "I told you I was coming. I caught the earliest flight I could get and with a layover. The things I do for you." She *tsk*ed. "I texted you my flight info. After waiting an hour, I took an Uber."

"Oh. Sorry." Darcelle scratched her head. It needed washing.

"Open these shutters." Shana spun around. "We have a problem. You and your place need a deep cleaning."

"Why didn't you use your key?"

"I didn't want any surprises—you and Evan." Shana gave her the side-eye.

"He's the least of my worries. Besides, we're not sleeping together."

"Well, I didn't know with your moodiness, weight loss, and constant sleepiness."

Although Shana's words weren't judgmental, Darcelle was surprised her friend would think such a thing. Placing her hands on her hips, she felt some fight stirring up. "Are you saying that because you go to church more than me? Church girls have sex outside of marriage."

"Lukewarm church folks. God is calling for holiness. Either you're in, or you're out. But God is no play toy. There's a difference between a practicing Christian to please God and a churchgoer to please men."

Shana stared Darcelle up and down. "I came too far to fight with you."

"Sorry." Darcelle sniffed. "I get so irritable. I don't like myself."

Shana hugged her, then stepped back. "You have to love yourself—that's the self-care rule. Now that's enough love without a toothbrush, a bath, and a shampoo." She took off for the bathroom.

Darcelle trailed, watching her friend rinse out the tub, then run warm water. "We'll start with a bath while I open these windows. I'll order some groceries and cleaning supplies to be delivered, then I'll be back in ten or fifteen minutes to wash your hair. After I get this place cleaned up, we need to talk." She spun on her heels and was gone.

Darcelle hated it when her friend acted like she was her mother. Like a two-year-old, she stomped her feet but did as Shana ordered.

Her friend reappeared and washed Darcelle's hair. The scalp massage was more relaxing than the bath.

After Darcelle's hair was rinsed and blow-dried, Shana left her to finish with her hair grooming. She glanced at her reflection and almost smiled—almost.

Darcelle walked into her bedroom to take a nap, but Shana had stripped her sheets. Looking over her shoulder, she grinned. "Bedtime is over for you. I threw away all that junk food and made you some oatmeal. And oh, you need to check your phone. You have messages and texts."

Grabbing her phone. Evan had texted her: **Have a safe flight, and tell Shana hi. Enjoy your stay in Texas, and I love you. See you when you come back.**

Sadness seemed to fill her.

"Call me nosey, but I read it. You need him." She tapped her foot and waited for Darcelle to respond.

"And he needs me to be someone I can't find myself. What is wrong with me?" Darcelle wanted to scream.

Shana hugged her as the intercom alerted them of the deliveries. "We'll find out. Let's get our food for fuel, because this place needs some attention."

By late afternoon, Darcelle's apartment resembled a home again. While Shana made chicken pasta, Darcelle put together a salad. After eating, they lounged in the living room. "Now, I see my friend." Shana grinned. "I'm glad because you looked scary."

After sticking out her tongue, Darcelle laughed too. "Amazingly, I feel like your friend. I've been feeling numb. I don't recognize myself."

"Hey, don't take this the wrong way, but I think you're suffering from depression."

Not that. Darcelle laughed to play off the warning from her mother not to claim or buy into that foolishness. "Me—" she patted her chest— "depressed? I'm a happy person."

"On most days, yes. Not lately. You haven't been yourself. I heard it over the phone and saw the evidence when I walked through the door."

"That doesn't mean I'm depressed," she argued for the sake of her mother being right.

"Listen, remember in college when I took an elective course that was for community service?" Shana didn't wait for Darcelle to acknowledge. "I was trained in mental health first aid, using the ALGEE plan."

"Mental health—please." Darcelle huffed. "What does my situation have to do with plant fungi?"

"Not algae. ALGEE is an acronym for an action plan— assess the risk, listen with godly love, reassure that this too will pass, encourage, encourage, and encourage. I added the extra 'e' for encourage. So, I'm here to listen, give reassurance or information, and strongly suggest you seek professional intervention."

"*Ummm-hmmm.* The risk of what?"

Shana rubbed her manicured nails against her teeth as she avoided eye contact. Some things never changed. It was a stall tactic.

"Hello." Darcelle tilted her head.

"Assess the risk of suicide or harm. Depression can lead to that."

"What?" Darcelle leaped to her feet. "You think I'm crazy enough to kill myself?" She was hot. "You flew all the way here to tell me that. I love you, Shana, but you can leave now." That sounded crazy to say those things to her best friend, but her mom said depression wasn't an option in Christians' lives, and Darcelle did attend church.

Shana didn't seem fazed as she leaned against the back of the sofa and crossed her legs. "I'm not going anywhere. You can't kick me out. I've got a key."

"The locks will be changed soon." She told her about her lease situation.

"The condo is definitely out. That's more stress on you. I have no problem taking a family leave of absence. You aren't going down like this."

"I'm not depressed. I'm mad. There's a difference." She jammed a fist in her side and waited for Shana to dispute it.

"*Ummm-hmmm.*" She rocked her leg over her knee. "To pass the class, I had to become a certified mental health first-aider. I didn't think any more about it until now. At first, I thought you could be pregnant, but I figured you would tell me."

"Is there such a thing?" Darcelle gave her a side-eye. "You're a public relations professional, not a psych specialist."

"Learning CPR isn't limited to doctors, neither is learning mental health first-aid. You're my best friend. I know you've been trying to hide your pain. I hear it in your voice, and you're not overcoming it—sleeping all the time, unconcerned about your appearance, and...I saw the wine bottles in the trash. You're irritable. This isn't you. Darcie, you need rescuing and professional help."

Shaking her head, Darcelle laughed. "No. I need a professional job, then I'll be back on track."

"Maybe, but I'm not sure." Pulling out her phone, Shana tapped away. "Some signs of depression: irritable—yep." She squinted at Darcelle. "Change in eating. Look at what you've been consuming. Trouble sleeping. You've been drinking. That borders on recklessness. Low energy. You can't clean behind yourself. These are symptoms on Google."

"For your information, I used shot glasses, not wine stemware. There's a difference in ounces." Darcelle couldn't look at her friend. Did she have those symptoms? Were they posted on the internet? She moved toward the nearest chair and collapsed, hiding her face in her hands. "So, I am nuts. Oh my God, I'm crazy. Van and my fam—"

"Don't need to know a thing. You can trust me. This is between you and me and a professional if you'll agree to be medically diagnosed and treated."

Tears flowed down Darcelle's cheeks as Shana pried her fingers from her face. "What happened to me. How did I become crazy?"

Squatting, Shana balanced on her knees until she was eye level with Darcelle, and the darts she shot at her conveyed she had crossed the line somewhere.

"You are part of the problem. Labeling people experiencing depression as crazy is a stigma that keeps people from seeking treatment. Some will try to harm themselves and succeed. I love you too much to let the devil take you out like that. Our mind is part of our body. God wants us whole—mind, body, and soul. If you had high blood pressure or diabetes, you would go to the doctor."

"Yep, but I'm healthy."

"For now, but not for long if you keep self-destructing, but you're stressed." Shana tilted her head and studied Darcelle. "Something is going on in your body that's making you unhealthy. Let's go through some things that have triggered your possible depression." She sat on the floor and started counting. "Mr. Price died unexpectedly, things changed at work, your perception that Evan wasn't supportive—your mom too."

"Okay, okay." Darcelle fanned her hand as if she was swatting a fly. "I'll talk to somebody to make you happy."

Shana shook her head. "Not how this works. You have to *want* to seek help."

"I'm craz… I'm stressed."

"A start. We'll both be unemployed because I'm not leaving here until you commit to go see a therapist—at least one visit. That's all I ask." Shana didn't call bluffs. She did exactly what she said she would.

Darcelle inched a finger up in the air. "One visit, and that's it."

"One more condition."

Resting her head on the back of the sofa, Darcelle groaned. "What now?"

"The therapist has to be a Christian counselor. Christ makes a difference in every situation."

Chapter Twenty-eight

*D*arcelle's lack of interest in their relationship was driving Evanston crazy. He refused to chase after her any longer. His heart mocked his boast when something would remind him of her and touch a soft spot. "It's been two weeks since she returned from visiting Shana in Texas," he rambled as Cedric half-listened, focused on the baseball game before them.

"Haven't heard from her, *huh*?"

"Nope." Evanston stared at the game, too, but his vision was blurred as his thoughts jumbled. What was the score anyway?

"It's not like she was into our relationship before she left. I called and suggested a date night—she was tired. I've wondered more than once if she's tired of me."

A player hit a homerun, judging by Cedric's sudden leap from the sofa.

Evanston didn't, as he continued his random thoughts. "I call and ask a simple question, 'How's your day, baby?' She's quiet and acts uninterested in any conversation. I love that woman like crazy, but it's only so much rejection a man can take."

"Hate to hear that, buddy. You were goofy with her. You two were in your own world. I thought she made you happy." Cedric settled down and faced Evanston. "I don't like seeing you miserable. So who's going to call it quits? The official breakup?"

Evanston's heart sank. He didn't want to be the one to walk away. That would make it final, which was why he hadn't stopped calling her, but not as much. With each phone call, he held out hope he could understand what was wrong, but it never came.

For her to agree to go their separate ways would be a blow to his heart where resuscitation would be ineffective.

"I think she's put the handwriting on the wall, and I don't want to see it." Evanston was disgusted with himself. "Why do I always pick the wrong ones?"

"Me too." Cedric shook his head. "I'm about done looking."

"There's no comparison. At least the chicks I date are gorgeous."

Cedric folded his arms. "*Humph*, and where has that gotten you? Looks matter, but I need something deeper— an emotional connection speaks volumes—and she has to be a sweet thing."

Evanston froze. Valencia's face flashed before him.

"What?" Cedric squinted. "What ya thinking?"

"Oh, nothing." Evanston shrugged.

"Your nothing is something. I can see it in your face. Spill it." Cedric didn't stand down.

"I thought about Darcelle's older sister, Valencia— she's pretty and a sweetheart."

"Go on." Cedric pointed his remote toward the flat screen to pause the game and give Evanston his full attention.

"She's a single mom with a quiet son and adorable daughter. They're the best. They eat up the attention."

The mention of children were a sore point for Cedric. His bout with childhood cancer cost him the chance to father an offspring. Women weren't the only ones who wanted children. Cedric Henson was a good guy and would make a great father. His heart was in the right place. "I'm interested. Set me up."

Cedric and Evanston were known as the last good guys. *I guess good guys finish last isn't just a cliché.*

"No can do, man." Evanston shook his head for emphasis. "Have you not heard anything I've said? Cece and I are done."

"Get out of here. I think you two should work it out." Where was friendship loyalty? His tune did a one-eighty without concern. He restarted the game and mumbled. "You're such a downer."

They finished watching the game in silence. Cedric was probably thinking about a chance meeting with Valencia while Evanston was trying not to think about Darcelle.

Counseling was Darcelle's secret. She was not about to tell anyone she had lost her mind. If the word got out, her mother would be livid and ready to cast out a legion of devils.

At least Darcelle hadn't called herself crazy in two days. That's the way society would label her if they knew.

She checked in at the desk for her appointment with Dr. Solomon Goodman, Shana's referral whom she'd found on the internet. Next, her friend personally called and vetted the office staff.

"Solomon is a biblical name. I figured you can't go wrong. I've prayed over this man—and you."

"Talk about intimidation. I don't live a Biblical lifestyle, although I have been reading and go to church with Mama more. She's none the wiser with my struggle."

"Let God judge you and not yourself or others." Shana took her to task from her home in Austin. "Luke in the Bible was a physician, and Jesus chose him to be a disciple. God is not against doctors, so go."

"You're right." Darcelle never thought of it that way.

Shana had threatened to return to St. Louis if Darcelle canceled her appointment. Her friend didn't bluff. Darcelle couldn't back out now. The man had been booked for three weeks, but Darcelle was a big girl. She could do this alone.

Then Shana had a change of heart and flew back in town the night before Darcelle's appointment. She was relieved not to do it alone. Sitting side by side, Shana held Darcelle's hand as if she were a child, and her mother had brought her to the doctor for vaccinations.

She thought about her mother and Evanston. If only they were here to hold her hands. Not that Shana wasn't a good substitute. They didn't understand her emotions and had judged her on how she handled the pre- and post-promotion situations at work. She untangled her hand from Shana and fumbled with her fingers as if she had mastered the art of crocheting.

People who sought mental help were weak.

I'm strong, God whispered.

Closing her eyes, Darcelle couldn't understand how she could be weak if Jesus loved her. "What am I doing here?"

No doubt, Evanston would have talked her out of this nonsense for good reason, she wasn't crazy, but on the other hand, Darcelle was curious if Shana's suspicions were on point. How had she gotten depression? Her mother believed Christians should claim no such thing. "Go to church, pray more, and you'll be fine," she said.

Darcelle was anxious and ready to leave. She did have other pressing matters—pack and move after she found a place to live.

A door opened.

"Darcelle Price," a tall, dark-skinned woman called, and Shana lifted her hand and pointed to Darcelle. The woman smiled. "I'm Amber, Dr. Goodman's assistant. He's ready for you."

Rubbing her jeans, Darcelle stood and glanced at her friend. Her heart didn't pound but slammed against her chest.

Her feet wouldn't move.

Her brain and body were out of sync.

"It's okay. Take your time," Amber said in a soft voice.

After a deep breath, Darcelle propelled her feet forward and followed the assistant to an office with wooden double doors. Double doors? What world was behind there? She had expected a clinical environment or a long sofa where she was supposed to stretch out and spill her guts.

The doors opened, and Darcelle couldn't be more wrong. She entered a place reminding her of someone's home with the plush carpet, healthy greenery here and there and even a fireplace. The walls were painted a soft pastel blue, and the lighting was cheerful and relaxing.

The psychiatrist rose from his spot in a plush cushion twin Queen Anne chair instead of behind a massive, imposing desk as she had imagined. He was short, white and had grayed hair, and she could pass him in a grocery store and not have given him a second look, so how was he going to help her?

"I'm Dr. Solomon Goodman." He smothered her hand with both of his. "Nice to meet you. Have a seat, and let's get to know each other."

Within minutes of their greetings, he stretched out his legs and folded his hands. "Now, Darcelle, tell me why you're here today." His voice was low and gentle.

"Evidently, my best friend thinks I need help coping."

"What about you? What do you think?" A smile formed on his otherwise blank expression.

Darcelle shrugged, not ready for someone to pick her brain.

"Are you tired—lack motivation, loss of appetite, problems with focusing or concentrating, struggle with insomnia?"

Her nights were sleepless because her mind kept replaying the fatal blow. Plus, she did eat, not the normal nutritious meals, but at least she ate. Pizza had proteins and carbs—both beneficial to the body.

She became absorbed in twirling her thumbs. "I don't think I'm depressed. I don't know what to think about my life right now."

"Tell me what's going on."

Dr. Goodman reached for his tablet. She guessed to record her answers. Now, she was feeling like a specimen.

Great.

She threw up her arms. "Everything at this point."

"What major events have led you to this place in your life? This is very important, and I need you to be honest with me. Are you having suicidal or homicidal thoughts or urges?" His intense expression caused fear to travel up her spine.

Was she? Darcelle swallowed hard before answering. "Even though life is bad right now, I don't want to end it. As far as killing somebody, I thought about my boss and the new assistant V.P., but it was only a fantasy."

For the next thirty minutes, Darcelle gave him a rundown of her life. "I think I've lived a happy life. When my dad died suddenly—he was my rock—I felt lost. Quitting my job was like filing divorce papers. Their betrayal was unbearable when I had been faithful."

Lastly, she described how she was annoyed, hurt, and confused by her mother's lack of support and pressure from her boyfriend about letting it go.

He pecked away, making notes and pausing at intervals to make eye contact. "Sounds traumatic. Sorry you had to experience that."

"Thank you. Me too. It was too much. I felt overwhelmed. " She appreciated the apology coming from a stranger. It sounded genuine. He placed the tablet back on the table, and they engaged in a casual dialogue about her passion beyond the promotion.

His empathy surprised her considering she expected him to ask a series of questions, check off the answers and tell her, "Time's up."

"That's a lot of stress, so how are you sleeping?"

"I'm not. My mind won't let me. I'm stuck in a place where I don't know how to get out. I'm always tired, so I take naps during the day and have a little wine at night—I'm not an alcoholic or anything—so I can sleep."

"Were you drinking before this crisis?"

"Not really. Evanston—Evan—my boyfriend, well I guess my ex, since we haven't spoken in over a month. Anyway, he brought a bottle over a couple of times for dinner," she shrugged, "but I've never developed a taste for it."

"Until now?" he prompted but didn't wait for an answer. "What about other sleep aids or drug use?"

Darcelle had bared her soul. Now, it was the doctor's turn. "So, what do you think? What's your professional opinion of my mental state—Am I crazy?"

"Crazy is defined in the dictionary as mentally deranged, manifested in a wild or aggressive way. That's not you. I hurt because you're hurting."

She had to blink to replay that statement. "Really?"

"Of course. I rejoice with those who rejoice and mourn with those who suffer. People who suffer can be made whole again."

That's promising. Darcelle felt encouraged.

"I want to see you another day this week, then I'll have a better idea of how to proceed. In the interim, I'm going to order blood work to check your serotonin level."

"What's that?" She frowned.

"Serotonin is an important chemical and neurotransmitter in our body. The medical profession believes it's linked to depression because it helps regulate our mood and social behavior, appetite, sleep, memory, and sexual desire. You said you had a boyfriend."

Darcelle twisted her lips. She couldn't be the perfect girlfriend Evanston was expecting.

"If your level is off, then I'll prescribe medicine. I'd prefer you're not alone the first couple of days in case there are side effects."

Side effects? That sounded scary, but she was too scared to ask what they were. Darcelle progressed from twirling her thumbs to twisting a strand of hair around her finger.

"My family doesn't know about this. Neither does my boyfriend—well, ex. It's kinda embarrassing to tell them I'm going to a..." She tried to find the right word not to belittle his profession. Darcelle didn't think he would appreciate the humor in being called a shrink or nut doctor.

"I see." Dr. Goodman nodded.

"My best friend is in the waiting room. I'm sure she can check on me."

"Good. Until we can properly diagnose you and get you on the right medication, I want you to avoid all stress-induced situations. All," he stressed with a pointed look as he closed his tablet. Linking his hands together, Dr. Goodman leaned forward.

"Darcelle, I didn't create you. God did that all by Himself. With that said, I can only guide you to a certain point, but the Lord Jesus can take you all the way, so I'm suggesting you let God treat your mind, body, and soul along with the medication. Are you willing?"

She thought about all the prayers her parents had prayed over the years for their daughters and how Shana had been praying for her now. "I guess."

"I'll take that as a yes." He stood and extended his hand. "I'm sorry you've been through a rough patch in the road, but I'm glad the road led you to me. Now, let's get your blood work done." His warm smile was reassuring. She was in good hands with Dr. Goodman.

Shana stood when Darcelle returned to the waiting room. "Well?"

"How much vacation time do you have? The nurse took my blood for tests. Dr. Goodman wants to put me on meds, but I can't be alone because of possible side effects."

"I'm on it. I'll email my boss and work remotely, then I'll take sick time and vacation time if I have to."

Shana's commitment brought tears to Darcelle's eyes. She hugged and thanked her friend.

When they stepped back, Shana told her. "Eventually—when you're comfortable—I think your family should know."

Darcelle nodded. She wasn't sure when that would be. "When I'm ready."

Lord, don't leave me now, she prayed as they left the doctor's office.

Chapter Twenty-nine

*T*he message was clear. After a month of Darcelle not calling Evanston and avoiding his calls, she had cut the ties on their relationship, and it hurt.

When a man finds that special woman, it's unbearable to part ways, but the choice was not his. Evanston's weekends were somber, replacing the special moments the two of them shared. A day hadn't gone by when he didn't wonder what she was doing. Was she working again? Had she moved to her mini-mansion condo?

Although their love affair was short-lived—almost ten months—the images of their emotional connection were waiting for him in his dreams.

It had been Valentine's Day when Evan kissed her soft hands. Her finger was void of a ring, but he had made up his mind to put one there before the year was out.

Why couldn't he detach his heart from Darcelle? He had prayed for the anguish to stop tormenting him. God had been silent to his pleas, except one time—only one time— the Lord whispered, *Who can find a virtuous woman? For her price is far above rubies.*

That had confused Evanston more than it helped. Was God telling him the woman for him didn't exist, or to keep looking? He found the Scripture in Proverbs 31. He read and re-read the entire chapter and was no closer to an understanding.

On a cool October morning, Darcelle's sweet giggles seemed to whisper in his ear, so he decided to make a surprise visit. Maybe all they needed was a cooling-off period. Six weeks were long enough. He came bearing gifts: day spa passes.

The surprise was on him. Darcelle was moving without telling him? There were so many emotions stirring in the pit of his stomach, he couldn't name them all.

First, he was stunned, then hurt, and now ticked off at her dismissing him from her life. But this was a peace visit. He didn't come to wage war, so he measured his steps toward her, hoping to leave his attitude behind him.

Darcelle didn't see him as she directed two bulky movers on how to pack her furniture in the truck.

After a deep breath, he guarded his words. "What's going on, Cece?" He studied her and noticed she had lost weight—not bad, but not necessary. She had been perfect without any need for adjustments.

Next, he scanned her features. Today, her fresh, youthful glow was missing. Her usual flawless skin held evidence of an allergic reaction to something.

Her eyes seemed happy to see him, but her lips twisted in annoyance at his presence. "What does it look like? I'm moving, Evan."

"I see that. I guess your condo is ready. I would have helped you, if you had called." Staring into her eyes, he saw an emptiness that lingered where a sparkle was always present. Who was this woman?

"We need to talk. Are you still upset about what happened at your job? I thought we moved past that."

"You did." An indignant attitude swelled up before his eyes. When Darcelle wagged her finger, he knew he must have struck a nerve. "Listen, Evanston Giles, when I wanted to talk about what was going on in my life, you couldn't bear to hear about my pain."

"So, this is my fault? I didn't know you were hurting like *that*." He pounded his chest as he towered over her. "I blame Reed and Meeks for any pain. You made the right decision to quit. I support that. Let's move on, babe." He tried to reason with her. Moisture welled in her eyes. This wasn't going as planned. "I don't want to fight."

"But that's all we do."

Evanston reached for her to apologize, but she stepped back. "Doesn't matter anymore. I have someone who listens when I talk." Twirling around, she started her trek back inside the apartment lobby.

Who? "Does he love you as hard as I love you?" Evanston was mad now at the thought that another man could make her happy. She needed to remember their love. He snaked his arm around her waist and spun her back to his chest, and kissed her. He needed to break the barrier between them, and she began to weaken in his arms.

When they parted, he rested his forehead on hers. "Baby, I do get it—how the demands of our job can consume us without us having any say about it. I went through that not long after your ordeal. I hear you. I'm sorry for what I did or didn't do, but you can talk to me."

Sadness filled her eyes. "I can't. I don't know how anymore." She broke free and continued toward the entrance.

Evanston didn't stop her this time. *You're begging, man. She doesn't want you.*

Accept it.

Move on.

Evanston wasn't a violent man—never. He preferred to walk away from a fight than start one, but knowing another man had come between him and Darcelle was unbearable. He thought about joining a boxing gym, because Evanston wanted to lash out at the interloper. Who was she talking to?

"Take a deep breath, man," Evanston coaxed himself, at times, when he heard himself growl and felt his fist clench.

Did losing Darcelle mean losing his connection to her family? He had thought about them often. What did they know that he didn't? He ached to pay a visit to Mrs. Price.

What if the guy Darcelle claimed was listening to her was there with her? Evanston would lose it.

Retreat and move on, he coaxed himself. He pounded his fist on his desk at work.

"They have gyms to work out that frustration," Lester said. "You okay?"

"Yeah, and, nah." Evanston whirled his chair to face him. "I just don't fathom what happened between us. It's mindboggling." He shook his head, still in disbelief. "What is it about Cece that makes me crazy?"

"Love. No man has lived life until we die from it. If Darcelle absolutely doesn't want to talk or be around you, move on. Get her out of your system by going out with other women, or hang around her like a lost puppy. I'm not feelin' the last one. Man up, my brother. You can drink your sorrows away, sex them away, or pray them away." He scrunched his nose at the last choice.

"What will give me the fastest relief?" Evanston asked as an email alerted him of a tech problem in the payroll department—a high priority.

At one time, he and Darcelle made each other a priority. If life truly goes on, he missed the bus.

Four weeks later and counting, Darcelle still hadn't adjusted.

Dr. Goodman had diagnosed her with situational depression, which she had never heard of. Her treatment was selective serotonin uptake inhibitors and supportive therapy.

"It could take up to thirty days for the anti-depressant to stabilize in your bloodstream," Dr. Goodman advised.

Shana stayed the first week while Darcelle struggled with the drowsiness—she couldn't get enough sleep and hated the smell of food.

How could she interview for a job—virtually or in-person—if she couldn't stay alert? Plus, she needed a new wardrobe. Her clothes hung off her body from weight loss. Her baby sister, Monique, would welcome the hand-me-downs. Without new employment, she didn't want to splurge. Darcelle had already lost her deposit on the condo.

At least she wasn't homeless. Brenda Horne from her apartment leasing office came through. She had persuaded her sister-in-law to allow Darcelle to rent a house based on her excellent payment history. She signed a one-year lease in hopes her life would be back on track in twelve months. Relocating to Austin, Texas, as Shana strongly offered, wasn't off the table.

Right now, Darcelle needed the familiar. Standing in the cramped space of her small two-bedroom bungalow, not the two thousand square feet condo she had hoped for, she admired the decor. The fireplace was the best feature, and she sat there every evening, writing in a journal to make sense of her life.

Her family knew she had moved and were waiting for an invite to her open house. She put them off, saying she would have an open house when everything was perfect. The Prices would be shocked that her living quarters were smaller than the space in their childhood home.

If they only knew her struggle. Darcelle had learned how to play the part to conceal her depression from her family. On autopilot, she smiled at the right moments, laughed, hugged on cue, and played with JJ and Zuri, yet she hadn't broken the threshold where she could absorb their warmth.

Her situation was so frustrating.

Annoying.

She always left her mother's before she became irritable.

None of them were the wiser of her struggle.

Mood swings were not her friend.

"Read your Bible," Dr. Goodman reminded her each visit.

"I do." Sometimes, the Scriptures were unfamiliar. Other times, words jumped off the pages: *For I know the plans I have for you, declares the LORD, plans to prosper you and not to harm you, plans to give you hope and a future* in Jeremiah 29, *and peace I leave with you, my peace I give unto you: not as the world giveth, give I unto you. Let not your heart be troubled, neither let it be afraid* in John 14.

One thing was for sure. She had to believe God at all costs for the breakthrough, no matter what.

Dr. Goodman reiterated no stressful situations.

Evanston showing up on moving day had threatened her peace. She wanted to close her eyes and disappear in his hugs and kisses, but what she needed now was more than physical affection. How could he understand her jumbled feelings, which she couldn't make sense of?

One evening as she relaxed by her fireplace, Shana called her.

Darcelle admitted, "I feel my confidence level is returning, and I'm not intimidated to begin the process of applying for jobs."

"Then it's time for you to come clean. It's November, and you've been in therapy for months. Tell your family. They love you, and you need them. If Miss Nellie knew, she'd be praying like crazy."

"Yeah, I wouldn't say crazy around her. I can see Mama now disappointed that I succumbed to the devil because I admitted I was depressed. I don't know." Darcelle gnawed on her lip thinking. "I don't want anyone's pity." The thought made Darcelle sad. "Or looking at me like I'm crazy. I mean, I still look the same."

"Almost. Get back on your health regimen."

"I know. Dr. Goodman says I need to make healthy eating and physical exercise a routine. He's right. When I was working, I volunteered and taught financial workshops. I walked and had a gym membership—the works. When Evan came along, we did a lot of things together every free weekend."

"Evan. I haven't heard you call him that in a while. He's someone else who needs to know." It wasn't the first time Shana had said that. "Ah, he's inboxed me on social media a couple of times, asking about you. I didn't break our confidence," Shana was quick to add, "but I reassured him there was nobody else. He was relieved."

Darcelle didn't know how she felt about that tidbit. Evanston downplayed her hurt feelings. Shana let her talk and probably took a nap while Darcelle rambled, but at least she allowed Darcelle to run out of steam. Dr. Goodman also listened, even though he was paid to do it.

"My family asks about Van every now and then. I think it's more for me not to forget him, but I offer them nothing encouraging. He was my hero, the man I desperately wanted to kiss my hurt, and make me feel better, but Darcelle needed to take care of Darcelle."

"Self-care is number one."

"Yep, and I'm not feeling divulging my illness. Plus, you said God knows, and that's all that matters."

"Yes—in the beginning."

"Shana, my first priority is a steady income. Landing another job while unemployed is stressful. I couldn't handle the job crisis and a relationship. I felt alone in my battle, and I'm still coping."

"Do you ever think about him?"

Darcelle smirked, and a tear fell. *I just did.* "All the time, it seems." She paused. "Things remind me of him. I liked us before the job situation, then it got to the point I didn't want to see him coming because I knew we weren't on the same page. Mental self-care means no stress. Our relationship became stressful. I don't regret quitting the company, though. No telling how toxic it would have become working with Hadley and his directives."

"I'm glad God put Dr. Goodman in your path."

"You mean the internet where you found him." Darcelle giggled.

"Also, you need to add church in the mix." Shana kept adding layers of what Darcelle should do next.

"I'll have you know I'm going more. I'm good with just reading passages for now. Sometimes I go with Mama. A few times, I've visited random churches."

"Oh, so now you're a pop-up churchgoer," Shana teased. "I'll take it."

They chuckled and chatted a few more minutes before Shana instructed Darcelle to grab her Bible. Scooping it up off the end table, Darcelle flipped through the pages as Shana waited patiently.

"Okay. I was reading Psalm 139 this morning and thought of you."

"Got it." In unison, they began at verse one and continued to the end. It reminded her of a silly task from grade school, but it brought the Scripture to life. "Thank you," Darcelle whispered. "Did I ever tell you how much I appreciate you being my best friend?"

"You don't have to. I already know." Seconds later, they ended their call.

Snuggling deeper into her throw blanket, Darcelle reached for her cup of tea, which she was sure was room temperature.

Would she ever share her bout with mental illness with anyone? Was it like attending an Alcoholics Anonymous meeting for the rest of her life?

Dr. Goodman had said a confidant would ensure Darcelle wouldn't go through it alone. Shana had been with her, but her friend could only do so much from afar. She wished Evanston understood.

I understand, God's voice sounded as if It was singing in the wind.

Chapter Thirty

Weeks later, Darcelle strolled into Dr. Goodman's office. She was happy. Darcelle had forgotten what that felt like.

"I see you're tolerating the medication, and you're looking healthier," he commented after she settled in her chair.

"Thank you." Darcelle gave him a genuine smile.

"I'm doing my part to bring you back to yourself. Are you letting God do His part regarding your holistic care?"

"Yes." She nodded, believing what she said.

Dr. Goodman smiled. "Good. Now, you've been under my care since September—almost three months. We'll recheck your serotonin levels next month. Depending on my findings, we'll begin to ween you off..."

Darcelle was about to do a happy dance. She always thought once she was on an antidepressant drug, she would always be reliant on the medicine. This was music to her ears.

"But, I want you to follow up with me every six months, sooner if you find yourself developing symptoms."

He rested his tablet on the table. "How you handle stressful situations or traumas, will determine if you need a selective serotonin reuptake inhibitor to manage the episode."

"I didn't even realize I was experiencing symptoms of depression. My friend noticed the signs. How am I to know if there is a next time?"

"Stress is part of our lives, and it's about getting you back into the place where you can handle it and bounce back correctly. Your family and friends are your best support system."

Darcelle was quiet. She was worried about her family's perception. "I'm not there yet."

Their judgment.

Others' stereotype.

"Talk to God about reconciliation. When you're ready to share, I believe God will be right there in the midst. He always sends help when we need Him."

"*Ooo-kay.*"

After her appointment, she stopped by her mother's house. *Is now the right time?* She wondered about having a talk.

She strolled into the kitchen, where her mom had already started baking desserts for Thanksgiving next week. Baking was her distraction when a lot was on her mind. Daddy's death was coming up.

Like her mother, Darcelle put on a brave face. "Hey, Mom." Darcelle gave her mother a kiss on the cheek.

Looking over her shoulder, Nellie smiled. It didn't reach her eyes. "Wow. You look nice today. Did you have a job interview?"

"Nope. Not yet."

"I still wish you didn't quit that good-paying job. Now, you're looking." Nellie tsked and shook her head.

That struck a nerve. That was in the past. Why couldn't her mother let it go?

Same reason you couldn't let your pain go. It hurts, she answered herself. They had switched places. Now, she understood a little better. "Need any help?"

"You can peel the sweet potatoes for the pie." She handed Darcelle the items.

They worked in silence, each in their own thoughts until her mother's voice was above a whisper. "Your dad will be gone a year this weekend, and it will be the second Thanksgiving without him."

What would Daddy say about being diagnosed with depression? Would he call her weak, a loser? Closing her eyes, Darcelle exhaled. "I know."

Valencia breezed through the door. "Hey, Mama. Hey, sis."

They hugged and kissed, and Darcelle relished in the comfort of love while their hug lasted, then it would be gone. When they released each other, Darcelle smiled, fighting to hold on to that sense of well-being.

Zuri screamed Darcelle's name and greeted her with a juicy kiss and hug.

Tell them, her mind urged at the same time a louder voice overruled. *Wait*. Darcelle didn't. She wanted to savor these happy moments with her family. An hour or so later, she was leaving as Monique was coming in from work.

"Hey. You look cute."

"Thanks. I feel cute too." The typical little sister, Monique, would borrow jewelry, clothes, and sometimes

Darcelle's car to be like her big sister. The sentiment flattered her.

"I still want to check out your new place," Monique reminded her.

"Soon."

"You're making me wonder if you've got a secret lover going on." Monique winked. "Poor Evan."

Darcelle still loved him. Too bad, she couldn't make him happy. When she got behind the wheel, she didn't drive off right away but stared ahead. A text jolted her from the trance.

Thinking about you and your family during this time of the year. Miss you and love you always. I'm here to listen if you need me, Cece. For anything.

Van. She whispered his name, and the floodgate broke seconds after she drove off. The tears and sniffs were her companions on the fifteen-minute ride home.

On Thanksgiving morning, Darcelle dressed to attend the holiday service. This was the old Darcelle Price who didn't step out of the house without stylish hair, polished makeup, and flattering clothes. She admired her cream sweater dress and cape in the mirror.

Memories flooded her mind when she last wore it. She and Evanston had attended a movie premiere.

Evanston Giles had all the qualities any woman, including her, would want in a man—financial stability, looks, a kind heart. None of that mattered when she was losing herself.

She took a deep breath to come out of her daze. She had to meet her family at church and hopefully God had a message for her.

The service was stirring as the praise team's selections were inspiring and had a spiritual depth to the words. Next, Pastor Clemons welcomed everyone to the annual Thanksgiving Day service.

"You're here today because you realize God's been good and merciful to you. Thanksgiving should be more than a holiday to eat turkey and dressing and to watch football. Every day should be a day of Thanksgiving—every day. God promises to supply your needs, which brings me to this morning's message taken from Philippians." He flipped the pages of his Bible.

"In chapter four, verse six: *'Be anxious about nothing; but in everything by prayer and supplication with thanksgiving let your requests be made known unto God.'* The key word is *thanksgiving*—thanksgiving when we ask and thanksgiving when we receive."

Darcelle repeated the verse as she read in her Bible.

"Everything in life isn't fair, according to *our* standards," he continued. "The Bible says in Psalm eighty-four, verse eleven, it reads, *'No good thing will God withhold from them who walk up righteously before Him.'* Check your walk today. Remember, Jesus has your best interest no matter what you go through."

Jesus has my best interest, she repeated to herself. Could she have stopped the Reed and Meeks situation from turning her life upside down? The short message was thought-provoking. She needed a spiritual stimulus to keep going.

I've always had your best interest, but you never came to Me, God spoke.

Not only did she feel the Lord's presence, but she heard His heavenly language speak to her soul. It was a reprimand of sorts. Maybe today would be the day she bared her soul.

That didn't happen when she and her sisters returned to the house. It was evident her mother was going through the motions. Her smiles were many, but the light in her eyes was little.

Darcelle saw her reflection. She wrapped her arms around her mother. "I miss Daddy too."

Before long, the entire family had a good cry. One by one, they took their seats at the table. Their mother led the prayer. "Lord, thank You for my daughters and the grandchildren Harold left me. This is hard, Jesus, so hard. We miss him." Nellie was silent. After a few moments, she continued. "Bless our food and those who are hungry. In Jesus' name. Amen."

Darcelle sniffed, and her heart was heavy, then she heard God's whisper.

And I shall wipe away all tears from your eyes; and there shall be no more death, neither sorrow, nor crying, neither shall there be any more pain: for the former things are passed away. Read Revelation 21:4.

Words of comfort settled in Darcelle's heart. She was sure if her family heard God's voice they'd feel the same, so she shared what the Lord had said. Her mother's face brightened, either from surprise, or God's presence amid their sorrow. Yes, everything would be alright. But to be sure, Darcelle wasn't going to reveal what she had experienced to add to their burden.

But soon.

Evanston never understood how people could be down around the holidays unless they missed the one they once loved. Who was he kidding? A part of him would always love Darcelle even though they had drifted apart. That truth annoyed him. Somewhat of good news, according to Shana, Darcelle didn't have a new boyfriend. That was all her friend was willing to divulge.

Dumbfounded—and it wasn't the first time, he chided himself to refocus. "It's the holidays." He forced a grin. Festive energy was all around him, the lights strung from buildings to buildings for blocks, the malls were packed, and bags weighed down shoppers—was anyone buying online this year? Invites to Christmas and holiday parties were already in the mail; he had received a couple. The bustle meant Christmas was around the corner.

Of course, he would never forget Christ's birth. His mother would give him a tongue-lashing for not putting Jesus number one on the list.

Yet, his holiday wasn't any brighter without having a special someone to share the moment with. He would rather be lonely than miserable with another woman. He should move on, the sensible part of his brain counseled him, but the other part said it was too soon to dismiss his feelings. So he was stuck in limbo.

His mind retreated back to Darcelle. It had been four months since he had last seen her. The out-of-sight, out-of-mind mantra never worked when you loved someone. His mind had been a constant rerun of their kisses, whispers, and smiles. He grimaced, missing it.

Her family was also part of the package. Evanston genuinely liked them. Reaching for his phone, he searched for a group text Darcelle had included him on—by accident— with her mother and sisters. That had been a happy time when she needed an old recipe to surprise him with a dish.

Evanston smiled. He had never let on as he saw the text and wished them a Happy Thanksgiving and letting them know he was thinking about them this time of year with Mr. Price's death. Her mother and sisters thanked him for his thoughtfulness. He never heard from Darcelle.

That stung, but he was a man. Evanston could take it. He was cool. No sweat. Life goes on. Everyone accepted that he had come to terms with his fate with Darcelle except his sister.

Jessica saw through his fake exterior when she came home for the holidays. "Bro, I guess you and Darcelle were never meant to be. You've been dumped."

"My relationship is not up for discussion." His tone was meant to drop the subject.

His sister didn't take the hint and retreat. "You need to get back in the game, because I'm not about to deal with your bad attitude this Christmas. I can set you up on a date. I've got connections." She grinned and winked.

"I'm not 'babysitting' your young friends." Evanston made air quotes with his fingers. "I happen to like my bad attitude for your info. Darcelle and I met this time last year. What do you think I am, a pick up a new woman for Christmas type of guy?"

Jessica jumped off the stool in the kitchen and lifted her chin. "Fine, if you want to be mopey, miserable, and sad during Christmas, don't wrap that up in a box and give it to me." She was heading out when she pivoted and returned to the table to deliver another blow.

"You know, for a man who says he's over a woman who dumped him, you protest too much. Prove it," Jessica dared him. "You don't have to date. How about going out on a business dinner at a table for two with a candle between you two?"

"Fine." Did that come out of his mouth? He squinted at Jessica's look of innocent triumph. This was stupid. Why did he let his sister bait him? Now, he had to prove himself, and that was beyond common sense.

A week later, on Friday evening, Evanston stared at his reflection as he shaved to go on a blind date "business" dinner. "Seriously?" He shook his head.

Evanston couldn't remember when and where Jessica had met Nyla Whitman, but he challenged any woman to get Darcelle out of his head. The more he went through the motions of getting dressed, the more he wasn't feeling it.

He called her to back out. She did have a lovely voice and Jessica showed him her picture—pretty, but not exquisitely unique like Darcelle.

Surprisingly, Nyla wasn't surprised when he canceled. "When you asked, I got the impression I was your charity case, but for Jessica's sake, I was going to give you the benefit of the doubt. I'm not desperate."

"I'm sorry. That wasn't my intention." Evanston felt like a jerk.

"From Jessica's point of view, you're right up there with the Marvel superheroes, so why isn't a man like you married?"

Evanston rubbed his freshly shaved face. He was glad that they weren't sitting across from each other where she could read his emotions. "Came close."

"What happened?" she pressed.

Evanston wasn't quick to answer. "I never got the chance."

"I never stand in the way of second chances. Happy holidays, Evan."

Chapter Thirty-one

Two weeks before Christmas

"Stop stalling," Shana fussed over the phone. "I've been your confidant for months. I've kept my peace while you recalibrated. But now, I'm threatening you. Darcie, tell your family, or I will."

Darcelle gritted her teeth while she and Shana were on FaceTime. "Okay, okay already. I was about to tell them on Thanksgiving, but remembering Daddy's death was too painful. I didn't want to add more pain." Darcelle would never forget the sadness that clung to the air like ice—it wouldn't melt away.

Heavy as a rock.

Yet invisible like gas.

Her father's absence couldn't be dismissed, but God did send comforting words, and she shared that with Shana.

"I do feel like I'm back to my old self, though. Valencia, Monique, and I went Christmas shopping for JJ and Zuri. I splurged like I usually do—from my savings. It felt good to be around other people for a change. The excitement of shoppers and children were contagious. I'm sinking, but Jesus rescued me like that song the choir sang a few Sundays back, 'Love Lifted Me.'"

"Yes, Thank You, Jesus. You're back. This is the last stage of your recovery, share your journey. I wish I was there."

"You've been with me every step, and I realize God too. I see I've taken Him for granted. The times when I could have gone to church freely, I opted out. You mentioned being lukewarm. I don't want to settle in my salvation. You and Dr. Goodman opened my eyes to see that Jesus will always send help when I need Him, which is what I'm praying for when I sent this invite to my Christmas dinner-slash-open house-slash-recovery celebration when we finish talking."

"In that case, bye."

Darcelle chose a group text to her family and typed: **Please share the Spirit of Christmas with me. Christmas Eve dinner at my new place, 7 p.m., 741 Whitby Court in Olivette.** She hit send.

Closing her eyes, her heart pounded. "Lord, please let them see my strength as an overcomer and not my weakness." A tear wormed its way down her cheek. "I need your help, Jesus, to do this."

Laying her phone on the table, she stared into the fireplace, and her mind drifted. The truth was she could be prone to bouts of depression again. Life was stressful. How was she to deal with everyday hiccups without needing medication, again?

To him who overcomes, I will grant to sit with Me on My throne, as I also overcame and sat down with My Father on His throne. God's voice wasn't a whisper, but strong. Defiant. Real. Revelation 3:21 came later as a hush.

Yes, an overcomer. Her depression had led her to reconcile with Christ, which made this Christmas more meaningful to her.

It was time to download Christmas music—worship, start cooking, and decorating—inside and out—to make her rental bungalow worthy to be on a holiday house tour. Bows. Garland. Ornaments. Lights. Black angels she had begun collecting as a little girl. Tons of presents. As the excitement built, she was about to go make her list. "Bring on the Prices, and please send Your peace. I'm ready for this. I celebrate You, Jesus, for the first time in a long time." Jesus was God's gift wrapped up.

Chapter Thirty-two

Christmas Eve

*D*arcelle's peephole didn't lie. Why was Evanston Giles—her heartthrob—standing on her doorstep? And her heart was pounding, poised to leap out of her chest.

She swallowed and stole a deep breath. Her fingers fumbled with the locks as she opened the door. Instantly, the magnetism of his brown eyes, the window to his soul, dared her to blink, so she didn't.

They were hypnotic whenever Evanston—her Van—conveyed his love for her, danced whenever he teased her, and indifferent whenever they argued, which was how they ended things.

At the moment, his eyes revealed nothing. Either it was deliberate on Evanston's part, or she had lost the ability to tap into his emotions. Her depression caused her to lose so much.

The strength of her deodorant was testing its claim to keep a person calm and dry. Darcelle could feel the heat and perspiration crawling up her back. She inhaled the chilly air, held it—counted to three, then exhaled it in an imperfect smoke cloud.

Darcelle trapped the smile that fought to surface as she admired his fedora. Sexy didn't begin to describe him. Hats were made for him, not the other way around: cowboy hats or baseball caps, even the top hat he wore at Lester's party.

Evanston could pull it off. His signature body language was powerful, confident, and commanding. Not tonight. His broad shoulders were slumped as if he was anything but sure of himself.

"What are you doing here?" she asked, although she was afraid of the answer.

"Wrong guy?"

What did he mean by that? Darcelle wondered. She hadn't even invited him, more or less, another man. This was a family gathering.

Lines folded between his brows. "You know, I asked myself that same question, more than once actually, on my drive over here. Why am I going to a Christmas Eve dinner given by my estranged girlfriend?"

Darcelle stood motionless, feeling his hurt. She wondered why too.

He twisted his lips as if he was disgusted with himself. "So are you rescinding the invitation you sent via group text?" he challenged, lifting one of his silky, thick brows. The steam that exhaled from his flared nostrils had the force of a cannon.

Group text? Had he been included? Darcelle recovered from the shock. "Of course not. Come in." Good thing he was her first guest, so the shock of his appearance would wear off on her before her family arrived.

She took one step back.

He took two steps forward. Once up close, Evanston towered over her. Brave. Strong. Handsome.

Her hero.

Some things never changed. Evanston never showed up without an offering. In one hand, a bouquet of festive red carnations—he used to bring her red roses. The other hand clutched a bottle of wine.

"I'll take the flowers, but not the wine."

"Oh? Since when?" He gave her a pinned look, expecting an answer.

Since my world spun out of control and I was tempted to dabble, and drink my sorrows away. "It's a long story." She shrugged and reached for the flowers. He put them behind his back and looked at her through the hood of his lashes, and more memories flashed before her eyes. His actions seemed to surprise him too.

Their relationship was what most couples envied. Their hide-and-seek antics were playful and teasing. Oh, if only his love had been strong enough for when she felt weak.

She missed their closeness. Darcelle didn't realize how much she craved it until tonight. Estranged was right. It had been so long since they were the loving couple most observers thought. She wondered if he had moved on. God knew, in her state, she had pushed him away.

If he had moved on, Evanston deserved the happiness she couldn't give him, and she refused to be one of those exes calling out of the blue when he was in a new relationship to say, "I want you back." Darcelle was not a drama chick. It was a loss, but she was broken, and she couldn't fix herself. The Lord was mending her.

"Darcelle, since when?" he urged, waiting for her to answer. Evanston watched her as if he was trying to read her mind.

Why did she cringe at the name he had once complimented? When did it get formal between them? She had come to expect his endearment, Cece.

"About three months ago."

Evanston squinted with such intensity as if to test her truth, then nodded and relinquished the flowers. "I see." He rested the bottle on a nearby table. "I'll take it back with me."

"Thank you." She hadn't become an alcoholic, but Dr. Goodman said self-destruction could act as a coping mechanism with the stress. Temptation hadn't gotten to that point. Praise God for Shana's intervention.

Where were her manners? She accepted his hat and waited for him to peel off his cashmere coat. His casual attire revealed he hadn't missed his workout regimen.

"Thanks. Nice place you have here. I didn't know if it was the condo you had planned to buy, then I noted this address and wondered." Evanston seemed relieved as he rocked on the back of his heels.

He studied her dining room to the left and the living room to the right, where her festive table was stacked with plates and silverware ready to be set to perfection. Stemware. China. Lit candles. Pinecones, and more. She was using every piece of decoration she had in storage from her larger apartment. She would grab one of two chairs from her café table in the kitchen. It was the same table they used for candlelight dinners on her balcony.

He slipped his hands in his pockets. His confident stride was in full force as he strolled to her fireplace, where stockings hung for her family. Evanston's name was absent. She had no idea he was coming.

After staring quietly at the roaring flames, Evanston whirled around. "Cece, I need closure. I can't move on until I know what happened between us. You knew I loved you like crazy, and I thought you loved me." He rushed to invade her space. "Maybe you didn't because you shut me out and never looked back."

"You have no idea of what I've gone through—alone." She gathered her emotions. It was supposed to be peace on earth, so she didn't want to argue, not tonight, on Christmas Eve.

"Funny." He rubbed his silky beard, then chuckled—it was fake. "I don't know what was stronger than our love that could separate us, so why don't you fill in the blanks?" He flopped in a nearby twin high-back chair, crossed his ankle over one knee, and made himself comfortable as if tonight was about them. It wasn't.

After taking a series of deep breaths as her heart pounded, Darcelle opened her mouth, "Back in July, I—"

A hard knock at her door offered perfect timing. Darcelle exhaled, relieved for the interruption. She only wanted to tell this story once tonight—to her family. They could all listen to her journey back together.

She swung open her door and squinted. Nobody was on her porch.

Frowning, she looked to Evanston. "Did you hear someone knock?" she asked to make sure she wasn't hearing things.

"Yeah." He stood and was by her side before she could blink twice. "What's going on?"

She stepped out in the light snowfall, half expecting a snowball coming her way from a prank. Darcelle spied a woman on the sidewalk, shivering in a red sweater, hardly warm enough from the elements in the distance. Where were her hat and coat?

No one else was in sight. It couldn't have been her at Darcelle's door because there were no footprints in the light snow. As a matter of fact, there were no footprints at all.

"Hmm. Maybe it was the wind," Evanston said.

"Maybe." She tilted her head, then stepped on Evanston's foot as she nudged him out of her way to grab her coat and a jacket for the woman.

"Where are you going?" he called after her.

She hurried down the stairs, careful of the slippery patches despite the snow pellets she had thrown down earlier. Darcelle approached the woman. "Excuse me, excuse me."

When she turned around, her smile was warm despite the blast of wind that slapped Darcelle on the cheek and made her shiver. "Can I help you? It's cold out here?" She wrapped the jacket around the woman's shoulders. "My name is Darcelle Price. I've only been in this house for a couple of months, so I don't know many of my neighbors."

"Thank you." The woman closed the jacket around her chest. "I don't live around here. I'm waiting for a ride."

Invite her to your home, God commanded her.

"Why don't you come inside...?" Darcelle pointed to her house, which she had decorated and strung with lights in every window and the porch rails. "You can wait here. I have hot chocolate, a warm fire, and plenty of food."

"I'm Miriam Peace. Thank you so kindly." The woman wasn't young, but Darcelle couldn't guess her age either. She held onto Darcelle's arm so as not to slip and fall. Evanston came out to the porch to assist.

"Thank you." The woman seemed out of breath.

"Let's get her by the fire," Evanston suggested.

"I'll get one of my blankets and some hot chocolate." The mention of the drink made her and Evanston pause. They stared, remembering that's how their love started.

Darcelle cleared her throat first and rushed off to get the items.

"Are you okay? Do you need a ride somewhere?" she heard Evanston ask Miriam.

"Oh, no. He's coming."

In the kitchen, Darcelle poured the hot chocolate from a carafe and spied the sole chair at the café table as if it had Miriam's name on it for Christmas dinner, if she was hungry.

She returned to the living room where Evanston was his charming self, entertaining Darcelle's guest.

The doorbell rang. From the loud, high-pitched child voices on her doorstep, she knew it was her family. Darcelle opened the door and smiled.

Nellie hugged and kissed her. "This is nice, Darcie. You have your home decorated like a gingerbread house neighborhood Winter Wonderland."

When JJ and Zuri saw Evanston, they made a beeline to him as her sisters brought up the rear.

It truly was about to become a night to remember.

Chapter Thirty-three

*T*he atmosphere shifted at the mention of hot chocolate, seeing JJ and Zuri, and Darcelle's vibes.

Evanston's plan was simple, or so he thought. Hear Darcelle out, then leave. Her text inviting him to Christmas dinner had come the morning after he backed out of a "business dinner date" with Nyla. What if he had taken her out, and things would have progressed? He didn't want to think about being trapped in a love triangle or something.

The timing of Darcelle's text had messed with his head. Did the woman have any idea how seeing her would stir up a longing only she could fill? Questions lingered as he drove to her house as if they were strapped into the passenger seat.

Where was the guy who stole Darcelle's affections? Had she broken up with him already?

"Mr. Evan." Darcelle's nephew and niece raced to him. Both vied to be first for his attention. He didn't disappoint. Evanston had missed them, too, and squeezed them tight. Had he come home for Christmas?

Next, Mrs. Price sniffed when she wrapped her arms around him. He didn't think she would let go. It was reminiscent of their family gatherings.

Valencia and Monique brought up the rear with smiles and hugs.

"'Bout time you got your act together and apologized."

Huh? What did he do?

Valencia winked at his perplexed look.

"Whew." Evanston was glad Valencia had been joking—he guessed. Valencia and Cedric would've hit it off—a missed opportunity.

"I'm so glad for my family." Darcelle beamed, and Evanston saw pure happiness pour over her when she nodded his way. "And friends who will share my first Christmas dinner on Christmas Eve. I wanted my place to be perfect on your first visit. I want to give the official tour. Oh, this is Miriam. She's waiting on her ride." Everyone greeted her. "You're welcome to join us for the tour."

"If you don't mind, dear, I'd rather stay warm by the fire." Miriam looked weary.

"Sure."

Odd. Was this Darcelle's family's first visit too? Was this her destination when he showed up at her last apartment on moving day? That was at least three months ago. What was going on? Things weren't adding up. She was close to her family. Had she been living in a bubble?

"It's small, but comfortable…" Darcelle led them from room to room, showcasing a spare bedroom she had set up as an office while the children did their own exploring. The next was the master bedroom, then they circled back to the cozy kitchen, moderate-sized dining room, and small living room.

"What happened to all your furniture?" Mrs. Price asked.

"It's in storage until I move, which I hope will be in a year."

Another tidbit Evanston tucked away as he folded his arms and leaned against the wall. Zuri and JJ amused him as they examined the pile of gifts under the tree. They called off names, and theirs came up several times.

Evanston hadn't thought about gifts for the family. His sole purpose hadn't been for a family reunion, but closure for a relationship he still wanted. Was he a fool or what?

"Now." Darcelle faced her guests. "Hope you're hungry. Let's eat. After that, there's something I want to tell you."

Fear crept up Evanston's back. What news needed a family meeting, and he happened to be included? He didn't care who was looking when he tugged her aside. "Cece, what is it?"

"You'll find out," she whispered.

Find out what? At one time, he was her confidant. There were no secrets between them. Guess he had to wait in line with the rest of her family.

"Do you have an extra seat for Miriam? If not, I can leave," he offered by proper etiquette but screamed, *Tell me to stay.*

She reached for his hand, and Evanston latched on and squeezed it. The spark was undeniable. "No, please stay. I'm glad you're here."

The way she said it—sweet, soft, and genuine—made him weak.

"I have two café chairs in the kitchen—"

"I'll get them." He smiled, and she returned it.

The vibes between them were real and strong. Had the barrier crumbled between them? It was like falling in love with her for the first time.

While he grabbed the chairs, Evanston heard the plates clinking as Darcelle's mother assisted her with rearranging the place settings. "Cece, where do you want me to put them?"

"I'm sure we can make room at the table, but it'll be tight. You decide."

Evanston did as he was instructed, then escorted Miriam into the dining room. The warm fire and hot chocolate seemed to revive the woman. Where was her ride? It was a good thing Darcelle had invited her inside.

They stood around the table as if they were waiting for seating arrangements.

"I want to sit by Mr. Evan." Zuri jumped in place as she waved her hand in the air.

Evanston smiled. He wanted a daughter as adorable as Zuri.

"Me too," JJ chimed in.

"If we're picking seats," Evanston mimicked the children. "I'll take the café chair next to Aunt DeeDee."

"Absolutely not. One of my grandbabies can sit in one," Mrs. Price said. "Miriam, since you're our guest, it only seems right for you to choose where you would like to sit."

Typical Mrs. Price—gracious at all times. He missed that. Evanston remembered when she had given him her late husband's seat at Christmas dinner.

"Thank you for asking." Their guest blushed. "Do you mind if I take the other middle seat?"

Everyone seemed pleased with the arrangements, so Evanston pulled back Darcelle's chair at the head of the table.

His reward was her smile. If only there was mistletoe. He glanced up just in case.

Once they were seated, Miriam asked, "May I offer the blessing, and can we sing a Christmas carol?"

"Yeah," Zuri shouted, bouncing in her chair.

Miriam waited for Darcelle's consent. "Of course."

When Miriam hit the first note to "Joy to the World," her voice had an angelic quality as if it coming through surround sound speakers. Soon the Prices hushed and listened while Darcelle closed her eyes. It was as if Miriam's melodious singular voice had the sound of a chorus singing three parts.

"...and the wonders of His love." Miriam held the last note.

Accolades filled the room. She nodded. "If everyone will join hands, close their eyes, and bow their heads in reverence. Father in heaven, Hallelujah to Your name Jesus. We thank You for the food we are about to eat for nourishment as we celebrate Your birth and Your presence tonight, giving us peace on earth. In Jesus' name. Amen."

"Before we eat, are you going to tell us what's going on?" Valencia asked.

"After," Miriam said as if she was the host, and Darcelle didn't push back. None of them did.

The serving dishes began to circulate around the table. Evanston fixed Zuri's plate to her delight.

Although he and Darcelle dined out a lot, they would sometimes prepare meals together. A great cook, she didn't need any assistance in the kitchen. He spied Darcelle a couple times. She watched him too.

What was the woman thinking? Did she still love him? Evanston hoped so. She scrunched her nose, a playful gesture he missed. Still, his appetite was on hold until he learned of her news.

Many topics floated around the table, from the tastiness of the meal to the light snowfall on Christmas Eve, but Darcelle gave no preview of what was to come. Once everyone finished, she rested her fork.

"Okay." Darcelle patted the table, then scooted back. All eyes followed her as she walked into the living room and returned with an armful of presents.

Evanston thought she was about to pass them out. Instead, she handed them all to JJ and Zuri. "These are for my favorite niece and nephew."

The children's eyes lit bright as they scooted back their chairs to receive them.

"I want you and your sister to go into my bedroom and open them, but don't come out until I tell you."

"Okay," they easily agreed and dashed off.

Now Evanston felt his heart palpitating. The woman was killing him softly and judging from her family's expressions—them too.

After the children had disappeared behind closed doors, Darcelle picked up her cell phone and tapped a number.

Shana's voice answered. "I'm here."

Darcelle took a deep breath and began to pace the limited space in the dining room. "Here goes. As you know, Daddy's death left a void in our lives. When I met Van, the pain subsided." She glanced at him and mouthed, *Thank you.*

"But," she lifted a finger, "I never healed, then with the stress on my job and other things, I was overwhelmed." She sniffed. "I got lost in a dark place, and there was no light to find my way out. I don't wish that experience on anybody."

"What are you saying, baby?" Mrs. Price didn't hide her concern.

Evanston held his breath as she continued without answering her mother.

"My thinking was off, my behavior was strange, and I started not to care about anything—myself, my relationships. I was in a bad place…" She lowered her lashes. "I needed mental health treatment for depression. Whew." She exhaled. "Shana flew in to check on me—"

"Hold up." Monique tilted her head. "Shana, why didn't you tell us? I'm feeling a certain kind of way about that."

"Don't blame Shana." Darcelle fumbled with her fingers. "I asked her not to say anything because at first, I wasn't convinced myself. I didn't think a strong Black woman could suffer from depression.

Depression? Evanston didn't personally know anyone who suffered from depression. He was speechless. Maybe he and Miriam shouldn't be there for this private confession. Yet, he couldn't desert her.

"Shana suspected something was wrong. In college, she did community service as a mental wellness aide trained in ALGEE. Anyway, she interrogated me based on her training. She led me to Dr. Goodman who led me to the cross of Jesus."

"I needed professional intervention. Dr. Goodman did blood work, and my serotonin levels had dropped, but—" she waved her hand in the air— "praise God, He pulled me

245

through. I've never been so scared." Tears welled in Darcelle's eyes.

Evanston stood. He wasn't going to let Darcelle continued this alone. He opened his arms, and Darcelle sought refuge in them. She sniffed against his chest until she composed herself, but Evanston wasn't going to let her go as she continued.

"After three months, Dr. Goodman gave me an early Christmas gift and released me from his care. As long as I manage my stress, I won't need to take medication long-term." She stepped away from the safety of his arms and exhaled. "I'm done."

"See there. You told them, sis," Shana said over the speaker. "Merry Christmas, everyone. Love you all. Evan, you better take care of her," she ordered.

"If she'll let me," Evanston said loud enough for Shana to hear but looked to Darcelle for permission.

"Let him Darcie. Bye." Shana ended the call.

Darcelle glanced around the room before she locked eyes with Evanston. "Please don't judge me. I need support, not denial."

"You should be in Hollywood because you had me fooled, sis." Valencia squinted.

Monique studied Darcelle. "I'm still suspect. I'm not buying those things you mentioned lead to depression. Although we struggle in this world, we deal with it and keep it moving. I was sad when Daddy died, too, but we still had Mama. I thought you were in control of your life."

"Baby, why didn't you say something?" Evanston frowned, thinking about her mood swings and the arguments. Were those signs?

Her eyes watered as she looked at him. "How could I ask for help when I didn't know I needed it?"

Mrs. Price shook her head. "I'm not judging you. God knows we've all been through a lot. Jesus is a keeper, and He would have kept you if you had asked. I'm not believing you had a bout with depression. You looked normal, not depressed. God's healing power is free. Doctors are always trying to get money..." Her mother ranted until she tired herself out.

"Mama, depression is real. If my body doesn't self-correct within a few weeks, then something is wrong, and something was wrong with me. Dr. Goodman explained how the brain malfunctions like high blood pressure, diabetes, and other medical conditions affect our bodies. He counseled me and put me on the path to Christ."

She squatted in front of her mother. "Mama. What does depression look like?" Darcelle raised her hand. "Me—for the past three months, I've been the face of mental illness."

"Don't say that word," Mrs. Price snapped. "I reared you to be a strong Black woman in a Christian home. You attend church with me. We don't have mental illness in our family. Hush."

"To be truthful, it was for show—for the sake of checking off a box that I went to church on Sunday. I tagged along because you asked me. I was hit and miss, depending on if I woke up on time. As I struggled with depression, I was desperate for help, help from God. I took the Lord Jesus for granted, casting Him aside in favor of my free will to do as I pleased. When I needed Him—I mean really needed Jesus—I didn't know how to find Him in here," she said, touching her chest. "I was the definition of a lukewarm Christian."

"Isaiah 55:6," Mrs. Price whispered, *Seek ye the Lord while he may be found, call ye upon Him while He is near.'"

Evanston witnessed Darcelle's torture as she explained how she started drinking to numb the pain from Reed and Meeks' betrayal, skipped meals, and put on a happy face around family and even him.

Valencia shook her head. "I'm not a psych doctor, but we're sisters. I'd have known if you were depressed. A woman I knew killed herself, and there were signs."

"God forbid." Mrs. Price sneered. "The devil is a lie."

Darcelle rubbed her temples. "Everyone has an opinion about mental illness, but Mama, when I read about healing in the Bible." She paused to recall which book. "It was in Matthew. Chapter eight stuck out when people went to Jesus with their issues. I noticed four things: they asked if it was Jesus' will, He spoke His Word, the people had the faith to believe it. If I don't admit I've got a problem, how can God heal me? This hasn't been easy. I'm sorry I kept this from you, but I was afraid of your reaction."

Evanston's heart ached as he heard the pleading in Darcelle's voice and her family's pushback. She was not winning them over as things became heated. Darcelle needed him on her team.

Miriam cleared her throat, reminding them of her presence and commanding their attention. "Let there be peace in your heart." Her soft voice seemed to amplify within the room. "Unto us a Savior is born to deliver His people for all manners of sickness and diseases. Celebrate His birth and rejoice in His death. Tonight, let all bickering and strife and jealousy be not named among you. The greatest commandment and gift is love. Love will cover a multitude of sins. Love on each other, and that will bring you peace. Celebrate Christ."

A loud honking blared outside Darcelle's door as if a vehicle was parked on her porch. Miriam stood. "That's for me. Thank you all for your kindness. Remember, the greatest gift we can give one another is love." She removed Darcelle's jacket and rubbed her arms on her sweater. She opened the door and stepped out into the howling wind, and a blast of snow swept onto the floor s if there was a blizzard outside.

"That poor woman is going to freeze out there with only a sweater." Mrs. Price moved to peep out the window. She spun around with a dumbfounded expression. "There's no sign of her."

"What?" Darcelle was the first to speak.

"What do you mean?" the sisters asked in unison and raced to the windows.

Darcelle opened the door. Evanston was behind her. There was no evidence of footprints or recent tire tracks in the street. The wind was calm, and there wasn't more than an inch of snow on the ground, not the snowstorm that seemed to have greeted Miriam when she opened the door. "It looks like she just disappeared as soon as she walked outside." Darcelle's confusion matched theirs.

"There was something about her. Miriam was like a fly on the wall. Quiet except when she had something to say." Mrs. Price chuckled and shook her head. "I wonder if we just entertained—" Her mother shrugged. "Never mind."

Darcelle gnawed on her lips that Evanston desperately wanted to kiss. "I did ask Jesus to send help when I broke the news to you all because I didn't know how you would respond."

Mrs. Price wrapped her arms around Darcelle. "Maybe, the Lord did. On the eve of celebrating His birth, this has been a night of miracles. I'm sorry. Please forgive me. I don't want any of my daughters to feel they can't come to me about anything. I'll try to understand this mental illness."

"Mama, Dr. Goodman said sometimes God heals in a blink of an eye. Other times, it's a process like the ten lepers, and until Jesus does His work, I should continue my treatment and medicine as he prescribes."

"He's a wise man." Mrs. Price nodded with a smile. "I guess if you're going to seek treatment, it should be with someone who knows Christ."

Evanston opened his arms. "Baby, I'm sorry for not understanding and not recognizing the signs and how to respond."

"I can't blame you for something I couldn't understand. I didn't mean to push you away, but at the time, everyone and everything made me irritable. I felt numb to emotions. I know it doesn't make sense, but I needed to talk, but no one was there to listen." Darcelle's frustration showed in her face and body language.

"I don't want this talk to stress you out." Evanston stepped into his protective role, whether she wanted approved, or not. This was the woman he loved.

Darcelle's warm smile melted his resolve. "It won't. I prayed with Shana earlier for peace to reign." She paused and gnawed on her lips. "Maybe God sent peace." She frowned, then shook her head. "I guess God hosted this party and sent out the invites."

Now that Evanston had the answers he needed, could they mend what was broken between them? "Do you have plans for tomorrow? It seems I'm going to do some late Christmas Eve shopping."

"All my presents are here with me."

"It's Christmas. She'll be spending the day with her family so we can love on her," Mrs. Price said. "I expect you at the head of the table again this year, Evanston Giles."

"Yes, ma'am." He turned to Darcelle. "I want another chance for us. I don't want to miss our first anniversary of when we met. I'm willing to listen and learn and fall asleep on the phone, if that what it takes, Cece."

She chuckled. "And, you snored."

Evanston was the last to leave that night, whispering, "Happy Anniversary" between kisses before leaving. Home truly was where the heart was, and Darcelle was here.

Chapter Thirty-four

*H*ad Christmas Eve dinner been a dream? Darcelle wondered the next morning as she hugged her pillow. Moments later, she scooted up in bed and stretched. Her mental restoration was nearing a hundred percent, and it had been a long time coming. The past six months had seemed like a lifetime.

Darcelle slipped out of bed and knelt. "Jesus, I thank You for new mercies this morning. Thank You for placing the right people in my life…" She petitioned God until His heavenly tongues flowed through her mouth, and she lifted up her hands and worshipped Him.

Even though she and Evanston talked for hours after he'd arrived home, the re-connection between them was immediate. She had sobbed, thinking about how she had hurt him.

"Cece, it's not okay for you to wait until I'm at home to start crying. Don't make me drive back over and wrap my arms around you."

That brought a smile to her face. Darcelle could see him doing just that. "I know."

"Cece, my life was terrible without you in it, and to learn that you went through that without me hurts. Honestly, I thought my love was stronger than any storm in our lives. How wrong I was. I want to learn and understand more about depression, so I can recognize the signs. I've heard about people with depression and suicide. I never thought it would hit so close to home."

Darcelle's phone beeped. "Listen, I'll see you later at Mama's. Shana's calling."

"Tell her Merry Christmas and thank you."

"Thank you?" Darcelle wracked her brain for a reason why.

"She was there for you, but I'm here now, and I'm not going anywhere."

Oh, how she missed him. And to think she almost lost him permanently as he considered going out with another woman.

When he told her that last night, it caused her to boo-hoo, and she admitted the possibility he had moved on stopped her from reaching out to him because she didn't want to interfere if he had found love again.

"How can I love another woman when I love you," he had said.

Darcelle ended the call with Evanston and switched over to Shana.

"I thought I was about to go to voicemail. Merry Christmas."

"Sorry...I was talking to Van." She giggled when her friend screamed.

"Yes. He was a Christmas surprise. I was calling to see how the Prices and Evan handled the news after I ended the call, but *girrl*, if Evanston Giles was in the house last night and you're talking to him this morning, I'd say everything is all right in your world. So...I want details."

"I got pushback from Mama, and I expected that." Darcelle remembered her own denial. "She's got to get over the idea that depression is a sign of weakness."

"Denial is big in the church and the Black community. But the thought of you getting worse, I don't want to think about it."

"I know. I have to thank God that you stepped in before I got worse." Darcelle would forever be grateful. "I can't believe I accidentally invited Van through an old group text."

Shana laughed. "Surprise on you and me. I was excited to know he was there. That reminds me of this white grandmother, Wanda, who sent out a text for a Thanksgiving dinner and invited a stranger, a Black teenager—Jamal somebody, thinking it was her grandson. They kept the tradition going until Wanda's husband passed away."

"*Awww.* Then I had another unexpected visitor. First, my doorbell rings—Evanston. Next, I hear a knock—nobody, then I see this woman..." She spared no detail, ending with the woman's disappearing within minutes without a trail in the snow.

"Sounds creepy. I'm shivering now. Sounds like she was an angel?" Shana laughed.

Darcelle wondered. Did God send an angel to her house for Christmas dinner?

"So," Shana continued, "back to you and Evan. Are you two dating again?" She didn't hide the glee in her voice.

"We're talking. I mean, it's hard to jump back into a relationship when stuff has happened—basically, another part of me happened."

"Now that Evan knows what happened to you, he's not going to let you go through anything else alone. I give you guys one year, and that man is going to ask you to marry him, and you're going to say yes, even if I have to hold your finger steady for him to slip on the big rock he'll probably buy you. Make sure you scream your answer for a more dramatic effect."

"My silly friend whom I love dearly." Darcelle broke out in a Hallelujah chorus and danced her way to the bathroom to shower and get ready for church. Shana had ended the call when Darcelle hit the wrong note the second time.

Thankful.

One word. So many emotions.

The group text changed everything. Evanston was thankful Darcelle sought treatment and...thankful he and Darcelle still loved and wanted to be together. Wrapped up in all thankfulness, he attended Christmas service with his family before he would go to the Prices later.

Back at his parents' house, Evanston and his family opened gifts, and he revealed the reason behind his big smile and humming. "Cece and I are working on getting back together."

His mother released an audible sigh. "'Bout time. Thank you, Jesus. It hurt me to see you so sad."

Langston grinned and patted his son's back. "I'm with your mom. You two were good together."

Jessica wasn't so fast with congratulations. "Wait a minute. Hold up. Did I miss something? A few weeks ago, you agreed to go out with Nyla, then you backed out—so not cool. Now," she snapped her fingers, "you and Darcelle are an item. Why? The one who hurt my big brother."

Evanston knew his sister was protective of him, but he had to get her straight about Darcelle. "Jess, there was never any Nyla and me. I love you, and I know how much you love me. But what I'm about to say stays here, and you'll not treat her any differently." He waited for each one to nod their agreement. "The job lost, among other things, caused Cece to fall into a deep depression."

"Oh, no." Sheila gasped and covered her mouth.

"Yes." His baby had suffered alone. "Her family didn't know, and I didn't know I was adding to her stress. If it weren't for her friend, Shana, she might have gotten worse."

"So, the chick is crazy?" Jessica rolled her eyes and folded her arms.

Evanston gritted his teeth and tamed the air leaving his nostrils. "Watch it. Mental illness isn't a crime unless we make it one, and I won't. I'll admit I don't fully understand it, but that's on me to learn all I can. I love Darcelle and want her to be a part of my life—healthy and happy. Respect that."

Jessica didn't say another word.

"I'm going to head over to the Prices, so Cece and I can celebrate our first anniversary, which was delayed."

"Tell her and her family Merry Christmas for us," her mother said, and father second.

Evanston spied Jessica. "Me too," she said in a low voice.

On the drive to Mrs. Price's house, Evanston wished he had sat in on Darcelle's therapies so he could be informed on how he could help. He wanted her to know he was here to stay. Instead of bumping heads and forcing her hand, Evanston should have backed down and listened. He repented for causing her pain and suffering.

Evanston planned to return to the jeweler where he'd stopped one day during his lunch break. It had been after their Valentine's Day dinner, and Evanston knew then he was going to ask Darcelle to be his wife. He felt it in his heart, so he picked out the ring. He bought it weeks before things started to go downhill.

But that's okay. He and Darcelle could only go uphill from now on. Evanston would hold on to that ring until they both were ready.

After Christmas, while Evanston was on vacation, he and Darcelle spent every day together rebuilding their love and trust.

He was with her when she got a job offer. Together they discussed how much stress would come with the position. His sole focus was to take care of her mental health, physical well-being, and for them to grow spiritually together. "The pay is comparable to what I was making, and I'll have a staff to delegate responsibilities."

Evanston squeezed her hands. "I promise you right now I'll be with you every step of the way, but if I recognize signs of stress, I'll step in to protect you. Will you give me permission to do that?"

"Yes. I'll call the company back to give them a verbal acceptance. I love you, Van." She leaned toward him.

"I love you more." He backed it up with the kiss she was asking for.

Christmas dinners would always hold a special place in their hearts. Now it was time to begin another chapter in their lives.

Author's Note

I hope you have enjoyed Evanston and Darcelle's journey to their love story. The Lord gave me the title long before he gave me the plot. Struggling with depression is real. If you or someone you know is experiencing symptoms, please reach out for help *and* seek mental health services at 1-(800)-662-HELP (4357).

A loved one left undiagnosed and not treated could lead to a person harming themselves or even considering death. Losing one soul to suicide is too many. The call for help is real in the church and within the community.

It's okay to feel depressed, but if you can't shake the gloom, please call the National Suicide Prevention Lifeline, 24 hours a day, seven days a week at 800-273-8255

Book Club Discussion Questions

- Discuss Evanston and Darcelle's attitude about church attendance.

- What is drawing people to church: Situations? Personal problems? Love for God?

- What are some signs of depression?

- Discuss Darcelle's response about not getting the promotion and compare it to a situation where you feel you were wronged.

- Talk about the things you liked and didn't like about Evanston.

- Discuss Darcelle's relationship with her family. Should she have confided in one of her sisters? Why or why not?

- Discuss Miriam's purpose at the Christmas Eve dinner.

- What does ALGEE stand for?

- Discuss depression in the Black community and how it is handled by society and in the church.

- How did you feel about Evanston confiding in his family about Darcelle's illness.

About the Author

Pat Simmons is a multi-published Christian romance author with more than thirty-five titles. She is a self-proclaimed genealogy sleuth who is passionate about researching her ancestors, then casting them in starring roles in her novels. She is a three-time recipient of the Romance Slam Jam Emma Rodgers Award for Best Inspirational Romance. Pat's first inspirational women's fiction, Lean On Me, with Sourcebooks, was the February/March Together We Read Digital Book Club pick for the national library system.

Pat describes the evidence of the gift of the Holy Ghost as a life-altering experience. She has been a featured speaker and workshop presenter at various venues across the country. Pat has converted her sofa-strapped sports fanatical husband into an amateur travel agent, untrained bodyguard, GPS-guided chauffeur, and administrative assistant who is constantly on probation. They have a son and a daughter. Pat holds a B.S. in mass communications from Emerson College in Boston, Massachusetts and worked in various positions in radio, television, and print media for more than twenty years. She oversaw the media publicity for the annual RT Booklovers Conventions for fourteen years. Visit her at www.patsimmons.net.

Other Christian Titles

The Jamieson Legacy series
Book 1: Guilty of Love
Book 2: Not Guilty of Love
Book 3: Still Guilty
Book 4: The Acquittal
Book 5: Guilty by Association
Book 6: The Guilt Trip
Book 7: Free from Guilt
Book 8: The Confession
Book 9: The Guilty Generation

The Carmen Sisters
Book 1: No Easy Catch
Book 2: In Defense of Love
Book 3: Driven to Be Loved
Book 4: Redeeming Heart

Love at the Crossroads
Book 1: Stopping Traffic
Book 2: A Baby for Christmas
Book 3: The Keepsake
Book 4: What God Has for Me
Book 5: Every Woman Needs a Praying Man

Making Love Work Anthology
Book 1: Love at Work
Book 2: Words of Love
Book 3: A Mother's Love

Restore My Soul series
Book 1: Crowning Glory
Book 2: Jet: The Back Story
Book 3: Love Led by the Spirit

Family is Forever:
Book 1: Lean on Me
Book 2: Here For You
Book 3: Stand by Me

God's Gifts:
Book1: Couple by Christmas
Book 2: Prayers Answered by Christmas

Perfect Chance at Love series:
Book 1: Love by Delivery
Book 2: Late Summer Love

Single titles
Talk to Me
Her Dress (novella)
Christmas Dinner
Christmas Greetings
Taye's Gift

Anderson Brothers
Book 1: Love for the Holidays (Three novellas): A Christian
Christmas, A Christian Easter, and A Christian Father's Day
Book 2: A Woman After David's Heart (Valentine's Day)
Book 3: A Noelle for Nathan (Book 3 of the Andersen Brothers)

PERFECT CHANCE AT *Love* SERIES

In *Love by Delivery*, Senior Accounts Manager Dominique Hayes has it all money, a car and a condo. Well, almost. She's starting to believe love has passed her by. One thing for sure, she can't hurry God, so she continues to wait while losing hope that a special Godly man will ever make his appearance. Package Courier Ashton Taylor knows a man who finds a wife finds a good thing. The only thing standing in his way of finding the right woman is his long work hours. Or maybe not. A chance meeting changes everything. When love finally comes knocking, will Dominique open the door and accept Ashton's special delivery?

In *Late Summer Love*, it takes strategies to win a war, but prayer and spiritual intervention are needed to win a godly woman's heart. God has been calling out to Blake Cross ever since Blake was deployed in Iraq and he took his safety for granted. Now, back on American soil, Blake still won't surrender his soul--until he meets Paige Blake during a family reunion. When the Lord gives Blake an ultimatum, is Blake listening, and is he finally ready to learn what it takes to be a godly man fit for a godly woman?

In *Crowning Glory*, Cinderella had a prince; Karyn Wallace has a King. While Karyn served four years in prison for an unthinkable crime, she embraced salvation through Crowns for Christ outreach ministry. After her release, Karyn stays strong and confident, despite the stigma society places on ex-offenders. Since Christ strengthens the underdog, Karyn refuses to sway away from the scripture, "He who the Son has set free is free indeed." Levi Tolliver, for the most part, is a practicing Christian. One contradiction is he doesn't believe in turning the other cheek. He's steadfast there is a price to pay for every sin committed, especially after the untimely death of his wife during a robbery. Then Karyn enters Levi's life. He is enthralled not only with her beauty, but her sweet spirit until he learns about her incarceration. If Levi can accept that Christ paid Karyn's debt in full, then a treasure awaits him. This is a powerful tale and reminds readers of the permanency of redemption.

Jet: The Back Story to Love Led By the Spirit, to say Jesetta "Jet" Hutchens has issues is an understatement. In Crowning Glory, Book 1 of the Restoring My Soul series, she releases a firestorm of anger with an unforgiving heart.

But every hurting soul has a history. In Jet: The Back Story to Love Led by the Spirit, Jet doesn't know how to cope with the loss of her younger sister, Diane. But God sets her on the road to a spiritual recovery. To make sure she doesn't get lost, Jesus sends the handsome and single Minister Rossi Tolliver to be her guide. Psalm 147:3 says Jesus can heal the brokenhearted and bind up their wounds. That sets the stage for Love Led by the Spirit.

In *Love Led By the Spirit*, Minister Rossi Tolliver is ready to settle down. Besides the outwardly attraction, he desires a woman who is sweet, humble, and loves church folks. Sounds simple enough on paper, but when he gets off his knees, praying for that special someone to come into his life, God opens his eyes to the woman who has been there all along. There is only a slight problem. Love is the farthest thing from Jesetta "Jet" Hutchens' mind. But Rossi, the man and the minister, is hard to resist. Is Jet ready to allow the Holy Spirit to lead her to love?

LOVE AT THE CROSSROADS SERIES

In *Stopping Traffic*, Book 1, Candace Clark has a phobia about crossing the street, and for good reason. As fate would have it, her daughter's principal assigns her to crossing guard duties as part of the school's Parent Participation program. With no choice in the matter, Candace begrudgingly accepts her stop sign and safety vest, then reports to her designated crosswalk. Once Candace is determined to overcome her fears, God opens the door for a blessing, and Royce Kavanaugh enters into her life, a firefighter built to rescue any damsel in distress. When a spark of attraction ignites, Candace and Royce soon discover there's more than one way to stop traffic.

In *A Baby For Christmas*, Book 2, yes, diamonds are a girl's best friend, but in Solae Wyatt-Palmer's case, she desires something more valuable. Captain Hershel Kavanaugh is a divorcee and the father of two adorable little boys. Solae has never been married and longs to be a mother. Although Hershel showers her with expensive gifts, his hesitation about proposing causes Solae to walk and never look back. As the holidays approach, Hershel must convince Solae that she has everything he could ever want for Christmas.

In *The Keepsake*, Book 3, Until death us do part…or until Desiree walks away. Desiree "Desi" Bishop is devastated when she finds evidence of her husband's affair. God knew she didn't get married only to one day have to stand before a judge and file for a divorce. But Desi wants out no matter how much her heart says to forgive Michael. That isn't easier said than done. She sees God's one acceptable reason for a divorce as the only opt-out clause in her marriage. Michael Bishop is a repenting man who loves his wife of three years. If only…he had paid attention to the red flags God sent to keep him from falling into the devil's snares. But Michael didn't and he had fallen. Although God had forgiven him instantly when he repented, Desi's forgiveness is moving as a snail's pace. In the end, after all the tears have been shed and forgiveness granted and received, the couple learns that some marriages are worth keeping

In *What God Has For Me*, Book 4, Halcyon Holland is leaving her live-in boyfriend, taking their daughter and the baby in her belly with her. She's tired of waiting for the ring, so she buys herself one. When her ex doesn't reconcile their relationship, Halcyon begins to second-guess whether or not she compromised her chance for a happily ever after. After all, what man in his right mind would want to deal with the community stigma of 'baby mama drama?' But Zachary Bishop has had his eye on Halcyon since the first time he saw her. Without a ring on her finger, Zachary prays that she will come to her senses and not only leave Scott, but come back to God. What one man doesn't cherish, Zach is ready to treasure. Not deterred by Halcyon's broken spirit, Zachary is on a mission to offer her a second chance at love that she can't refuse. And as far as her adorable children are concerned, Zachary's love is unconditional for a ready-made family. Halcyon will soon learn that her past circumstances won't hinder the Lord's blessings, because what God has for her, is for her...and him...and the children.

In *Every Woman Needs A Praying Man*, Book 5, first impressions can make or break a business deal and they definitely could be a relationship buster, but an ill-timed panic attack draws two strangers together. Unlike firefighters who run into danger, instincts tell businessman Tyson Graham to head the other way as fast as he can when he meets a certain damsel in distress. Days later, the same woman struts through his door for a job interview. Monica Wyatt might possess the outwardly beauty and the brains on paper, but Tyson doesn't trust her to work for his firm, or maybe he doesn't trust his heart around her.

In *A Christian Christmas*, Book 1, Christian's Christmas will never be the same for Joy Knight if Christian Andersen has his way. Not to be confused with a secret Santa, Christian and his family are busier than Santa's elves making sure the Lord's blessings are distributed to those less fortunate by Christmas day. Joy is playing the hand that life dealt her, rearing four children in a home that is on the brink of foreclosure. She's not looking for a handout, but when Christian rescues her in the checkout line; her niece thinks Christian is an angel. Joy thinks he's just another man who will eventually leave, disappointing her and the children. Although Christian is a servant of the Lord, he is a flesh and blood man and all he wants for Christmas is Joy Knight. Can time spent with Christian turn Joy's attention from her financial woes to the real meaning of Christmas—and true love?

In *A Christian Easter*, how to celebrate Easter becomes a balancing act for Christian and Joy Andersen and their four children. Chocolate bunnies, colorful stuffed baskets and flashy fashion shows are their competition. Despite the enticements, Christian refuses to succumb without a fight. And it becomes a tug of war when his recently adopted ten year-old daughter, Bethani, wants to participate in her friend's Easter tradition. Christian hopes he has instilled

Proverbs 22:6, into the children's heart in the short time of being their dad.

In *A Christian Father's Day*, three fathers, one Father's Day and four children. Will the real dad, please stand up. It's never too late to be a father—or is it? Christian Andersen was looking forward to spending his first Father's day with his adopted children---all four of them. But Father's day becomes more complicated than Christian or Joy ever imagined. Christian finds himself faced with living up to his name when things don't go his way to enjoy an idyllic once a year celebration. But he depends on God to guide him through the journey.

(All three of Christian's individual stories are in the Love for the Holidays)

In *A Woman After David's Heart*, Book 2, David Andersen doesn't have a problem indulging in Valentine's Day, per se, but not on a first date. Considering it was the love fest of the year, he didn't want a woman to get any ideas that a wedding ring was forthcoming before he got a chance to know her. So he has no choice but to wait until the whole Valentine's Day hoopla was over, then he would make his move on a sister in his church he can't take his eyes off of. For the past two years and counting, Valerie Hart hasn't been the recipient of a romantic Valentine's Day dinner invitation. To fill the void, Valerie keeps herself busy with God's business, hoping the Lord will send her perfect mate soon. Unfortunately, with no prospects in sight, it looks like that won't happen again this year. A Woman After David's Heart is a Valentine romance novella that can be enjoyed with or without a box of chocolates.

In *A Noelle for Nathan*, Book 3, is a story of kindness, selflessness, and falling in love during the Christmas season. Andersen Investors & Consultants, LLC, CFO Nathan Andersen (A Christian Christmas) isn't looking for attention when he buys a homeless man a meal, but grade school teacher Noelle Foster is watching his every move with admiration. His generosity makes him a man after her own heart. While donors give more to children and families in need around the holiday season, Noelle Foster believes in giving year-round after seeing many of her students struggle with hunger and finding a warm bed at night. At a second-chance meeting, sparks fly when Noelle and Nathan share a kindred spirit with their passion to help those less fortunate. Whether they're doing charity work or attending Christmas parties, the couple becomes inseparable. Although Noelle and Nathan exchange gifts, the biggest present is the one from Christ.

MAKING LOVE WORK SERIES

This series can be read in any order.

In *A Mother's Love*, to Jillian Carter, it's bad when her own daughter beats her to the altar. She became a teenage mother when she confused love for lust one summer. Despite the sins of her past, Jesus forgave her and blessed her to be the best Christian example for Shana. Jillian is not looking forward to becoming an empty-nester at thirty-nine. The old adage, she's not losing a daughter, but gaining a son-in-law is not comforting as she braces for a lonely life ahead. What she doesn't expect is for two men to vie for her affections: Shana's biological father who breezes back into their lives as a redeemed man and practicing Christian. Not only is Alex still goof looking, but he's willing to right the wrong he's done in the past. Not if Dr. Dexter Harris has anything to say about it. The widower father of the groom has set his sights on Jillian and he's willing to pull out all the stops to woo her. Now the choice is hers. Who will be the next mother's love?

In *Love at Work*, how do two people go undercover to hide an office romance in a busy television newsroom? In plain sight, of course. Desiree King is an assignment editor at KDPX-TV in St. Louis, MO. She dispatches a team to wherever breaking news happens. Her focus is to stay ahead of the competition. Overall, she's easy-going, respectable, and compassionate. But when it comes to dating a fellow coworker, she refuses to cross that professional line. Award-winning investigative reporter Bryan Mitchell makes life challenging for Desiree with his thoughtful gestures, sweet notes, and support. He tries to convince Desiree that as Christians, they could show coworkers how to blend their personal and private lives without compromising their morals.

In *Words of Love*, call it old fashion, but Simone French was smitten with a love letter. Not a text, email, or Facebook post, but a love letter sent through snail mail. The prose wasn't the corny roses-are-red-and-violets-are-blue stuff. The first letter contained short accolades for a job well done. Soon after, the missives were filled with passionate words from a man who confessed the hidden secrets of his soul. He revealed his unspoken weaknesses, listed his uncompromising desires, and unapologetically noted his subtle strengths. Yes, Rice Taylor was ready to surrender to love. Whew. Closing her eyes, Simone inhaled the faint lingering smell of roses on the beige plain stationery. She had a testimony. If anyone would listen, she would proclaim that love was truly blind.

In *Talk To Me*, despite being deaf as a result of a fireworks explosion, CEO of a St. Louis non-profit company, Noel Richardson, expertly navigates the hearing world. What some view as a disability, Noel views as a challenge—his lack of hearing has never held him back. It also helps that he has great looks, numerous university degrees, and full bank accounts. But those assets don't define him as a man who longs for the right woman in his life. Deciding to visit a church service, Noel is blind-sided by the most beautiful and graceful Deaf interpreter he's ever seen. Mackenzie Norton challenges him on every level through words and signing, but as their love grows, their faith is tested. When their church holds a yearly revival, they witness the healing power of God in others. Mackenzie has faith to believe that Noel can also get in on the blessing. Since faith comes by hearing, whose voice does Noel hear in his heart, Mackenzie or God's?

TESTIMONY: If I Should Die Before I Wake. It is of the LORD's mercies that we are not consumed, because His compassions fail not. They are new every morning, great is Thy faithfulness. Lamentations 3:22-23, God's mercies are sure; His promises are fulfilled; but a dawn of a new morning is God' grace. If you need a testimony about God's grace, then If I Should Die Before I Wake will encourage your soul. Nothing happens in our lives by chance. If you need a miracle, God's got that too. Trust Him. Has it been a while since you've had a testimony? Increase your prayer life, build your faith and walk in victory because without a test, there is no testimony. (eBook only)

In *Her Dress*, sometimes a woman just wants to splurge on something new, especially when she's about to attend an event with movers and shakers. Find out what happens when Pepper Trudeau is all dressed up and goes to the ball, but another woman is modeling the same attire. At first, Pepper is embarrassed, then the night gets interesting when she meets Drake Logan. Her Dress is a romantic novella about the all too common occurrence—two women shopping at the same place. Maybe having the same taste isn't all bad. Sometimes a good dress is all you need to meet the man of your dreams. (eBook only)

In *Christmas Greetings*, Saige Carter loves everything about Christmas: the shopping, the food, the lights, and of course, Christmas wouldn't be complete without family and friends to share in the traditions they've created together. Plus, Saige is extra excited about her line of Christmas greeting cards hitting store shelves, but when she gets devastating news around the holidays, she wonders if she'll ever look at Christmas the same again. Daniel Washington is no Scrooge, but he'd rather skip the holidays altogether than spend them with his estranged family. After one too many arguments around the dinner table one year, Daniel had enough and walked away from the drama. As one year has turned into many, no one seems willing to take the first step toward reconciliation. When Daniel reads one of Saige's greeting cards, he's unsure if the words inside are enough to erase the pain and bring about forgiveness. Once God reveals to them His purpose for their lives, they will have a reason to rejoice.

In *Guilty of Love*, when do you know the most important decision of your life is the right one? Reaping the seeds from what she's sown; Cheney Reynolds moves into a historic neighborhood in Ferguson, Missouri, and becomes a reclusive. Her first neighbor, the incomparable Mrs. Beatrice Tilley Beacon aka Grandma BB, is an opinionated childless widow. Grandma BB is a self-proclaimed expert on topics Cheney isn't seeking advice—everything from landscaping to hip-hop dancing to romance. Then there is Parke Kokumuo Jamison VI, a direct descendant of a royal African tribe. He learned his family ancestry, African history, and lineage preservation before he could count. Unwittingly, they are drawn to each other, but it takes Christ to weave their lives into a spiritual bliss while He exonerates their past indiscretions.

In *Not Guilty*, one man, one woman, one God and one big problem. Malcolm Jamieson wasn't the man who got away, but the man God instructed Hallison Dinkins to set free. Instead of their explosive love affair leading them to the wedding altar, God diverted Hallison to the prayer altar during her first visit back to church in years. Malcolm was convinced that his woman had loss her mind to break off their engagement. Didn't Hallison know that Malcolm, a tenth generation descendant of a royal African tribe, couldn't be replaced? Once Malcolm concedes that their relationship can't be savaged, he issues Hallison his own edict, "If we're meant to be with each other, we'll find our way back. If not, that means that there's a love stronger than what we had." His words begin to haunt Hallison until she begins to regret their break up, and that's where their story begins. Someone has to retreat, and God never loses a battle.

In *Still Guilty*, Cheney Reynolds Jamieson made a choice years ago that is now shaping her future and the future of the men she loves. A botched abortion left her unable to carry a baby to term, and her husband, Parke K. Jamison VI, is expected to produce heirs. With a wife who cannot give him a child, Parke vows to find and get custody of his illegitimate son by any means necessary. Meanwhile, Cheney's twin brother, Rainey, struggles with his anger over his ex-girlfriend's actions that haunt him, and their father, Dr. Roland Reynolds, fights to keep an old secret in the past.

In *The Acquittal*, two worlds apart, but their hearts dance to the same African drum beat. On a professional level, Dr. Rainey Reynolds is a competent, highly sought-after orthodontist. Inwardly, he needs to be set free from the chaos of revelations that make him question if happiness is obtainable. To get away from the drama, Rainey is willing to leave the country under the guise of a mission trip with Dentist Without Borders. Will changing his surroundings really change him? If one woman can heal his wounds, then he will believe that there is really peace after the storm.

Ghanaian beauty Josephine Abena Yaa Amoah returns to Africa after completing her studies as an exchange student in St. Louis, Missouri. Although her heart bleeds for his peace, she knows she must step back and pray for Rainey's surrender to Christ in order for God to acquit him of his self-inflicted mental torture. In the Motherland of Ghana, Africa, Rainey not only visits the places of his ancestors, will he embrace the liberty that Christ's Blood really does set every man free.

In *Guilty By Association*, how important is a name? To the St. Louis Jamiesons who are tenth generation descendants of a royal African tribe—everything. To the Boston Jamiesons whose father never married their mother—there is no loyalty or legacy. Kidd Jamieson suffers from the "angry" male syndrome because his father was an absent in the home, but insisted his two sons carry his last name. It takes an old woman who mingles genealogy truths and Bible verses together for Kidd to realize his worth as a strong black man. He learns it's not his association with the name that identifies him, but the man he becomes that defines him.

In *The Guilt Trip*, Aaron "Ace" Jamieson is living a carefree life. He's good-looking, respectable when he's in the mood, but his weakness is women. If a woman tries to ambush him with a pregnancy, he takes off in the other direction. It's a lesson learned from his absentee father that responsibility is optional. Talise Rogers has a bright future ahead of her. She's pretty and has no problem catching a man's eye, which is exactly what she does with Ace. Trapping Ace Jamieson is the furthest thing from Talise's mind when she learns she pregnant and Ace rejects her. "I want nothing from you Ace, not even your name." And Talise meant it.

In *Free From Guilt,* it's salvation round-up time and Cameron Jamieson's name is on God's hit list. Although his brothers and cousins embraced God—thanks to the women in their lives—the two-degreed MIT graduate isn't going to let any woman take him down that path without a fight. He's satisfied with his career, social calendar, and good genes. But God uses a beautiful messenger, Gabrielle Dupree, to show him that he's in a spiritual deficit. Cameron learns the hard way that man's wisdom is like foolishness to God. For every philosophical argument he throws her way, Gabrielle exposes him to scriptures that makes him question his worldly knowledge.

In *The Confession,* Sandra Nicholson had made good and bad choices throughout the years, but the best one was to give her life to Christ when her sons were small and to rear them up in the best Christian way she knew how. That was thirty something years ago and Sandra has evolved from a young single mother of two rambunctious boys, Kidd and Ace Jamieson, to a godly woman seasoned with wisdom. Despite the challenges and trials of rearing two strong-willed personalities, Sandra maintained her sanity through the grace of God, which kept gray strands at bay.

Now, Sandra Nicholson is on the threshold of happiness, but Kidd believes no man is good enough for his mother, especially if her love interest could be a man just like his absentee father.

In *The Guilty Generation,* seventeen-year-old Kami Jamieson is so over being daddy's little girl. Now that she has captured the attention of Tango, the bad boy from her school, Kami's love for her family and God have taken a backseat to her teen crush. Although the Jamiesons have instilled godly principles in Kami since she was young, they will stop at nothing, including prayer and fasting, to protect her from falling prey to society's peer pressure. Can Kami survive her teen rebellion, or will she be guilty of dividing the next generation?

In *Fun and Games with the Jamieson Men*, The Jamieson Legacy series inspired this game book of fun activities:• Brain Teasers• Crossword Puzzles• Word Searches •Sudoku •Mazes •Coloring Pages. The Jamiesons are fictional characters that put emphasis on Black Heritage, which includes Black American History tidbits, African American genealogy, and strong Black families. Relax, grab a pencil and play along.

THE CARMEN SISTERS SERIES

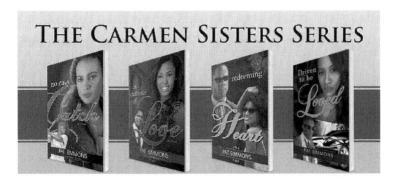

In *No Easy Catch*, Book 1, Shae Carmen hasn't lost her faith in God, only the men she's come across. Shae's recent heartbreak was discovering that her boyfriend was not only married, but on the verge of reconciling with his estranged wife. Humiliated, Shae begins to second guess herself as why she didn't see the signs that he was nothing more than a devil's decoy masquerading as a devout Christian man. St. Louis Outfielder Rahn Maxwell finds himself a victim of an attempted carjacking. The Lord guides him out of harms' way by opening the gunmen's eyes to Rahn's identity. The crook instead becomes infatuated fan and asks for Rahn's autograph, and as a good will gesture, directs Rahn out of the ambush! When the news media gets wind of what happened with the baseball player, Shae's television station lands an exclusive interview. Shae and Rahn's chance meeting sets in motion a relationship where Rahn not only surrenders to Christ, but pursues Shae with a purpose to prove that good men are still out there. After letting her guard down, Shae is faced with another scandal that rocks her world. This time the stakes are higher. Not only is her heart on the line, so is her professional credibility. She and Rahn are at odds as how to handle it and friction erupts between them. Will she strike out at love again? The Lord shows Rahn that nothing happens by chance, and everything is done for Him to get the glory.

In *Defense of Love*, Book 2, lately, nothing in Garrett Nash's life has made sense. When two people close to the U.S. Marshal wrong him deeply, Garrett expects God to remove them from his life. Instead, the Lord relocates Garrett to another city to start over, as if he were the offender instead of the victim. Criminal attorney Shari Carmen is comfortable in her own skin—most of the time. Being a "dark and lovely" African-American sister has its challenges, especially when it comes to relationships. Although she's a fireball in the courtroom, she knows how to fade into the background and keep the proverbial spotlight off her personal life. But literal spotlights are a different matter altogether. While playing tenor saxophone at an anniversary party, she grabs the attention of Garrett Nash. And as God draws them closer together, He makes another request of Garrett, one to which it will prove far more difficult to say "Yes, Lord."

In *Redeeming Heart*, Book 3, Landon Thomas (In Defense of Love) brings a new definition to the word "prodigal," as in prodigal son, brother or anything else imaginable. It's a good thing that God's love covers a multitude of sins, but He isn't letting Landon off easy. His journey from riches to rags proves to be humbling and a lesson well learned. Real Estate Agent Octavia Winston is a woman on a mission, whether it's God's or hers professionally. One thing is for certain, she's not about to compromise when it comes to a Christian mate, so why did God send a homeless man to steal her heart? Minister Rossi Tolliver (Crowning Glory) knows how to minister to God's lost sheep and through God's redemption, the game changes for Landon and Octavia.

In *Driven to Be Loved*, Book 4, on the surface, Brecee Carmen has nothing in common with Adrian Cole. She is a pediatrician certified in trauma care; he is a transportation problem solver for a luxury car dealership (a.k.a., a car salesman). Despite their slow but steady attraction to each other, neither one of them are sure that they're compatible. To complicate matters, Brecee is the sole unattached Carmen when it seems as though everyone else around her—family and friends—are finding love, except her. Through a series of discoveries, Adrian and Brecee learn that things don't happen by coincidence. Generational forces are at work, keeping promises, protecting family members, and perhaps even drawing Adrian back to the church. For Brecee and Adrian, God has been hard at work, playing matchmaker all along the way for their paths cross at the right time and the right place.

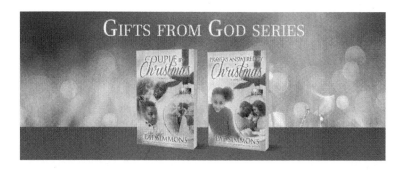

In *Couple by Christmas*, five year old Tyler Washington wants his daddy to marry this mother. The problem is both his parents were once married, then divorced two years ago. But it's Christmas time and the holidays are not the same. This year, Derek has custody, and he knows the loneliness his ex-wife will face on Christmas Day without their son. He experienced it the previous year. His past regrets and Tyler's request have Derek thinking. Maybe, just maybe, Robyn would be willing to do things as a family again for Tyler s sake. At best, act as a couple for Christmas.

In *Prayers Answered by Christmas*, Christmas is coming. While other children are compiling their lists for a fictional Santa, eight-year-old Mikaela Washington is on her knees, making her requests known to the Lord: One mommy for Christmas please. Portia Hunter refuses to let her ex-husband cheat her out of the family she wants. Her prayer is for God to send the right man into her life. Marlon Washington will do anything for his two little girls, but can he find a mommy for them and a love for himself? Since Christmas is the time of year to remember the many gifts God has given men, maybe these three souls will get their heart s desire.

Lean on Me, Book 1. No one should have to go it alone... Caregivers sometimes need a little TLC too.

Tabitha Knicely believes in family before everything. She may be overwhelmed caring for her beloved great-aunt, but she would never turn her back on the woman who raised her, even if Aunt Tweet's dementia is getting worse. Tabitha is sure she can do this on her own. But when Aunt Tweet ends up on her neighbor's front porch, and the man has the audacity to accuse Tabitha of elder abuse, things go from bad to awful. Marcus Whittington feels a mountain of regret at causing problems for Tabitha and her great-aunt. How was he to know the frail older woman's niece was doing the best she could? As Marcus gets to know Aunt Tweet and sees how hard Tabitha is fighting to keep everything together, he can't walk away from the pair. Particularly when helping Tabitha care for her great-aunt leads the two of them on a spiritual journey of faith and surrender.

Here For You, Book 2. Rachel Knicely's life has been on hold for six months while she takes care of her great aunt, who has Alzheimer's. Putting her aunt first was an easy decision—accepting that Aunt Tweet is nearing the end of her battle is far more difficult. Nicholas Adams's ministry is bringing comfort to those who are sick and homebound. He responds to a request for help for an ailing woman but when he meets the Knicelys, he realizes Rachel is the one who needs support the most. Nicholas is charmed by and attracted to Rachel, but then devastating news brings both a crisis of faith and roadblocks to their budding relationship that neither could have anticipated. This beautifully emotional and clean story contains a hero and heroine who are better at taking care of other people than themselves, a dark moment that shakes their faith, and a well-earned happily ever after.

Stand by Me, Book 3 (Coming November 2021)